The Italian Fiancé

T0345482

Victoria Springfield inherited a passion for Italy from her father who loved visiting Tuscany, particularly the tiny village of Gioviano and the walled city of Lucca – the setting for *The Italian Fiancé*.

Victoria grew up in Upminster, Essex. After many years in London, she now lives in Kent with her husband in a house by the river. She likes to write in the garden with a neighbour's cat by her feet or whilst drinking cappuccino in her favourite café. Then she types up her scribblings in silence whilst her mind drifts away to Italy.

Also by Victoria Springfield

The Italian Holiday
A Farmhouse in Tuscany

THE
ITALIAN FIANCÉ

Victoria Springfield

First published in Great Britain in 2022 by Orion Dash,
an imprint of The Orion Publishing Group Ltd,
Carmelite House, 50 Victoria Embankment
London EC4Y ODZ

An Hachette UK company

1 3 5 7 9 10 8 6 4 2

A CIP catalogue record for this book
is available from the British Library.

ISBN (eBook) 978 1 3987 1248 5
ISBN (Paperback) 978 1 3987 1249 2

www.orionbooks.co.uk

For John and Susan Neville, lovers of Lucca

Chapter One

Dozens of tiny golden hearts were scattered across the floor. Lisa had to use a stubby fingernail to prise them off the coir doormat, one by one. She popped them back into the hastily torn-open envelope and studied the invitation: two gold hearts entwined, a simple border and elegant script. It was quite modern, not the sort of design she imagined her elderly aunt would choose.

The doorbell rang. Lisa didn't need to look up to know who was standing on her doorstep. She opened the front door. Her younger sister marched straight in, a frown etched on her beautiful forehead.

'So, you've had yours too.' Cassie pointed the toe of her shoe at an errant gold heart wedged in the doormat's bristles.

'And good morning to you,' Lisa murmured.

Cassie brushed past her into the kitchen, turned on the cold tap at full strength and began filling Lisa's kettle.

'Coffee?' Lisa said. She reached into an overhead cupboard for her cafetière and two mugs.

'So, what are we going to do about it?' Cassie said.

'Do about it? What do you mean?'

'This is a wedding invitation, Lisa,' Cassie said.

'I realise that,' Lisa said slowly.

'Aunt Jane thinks she's going to marry this Italian fellow. He's an artist, for goodness' sake! And he's called Luciano

– what a ridiculous name. She can't marry him, Lisa. We've got to stop her.'

Lisa pressed the plunger down on the coffee pot. She fetched the milk from the fridge, buying time. Cassie drummed her French-manicured fingernails on the wooden table. Tiny beads of perspiration glistened above her upper lip.

'Don't you think Aunt Jane is old enough to do what she likes?' Lisa said. She put the two coffees on the table and waited for the explosion.

'She's not choosing a new hearth rug, Lisa. This is serious.' Cassie snapped a chocolate digestive in half viciously.

'She's in love,' Lisa said.

'In love? She's seventy!' Cassie sprayed a fine mist of biscuit crumbs across the table.

'There's no age limit on falling in love,' Lisa added.

'She hardly knows him. She met him on holiday – a holiday romance at her age, for heaven's sake! Now she's living out in Italy and she's talking about putting Sundial Cottage on the market. She says she's going to move to Italy for good. It's obvious she's not thinking straight.'

'Perhaps it was love at first sight,' Lisa said.

'I didn't think you believed in that sort of nonsense.'

'I don't. But other people do.'

'Aunt Jane isn't *other people*. Things like that don't happen to Jane. She's always been so sensible.'

Lisa looked at her sister. 'Seventy years of being sensible is enough for anyone.'

'Don't be flippant, Lisa. Aunt Jane is being exploited. This man is manipulating her.' Cassie twisted the end of her fishtail plait violently; tears formed in her clear blue eyes.

Lisa touched her sister's arm. 'It's been nearly ten years since she lost Uncle Eddie. She's probably lonely. This Luciano chap . . .'

'She's got us,' Cassie interrupted.

'That's not the same thing at all. Now she's found herself a partner – someone to share her life with. And if it doesn't work out, so what? Not everything lasts for ever.'

'What do you mean, *so what*? We're not all like you, Lisa, drifting from one disastrous love affair to another.'

'Thanks a lot.'

'Sorry, I shouldn't have said that,' Cassie said. She glanced down at the table.

'What does Paul say about it?' Lisa did not want to dwell on her own situation.

'Paul says we shouldn't interfere, but I know he agrees with me that this whole marriage idea is ridiculous,' Cassie said, but she avoided meeting Lisa's eyes.

'Hmm.' Lisa wasn't surprised; Cassie would never admit that she and Paul weren't in total agreement.

'Since we got married, Paul and I haven't spent a night apart, but this is an emergency,' Cassie said. 'Besides, someone needs to stay at home; we've got three sets of builders coming round to quote for the kitchen extension.'

'Stay at home?' Lisa was confused.

'When you and I go to Italy.'

'The wedding's not 'til after Christmas. Even you don't need to start planning yet,' Lisa said.

'We're not going to sit back and wait until December!' Cassie's voice rose at least an octave. 'We've got to go to Italy now. We've got to go and put a stop to this.'

'It would be nice to go and meet Luciano, I suppose,' Lisa said. 'But I thought Aunt Jane said the apartment was quite small. We don't want to impose . . .'

'We're not going to stay with them – that would imply we approve. I've asked Paul to research a small hotel in Lucca for us; he likes doing that kind of thing.'

'And getting a bargain,' Lisa said.

'There's nothing wrong with that.'

'Of course not,' Lisa said quickly. 'Okay, you can count me in. Let me know when you've checked on the flights. Lucca is in Tuscany, isn't it? It's supposed to be a beautiful part of Italy – I've always wanted to go.'

'It's not a holiday,' Cassie said. She picked up her tan leather shoulder bag.

'Of course not,' Lisa said. She kissed her sister on both cheeks, inhaling Cassie's fresh, floral scent.

Cassie reversed her hatchback down the drive. Lisa stood on the doorstep, smiling and waving. The car disappeared; Lisa let out a sigh of relief. She had begun to find Cassie's visits increasingly draining, even when they were as short as this one.

How different things used to be. Lisa still remembered the day that her parents had brought Cassie home wrapped in a cream waffle blanket edged in satin. Aunt Jane had told her that Cassie was Mum and Dad's new baby, but three-year-old Lisa knew better. Cassie belonged to Lisa – a gorgeous pink present, a funny little real-life doll.

As they were growing up, Cassie granted Lisa almost God-like status. Cassie wanted to walk like her, talk like her and dress like her. Even at the age of ten, Cassie only wanted to wear the clothes that Lisa picked out and she begged her older sister to style her hair with Lisa's prized straighteners. And when Lisa was a gawky, knock-kneed thirteen-year-old with a smattering of spots, in Cassie's eyes she was still the epitome of sophistication.

Lisa no longer wanted, or needed, Cassie to hang on her every word but it would be nice if – just sometimes – her younger sister would treat Lisa as a woman of nearly thirty who was capable of making her own life choices, not as some errant teenager in need of guidance. Cassie didn't seem to realise that not everyone aspired to a spanking new semi-detached house and a husband who worked in finance.

'*We're not all like you, Lisa, drifting from one disastrous love affair to another,*' Lisa mimicked under her breath. So what if her life was shambolic by her younger sister's standards; that didn't give Cassie the right to judge. She knew she should try to shrug it off, but the comment still stung.

Lisa put the two used coffee mugs by the side of the kitchen sink; she would wash up later. A week in Italy sounded wonderful. But a whole week with her sister – that would be hard. Lisa loved her sister, of course she did. But she wasn't sure she liked her very much.

Cassie parked her little red car and double-checked she had engaged the handbrake. She opened her front door; there was a pleasing scent of wood polish in the hallway. It was so nice to be home. Lisa's flat was so untidy and it certainly wasn't Cassie's idea of clean. She'd spotted a cobweb clinging to the corner of Lisa's kitchen this morning. A cobweb! Cassie shuddered. She didn't know how her older sister could live like she did. No spider would dare set up home in *her* house.

Cassie picked up her pen and crossed *Visit Lisa* off her to-do list. *Marinade beef, put on dark wash, weed front border . . .* it didn't promise to be a terribly exciting Saturday morning but it made sense to get those jobs out of the way whilst Paul was out playing golf. She looked longingly at the pile of glossy brochures lying on the kitchen counter. She could spend hours flicking through the pages of shiny new appliances – those big American-style fridges were the stuff of fantasies. It was a good thing she had Paul to rein her in; her initial plans for the house extension were way over budget.

The thought of Paul made Cassie smile. It was unusual to marry at twenty-three these days, but Paul ticked all the right boxes: he was tall, well spoken, had a job with good prospects, and he was also kind and caring. Moreover, though she hated herself for being so shallow, he was so very good-looking. They had met five years ago at a black-tie charity dinner where she had been handing out the laminated name badges. She could not help noticing the way Paul's broad shoulders filled out his tuxedo as she helped him fasten the safety pin. A little thrill had made her shiver as she looked up into his piercing blue eyes and said to herself *James Bond*.

Paul was an accountant, not a government agent, but at least he didn't have to go away on any secret assignments. It was a shame he didn't get to wear a dinner jacket very often but he was still just as handsome, even in his Dad-style V-neck golfing sweater. She hummed along to Radio 2 as she mixed half a teaspoon of crushed garlic into the marinade. Paul would open a nice bottle of red tonight. After three years of marriage, she knew him inside out. How lucky she was to have such an ideal husband. If only she could find a man like Paul for Lisa.

Lisa was nearly thirty but she was still running around with unsuitable men. Her last partner was a poet. All he seemed to do all day was stare out of the window and scribble whimsical thoughts. Max was thirty-six; surely that was old enough to realise he should go out and get a proper job. But worse than that, Max was always late, he rarely returned texts and when he and Lisa had rented a cottage in Cornwall with Cassie and Paul, he had worn the same floral shirt three days in a row. Cassie wrinkled her nose. Thank goodness he'd gone. Lisa claimed she wasn't too bothered. She always said that she never wanted to settle down.

Cassie hadn't worried too much about her sister; she had always believed that people became more sensible with each passing year. Then Aunt Jane took up with an Italian artist and blew that theory out of the water. Poor Aunt Jane. They should have realised how vulnerable she was now that Mum and Uncle Eddie were gone. Jane truly believed this Luciano fellow was in love with her – but what was he really like? Only last week, Cassie had read a dreadful story in the *Daily Mail*. A dear old soul had been taken in by a smooth-talking Sardinian waiter. She believed they were going to be together for ever until he was unmasked as a bigamist. When she thought of the cruel way he had manipulated a sweet old lady's emotions, it brought tears to Cassie's eyes. She couldn't bear to think of Jane's heart being broken. If only she or Lisa had taken Mary's place and accompanied Jane to Florence, her aunt would never have got into this predicament.

Cassie stretched a piece of cling film over the surface of the beef and put the dish on the bottom shelf of the fridge. She climbed the stairs to the spare bedroom, began to sort the dark clothes from the whites and piled them into her woven plastic laundry basket.

Chapter Two

The tall yellow buildings were casting long shadows on the far side of the Piazza Anfiteatro. The waiting staff stood gossiping outside Pizzeria Za Za, resigned to their dwindling clientele. The tourists and locals were now congregating on the sunny side of the oval-shaped piazza where the bars were doing a brisk trade and only the odd puddle attested to the afternoon's showers.

Jane arrived at Galleria Guinigi just as Viviana was pulling the dark green metal shutter down over the door. She was always glad to see the gallery's young manageress. Viviana and her mother Livia had been so kind since Jane's arrival in Lucca, helping her with all kinds of practicalities and lifting her with their wise words when Jane was having a wobble about the huge life change she had set in motion.

'*Ciao!*' Jane called.

Viviana straightened up. She smoothed down her black tunic and tucked her short, chic hair behind her ears.

'*Ciao*, Jane. Luciano asked me to tell you he's gone straight to the studio.'

Jane smiled. Studio was rather a grand description of the spare room on the top floor of Luciano's split-level apartment. 'Thank you, Viviana. I mean *grazie*. How was today?'

'Surprisingly busy. We've sold two of Luciano's pencil sketches and a pair of Alonzo's earrings.'

'*Fantastico!*' Jane said. The word sounded so ridiculous. She wondered how long it would take her to say anything in Italian without feeling horribly self-conscious.

'Are you okay, Jane?' Viviana asked.

'Yes . . . yes, of course.' Jane's hand instinctively tightened around the leather handle of her nylon tote bag. The mobile phone inside vibrated gently. Jane ignored it. She would answer Cassie's latest message in her own good time.

'But there is something on your mind,' Viviana said.

'Yes, my two nieces are coming to visit,' Jane said.

'That's wonderful news!'

'Yes, of course it is.'

'But there is a problem.' Viviana was eyeing Jane with concern.

'It's nothing,' Jane said.

'Of course, I do not mean to pry.'

Jane sighed; keeping her feelings to herself didn't seem to be the Italian way.

'I'm terribly fond of Lisa and Cassie. They're lovely girls. They were a tower of strength after Eddie passed away. I don't know what I would have done without them, and we've been even closer since my dear sister died. They always supported me, whatever I decided to do. But since I moved here . . .'

'They don't approve?'

'They act as if it's a phase I'm going through. They don't trust me to make my own decisions.'

'Aah . . . And now you are getting married . . .'

'I'm so happy, Viviana, but it *is* a big decision; perhaps they are right to be concerned.'

'They have their own families?'

'Cassie's been married three years, but no children yet. She's twenty-six, about your age. Lisa's nearly thirty

9

now, she's not the type to settle down – at least that's what she says.'

'When they come here, they will meet Luciano and see how happy you are. Then they will be happy too.' The younger woman beamed.

'Of course, you're right,' Jane said. She had a feeling it wasn't going to be quite that simple.

Jane unlocked the door to Luciano's apartment, *their* apartment she had to remind herself. She dropped her tote bag onto the kitchen table. The smell of oil paint hung in the hallway. Puccini's 'Nessun Dorma' was blasting from the ancient turntable in the attic studio on the top floor. Her sandals made a clip-clopping sound as she climbed the bare wooden stairs.

Luciano was standing at his easel, his bulky frame and wild explosion of steel-grey hair half obscuring the large canvas he was daubing with blue paint.

'Chiesa San Michele,' Jane said, above the music.

Luciano spun around. Flecks of paint splattered onto the terracotta tiled floor. He wiped his brush on the front of his trousers.

'Yes, you are right. The façade of this church is unmistakable, however poor the artist's work.'

'No, this is good,' Jane said.

'It is not too bad, I admit, but however many times I try to capture this church, there is a certain something that eludes me.' He turned down the volume on the record player.

'I didn't mean to interrupt you.'

'But I am glad that you did. Come here . . .' He put his arms around her and brushed his lips against hers. His beard felt rough against her cheek.

'Let us go out, I have done enough for today,' he said. 'No . . . wait.' He turned up the music. 'This is my favourite part. We must dance. Let me clean my hands.' He picked up a well-used rag. 'Now put your feet on top of mine and lean against me. You will not fall; I shall hold you.'

Jane laughed. She stepped onto Luciano's paint-splattered boots and balanced precariously as he began to waltz her around the room. She never ceased to be surprised at how small and slight she felt when he held her against him. And how safe.

'*Dilegua, o notte!*' he sang in his deep baritone, twirling them both around, missing the easel by inches.

'Stop!' she laughed. 'You're making me dizzy.'

He stopped dancing, gripped both sides of her waist and lifted her up until her head nearly touched the sloping ceiling. She caught sight of herself in the large gilt mirror on the wall behind them. Her face was red, her newly dyed hair all mussed up. She hardly recognised herself.

'*Vincerò! Vincerò! Vincerò!*' he sang the final words. The record player clicked off, signalling the end of Side One.

'You're crazy!'

'But that is what you like about me.' He grinned. 'So, shall we go out? Where shall I take my beautiful fiancée this evening?'

'We could try Da Giocomo, but I must get changed – just look at me!' Jane patted her hair.

'Nonsense! One cannot improve on perfection.' He kissed her again. 'I, on the other hand, must change out of these trousers. I cannot be seen in such a state with the most beautiful woman in Lucca.'

Jane laughed. At first she'd been embarrassed by Luciano's effusive compliments, had even suspected them to be a form of gentle mockery but it didn't take long for her to realise that his over-the-top words were an expression of his zest for life. Wherever he went, friends, neighbours and the local dogs were met with expansive gestures and joyful greetings.

Luciano reappeared in clean, red trousers. He'd changed his shirt too. The striped linen gaped slightly where the material struggled to contain his soft, brown belly. There was a streak of green paint in his hair.

'Will I do?' he asked.

'Perfectly,' Jane said. She'd decided not to get changed. Her blue shirt dress was cool and comfortable, so she'd contented herself with smoothing down her rumpled skirt and reapplying her pink lipstick and a dusting of face powder.

They walked through the shady, narrow streets, her hand in his. The hem of her calf-length dress swished against her bare legs. She glanced up at him. He was a big bear of a man whose physique paid tribute to a lifetime of red wine and pasta. His clothes were unapologetically loud and his unruly salt-and-pepper hair lapped the edge of his shirt collar. Perhaps they looked like an odd couple; she was sure Cassie and Lisa would think so.

Jane and Eddie had been made for each other; everybody said so. Her late husband had shared her equitable temperament and her love of books and European travel. As the years went by, they had become more and more alike, pottering in the garden, enjoying the same television series and finishing each other's sentences. They looked similar too, with their clear blue eyes, slim figures and neat button noses.

Jane had never expected to meet somebody else; she certainly wasn't looking to replace the kind, loving scientist with whom she had shared four decades. There would never be another Eddie. But her relationship with Luciano was something entirely different. To compare the two men would be as pointless as debating the respective merits of Constable versus Picasso or weighing up the tastiness of a bowl of spicy *spaghetti puttanesca* against a Sunday roast with all the trimmings.

Luciano was different from any man – any person – she had ever met. And she was different too. From the day they met, he had uncovered a whole other side to her – a more daring, adventurous side. And now, at seventy, she was embarking on the biggest change of her life – a new husband, a new country, new blank chapters to fill with the story of the rest of her life. She had reinvented herself and no matter how disapproving Lisa and Cassie might prove to be, she wouldn't – couldn't – go back to being the person she had been before she and Luciano met.

They passed in front of the red brick Guinigi Tower. The eccentric-looking tower, crowned with a roof terrace of leafy holm oak trees, was the sole survivor of the four erected by the wealthy merchants and bankers of the Guinigi family. Two hundred and thirty-two steps led to the viewing platform on the tower's top. Jane made a mental note to add it to the list of things that might entertain her visitors. It would certainly appeal to Lisa, though it was unlikely she would be able to persuade Cassie to climb up there; her younger niece had never had a head for heights.

They cut through the streets and entered the top end of Piazza Napoleone, the largest square in the town. Da Giocomo was tucked just off the square in a corner shaded by a thick canopy of trees. A couple sitting in the corner gave them a friendly wave and the waiter gave Luciano a hearty slap on the back. He seemed to know everybody. Luciano pulled back a white metal chair for Jane.

'May I suggest a negroni?' The waiter smiled encouragingly. 'Jane?'

'That sounds wonderful.'

'Two please, Gianni,' Luciano said. He unwrapped a wooden toothpick and speared one of the green olives in the glass dish in the centre of the table.

The waiter returned with two large, etched tumblers accessorised with a twist of lemon peel, a glass bowlful of crisps and an oval platter of *crostini* arranged on a scallop-edged doily. Luciano crunched into a *crostino* topped with black olive tapenade. 'How was your day, my love?'

'Successful, I think. I've repotted those herbs on the balcony and finally learnt all the words of the Beatitudes.'

'Well done, you are ready for choir practice tomorrow.'

'As ready as I can be.' Jane smiled.

'But there is something else? You mentioned you had some news for me.'

Jane fiddled with the stem of her cocktail stirrer, prodding the ice at the bottom of her glass. 'My niece Cassie contacted me today. She and her older sister, Lisa, are coming to visit.'

'That's marvellous! They are like daughters to you, are they not? And now, at last we will meet. When are they coming?'

'The day after tomorrow.'

'Such short notice! Still, we shall manage. I shall move those boxes out of the spare room and up to the studio. The lamp is still broken but we do not really need two in the living room . . .'

'They're not going to be staying with us. They've booked a room at the Hotel Tosca.'

Luciano's eyes widened. 'No. This is not right. You are their aunt; they must stay with us.'

'Cassie says that they did not want to put us to any trouble. She was most insistent. Besides, they received a special discount from the hotel for paying in advance, so now it's too late.'

Luciano shook his head and tutted. 'Not staying with family! Sometimes I do not understand these English ways. But I am glad not to spend tomorrow moving boxes. I am determined to finally capture the façade of Chiesa San Michele.'

'And I am going to walk the length of via Fillungo and find my wedding shoes.'

'You are happy to do that alone?' Luciano asked.

'Oh, yes.'

'I am rather glad you said that. I feel I would be of no use on such a quest.' Luciano smiled. 'So, how long will your nieces be staying in Lucca?'

'About a week, I believe.'

'Good. That is plenty of time for them to see everything. But they are young. Perhaps they will not want to spend all their time with two old folk.'

'I could ask Viviana's advice. She's about the same age as Cassie; she is sure to think of some things they will enjoy.'

'An excellent idea.'

'It will be good to find something to distract them.'

'To distract them from what?'

'Checking up on me,' Jane said.

'Checking up on you? What on earth are you likely to get up to?'

Jane flexed her left hand. Three small diamonds sparkled in the light.

Luciano linked his fingers between hers. His gaze fell on her unusual star-shaped ring. 'Aah . . . now I understand. But I think it's me they've come to check up on.'

'I'm afraid so,' she said quietly.

He squeezed her hand. 'Am I so bad?'

'Not at all. I'm sure they'll like you very much. But . . .'

'But they may not approve of us getting married?'

'Lisa is very easy-going; I can't imagine her trying to tell me what to do, but Cassie can be very judgemental. I'm afraid they both think I'm a daft old lady who's fallen for a smooth-talking Italian playboy.'

'I'm sure one look at me will dispel them of that illusion,' Luciano chuckled. 'But why are you looking so serious? You are not having second thoughts, are you?'

'Of course not. You've changed my life.'

Luciano caught the eye of the waiter. 'A glass of red wine, I think. Those cocktails are rather dangerous. I do not want my fiancée to have to carry me home.'

'*Signora*?'

'Just a mineral water please.'

'*Saluti!*' Luciano raised his glass. 'I love you, Jane.'

'I love you too,' Jane said. 'And that's all that matters.'

Chapter Three

Jane paused in front of the church of Saint Francis. The stark limestone façade, enlivened only by two blind arches and a single rose window, gave no hint of the loveliness beyond. Jane passed to the side of the church and entered the cloisters.

She stopped in front of the frescoed lunette above the tomb of Tignosini. There were hundreds of depictions of the Holy Mother and Child in the churches and galleries of Lucca, but this was her favourite. She never grew tired of looking at the butterscotch-coloured haloes above the heads of Mary and Jesus, the soft brown robe of St Francis and the merchant, Tignosini, kneeling to receive the Holy Mother's blessing.

Jane came to the cloisters at least twice a week; it was such a peaceful place. She loved it when no one else was around and she could imagine the days when the monks had grown food for the poor in one cloister, feed for the mules in another and herbal remedies for the monks' apothecary in the last. Now those industrious spaces were replaced by neat, manicured lawns.

The scent of freshly mown grass was in the air. If she closed her eyes, she could be back in England watching Eddie cutting the lawn in his slip-on leather shoes with the sleeves of his old work shirt rolled up to the elbows. She felt a pang of nostalgia. How different her life was now to the years she and Eddie had spent in Honeypot Lane. She had changed too. What would Lisa and Cassie make of it all? She could hardly believe they would be arriving tomorrow. She couldn't wait to see them, but the niggling worries remained. What would they think of Luciano? Would they compare him to their dear Uncle Eddie and find him wanting?

Jane left the cloisters, passed the piazza in front of the church and crossed over the canal that ran along a narrow channel cut into via del Fosso. She would soon reach the heart of the old town. She tried to push her cares aside and concentrate on the task ahead: shopping for her wedding shoes. Who would have believed she would be doing that at the age of seventy? In a few months' time she would be married to Luciano Zingaretti. Sometimes it seemed like a dream.

She turned into the elegant shopping street that snaked its way behind the Piazza Anfiteatro. There was only a handful of shoe shops on via Fillungo but Jane had allocated the rest of the morning to her quest. Even though she had only moved to Lucca a few months before, she knew that it was impossible to walk down the winding shopping street without bumping into some acquaintance who would waylay her for a long conversation in rapid Italian that Jane could just about follow now that she understood about two out of every three words. And afterwards, whilst her head was still spinning, she would seek out a restorative cappuccino in one of the nineteenth-century cafés where the literary giants of Lucca once gathered. She would work her way through the stories in last night's *Corriere della Sera*, with her little green leather dictionary to hand, and wonder if she would ever understand enough of the language to tackle a novel.

So far today, the only person she recognised was Viviana's mother, Livia, who waved and called 'see you at choir practice' as she wobbled past on her bicycle. It was a shame she hadn't stopped to chat. Jane carried on up the road, stopping to look in the window of a smart menswear shop. Luciano would look so handsome in the cappuccino-coloured linen jacket in the window, but she knew he would be happier in his old purple number even though it was dotted with flecks of paint that wouldn't wash out. It would be nice if Luciano dressed up a little, but Jane knew there were benefits to being with a man who was confident in his own skin rather than one who fussed about in front of the mirror. Besides, she was old enough to appreciate what she had. There were too many women who found a man, then set about trying to change him.

Reluctantly, she tore her eyes away from the linen suits in the window. She had to step around two women who were standing in the middle of the pavement-less street showing each other photos on their mobile phones – an activity that apparently required a lot of hand-waving and loud exclamations of delight. Jane picked her way past them, avoiding two elderly gents in neatly pressed polo shirts and belted knee-length shorts who were standing in the road munching chocolate-flecked ice-creams. One had a small, white terrier under his arm which was sticking out its pink tongue and trying to wriggle its way towards its owner's dripping cone.

She stopped outside a small shoe shop with most of its wares crammed into the window. Browsing took place in the street; there was no need to step inside without an intent to purchase something. Jane scanned the display, which seemed to have been arranged with no notice-able concession to theme or colour. She needed white or neutral to go with the pale pink suit she had picked out, but nothing here looked right.

She stared at the window and sighed. There was no point in going inside; the small interior contained only a few shoes and sandals on individual, wall-mounted perspex shelves, a couple of bench seats for trying on, and a wooden counter behind which the white-haired proprietor perched on a rickety wooden chair whilst shaking his head in disgust at the contents of the local edition of *Il Tirreno*.

Jane walked on until she came to the corner of via San Giorgio. Carlo Alessi was one of the larger shops on the street. A bell rang as Jane pushed open the door. The proprietor was by her side in an instant. The woman was warm and friendly but quite insistent that Jane could not possibly reject any of her suggestions without trying on the proffered shoes. Jane found herself walking back and forth to the mirror whilst empty cardboard boxes piled up around her. Everything was too high or too low, too plain or too fancy. She was past the age of teetering on spindly heels, but she still wanted something special. Eventually the saleswoman admitted defeat and turned her attention to two other customers trying on matching stilettos. As Jane left the shop, one of the women struck a pose, the other laughed loudly and clapped her hand to her mouth. Jane felt a pang of loneliness. Looking for shoes by herself wasn't as exciting as she had anticipated. If only her best friend, Mary, was here – what fun they would have together looking for all the finishing touches to Jane's outfit.

Jane turned away from the shop window. She would treat herself to a cup of coffee in her favourite café before she tried any more shops. She dropped a couple of coins into the upturned hat of a young girl who was playing a portable keyboard nearby, pushed open the glass doors and inhaled the aroma of freshly ground coffee and the sweet scent of sugar-dusted pastries. Jane took a seat and ordered a cappuccino. It was cheaper to drink her coffee standing at the bar as Luciano always did, but whenever Jane sank into the comfortable dark red leather banquette at Café Patrizia she felt the extra euro was money well spent.

She sat for a while toying with her cup and saucer. There were a couple more shoe shops at the other end of via Fillungo; she knew Viviana favoured a small establishment not far from the clock tower. She would try there and if she had no luck, she could always take the train into Florence. Perhaps she could persuade Livia to go with her, though she was bound to try to talk Jane into something far too glamorous, unlike dear Mary who would steer her towards something practical with a capital P.

It would be nice to have an excuse to visit Florence again. It was the city where she and Luciano first met so it held a special place in her heart. Jane had been to Italy several times before; she and Eddie had travelled all over Europe, but on their visits to Italy, they had always stayed by the lakes and mountains that Eddie loved. Jane had ventured abroad occasionally since Eddie's death: a tour of Andalucia; a trip with Mary to see the tulip fields of Holland; a river cruise along the Rhine. But she had never returned to Italy.

With her seventieth birthday fast approaching, Jane had decided she must, at last, visit Florence, and do so at her own pace with no set itinerary to follow. Mary had been due to accompany her. The two of them had had so much fun brushing up their Italian together, researching the places they might see and sighing over the scenery and costumes in *A Room with a View*. At the last minute,

Mary's granddaughter had gone into premature labour. Mary didn't want to leave England and Jane respected her old friend's point of view. It was too late to cancel their trip so, despite Lisa and Cassie's strongly expressed misgivings, Jane had summoned up a determination she didn't know she possessed and went alone.

Jane's courage had almost failed her when she crossed the piazza in front of the Santa Maria Novella railway station and found herself in a wave of baseball caps and backpacks heading for the streets surrounding the cathedral and the baptistry. But the small hotel she and Mary had chosen was situated in a quiet residential street on the south side of the river, far from the crowds. Despite the sultry weather, the language barrier and the almost indecent excess of statues and architectural treasures that surrounded her at every turn, Jane felt almost immediately at home.

On her second morning she strolled across the Ponte Vecchio past the tourists ogling the jewellery shops that lined the old bridge. Jane had never seen so much gold in one place. She turned towards the grey bulk of the Uffizi, the most famous art gallery in the world. A queue was already forming outside; some were distracted by a busker with a dancing marionette but most stared down at their phones.

Jane wandered around the perimeter of the building watching the street artists who made a living from selling their watercolours and sketching the portraits of the passing tourists. Jane hadn't planned to linger but she was soon drawn into conversation by a scruffy young man standing by a display of fine sketches of Hollywood actresses whom Jane recognised immediately. The man chatted pleasantly enough until she politely declined his suggestion that she might pose for a portrait. His intense green eyes turned cold. Ignoring her refusal, he picked up a soft brown pastel stick and began to sketch. The approximate outline of Jane's face began to materialise on a sheet of cream paper.

Jane tried to move away. The man shifted position. Jane tensed. She was trapped between the man and his easel. She looked around. It was broad daylight, and she was surrounded by dozens of people, but everyone was in their own little world. No one noticed her distress. She felt very vulnerable and very alone.

'Is that man bothering you?' a voice said. A man stepped out from behind one of the pillars. He was an imposing figure, tall and broad, dressed in old jeans and a loose purple top, something between a shirt and a smock.

'Oh, no, I'm . . .' she murmured; she hated to make a fuss.

The artist stepped away from his easel advancing on the stranger, spitting out a string of rapid Italian. The two men's voices rose. Jane seized her chance. She walked away quickly, gripping the handle of her shoulder bag. She didn't look back.

Jane walked as fast as she could. She had no idea where she was going, but she was confident that she couldn't get lost if she followed the path of the river. Soon the Uffizi Gallery and Ponte Vecchio were far behind her. The sun was hot, she had left her straw hat back at the hotel, and her silky blouse was clinging to her back. She crossed the road to take advantage of the shade. A van hooted, making her jump.

She had almost reached the next bridge, the pretty Ponte Santa Trinita, when she heard the stranger's voice: '*Signora*, please wait!'

Jane stopped, reluctantly. The man was breathing heavily in the heat. She waited for him to catch his breath.

'I could not let you go without checking that you are okay.' His dark eyes were full of concern.

'I'm quite all right now, thank you,' Jane said, although she was still feeling quite shaken up. She was about to walk away but something stopped her. 'It was very kind of you,' she added.

'Young Luigi Vasari is a talented artist, but he is a most unpleasant fellow. His grandfather, Old Luigi, was just the same.'

'You know him?'

'All of us artists know each other.'

'You're an artist?'

'Yes. Luciano.' He held out his hand. Jane took it. His handshake was warm and firm.

'Jane. I suppose that you want to draw my portrait now.'

'Not at all.'

Jane had no desire to own a portrait of herself, but she felt inexplicably disappointed by the man's reaction.

'I don't draw portraits. But even if I did, I do not think I could do justice to your beautiful face. My easel is over there . . .' He waved an arm in the direction of the river. 'The great buildings, the churches, the bridges over the Arno — these are my subjects. I have drawn and painted them all a dozen times.'

'Like Monet with his views of the Thames.'

Luciano laughed. 'Aah, Claude Monet. I'm afraid my daubings wouldn't stand comparison.'

'Well, thank you again. I mustn't keep you,' Jane said.

'But you must,' Luciano said. 'I must buy you a drink to make up for that man's behaviour. My friend is keeping an eye on my easel.'

'I . . .' Jane began.

'I absolutely insist.' Luciano's voice was firm but his eyes were twinkling.

'Okay,' Jane said. 'But just a cup of tea.'

'A fine English tradition.' Luciano smiled. So, with Lisa and Cassie's dire warnings echoing in her ears, Jane allowed Luciano to lead her through the city streets. After their tea, they walked further along the River Arno and before she knew it, Jane found herself in a cosy trattoria down a side street lined with parked mopeds that she would never have discovered herself.

'Shall we order more tea?' Luciano said.

'Wine, please – but on one condition,' Jane said.

'And what is that?' he asked.

'That you choose.'

Luciano raised his glass. 'To new friends.'

'New friends.' Jane echoed his words.

How quickly the evening had flown by; Jane was shocked to realise it was starting to get dark as Luciano walked her back to her hotel. He hummed to himself as they crossed the Ponte Santa Trinita back to the south side of the city.

'*Firenze è come?*' Jane recognised the tune at once.

Luciano stopped walking. 'Yes, from *Gianni Schicchi*. You like Puccini? That is marvellous.' He began to sing the lyrics. He had a clear, deep voice. People were turning and staring. Jane was shocked to realise that she didn't care.

Luciano stopped singing as suddenly as he began.

'Don't stop!' Jane said.

'I cannot reach the high notes. You must sing the next part!'

Jane clapped her hand over her mouth. She enjoyed singing in the church choir, hidden away in the chorus, but a solo serenade in the street was quite another matter. 'No, no!' she laughed.

'Then you must do the next best thing. Come and listen to Puccini with me. There is a concert tomorrow in Lucca. It is the town where Puccini was born and the place where I live.'

'Oh, I couldn't,' said Jane. But she knew that she would. And that was how it began.

Jane picked up her bag. She had whiled away half an hour drinking coffee and reminiscing. She handed a five-euro note to the man behind the till and waited for her change. She looked in the mirror behind the row of bottles lined up against the wall and patted her auburn hair into place. She was glad her new Italian hairdresser had persuaded her to tint her hair back to a softer version of its original colour.

Behind Jane, another woman's face was reflected in the glass: a woman in her sixties sitting alone. The woman's hair was pulled back into a rather severe ponytail; it was jet-black save for a solitary streak of white. An orb-shaped gold pendant nestled between the wide lapels of her violet jacket. An emerald-green handbag with a bamboo handle was perched on the table in front of her. Jane's pastel-pink floral blouse suddenly seemed frumpy and dull.

The man behind the counter was speaking, but Jane hadn't heard a word.

'*Il suo resto, signora,*' he repeated in Italian, then loudly, in English: 'Your change, madam!'

'So sorry, please excuse me,' Jane said. She put the coins in her leather purse and snapped it shut. The woman with the white streak in her hair was tipping a sachet of sugar into her coffee. How confident she looked. How Italian. So unlike Jane. Would she ever really fit in? But she loved Luciano and he loved her. She knew he did. When they were alone, she had no doubts.

26

Jane let the glass door swing shut behind her. She stepped out into the street and turned back the way she had come. She didn't feel like shopping anymore. She wanted to go home to the familiar comfort of the apartment and potter in the living room with the smell of oil paint in the air and the sound of Luciano's singing drifting down the stairs.

Chapter Four

Cassie had to admit that Aunt Jane looked well. Italy suited her, or perhaps it was just the soft light cast by the wall lamps in the cosy lounge of the Hotel Tosca that was responsible for her glowing complexion.

'I would have brought Luciano to meet you straight away, but I thought you'd rather get settled in first.'

'Yes, you're quite right. We'll need a chance to freshen up,' Cassie said.

'But we're so looking forward to meeting Luciano, aren't we, Cassie,' Lisa said.

'Of course we are,' Cassie said. She took a sip of her fizzy water and shot her sister a look. Lisa didn't seem to notice.

Jane shifted awkwardly on the damask couch. She twisted the delicate star-shaped ring on her left hand.

'Oh, let me see!' Cassie took hold of Jane's hand and examined the ring. It was dwarfed by Cassie's huge emerald-cut sparkler. 'It's lovely,' she said truthfully.

'White gold. Luciano chose it himself.'

'I've never seen anything quite like it,' Cassie said.

'A young man, Alonzo, designed it. He sells some of his jewellery through the gallery where Luciano sells his paintings.'

'He's obviously very talented,' Lisa said. 'The gallery sounds wonderful – I hope we get the chance to visit.'

'Of course. In fact, I thought we would meet Luciano there before we head out for dinner.'

'Won't it be closed?' Cassie said.

'Oh, no. The shops here don't close until seven-thirty or eight at night but they shut for a couple of hours or more in the middle of the day.'

'How odd.'

'It's the traditional way. Luciano swears by a proper lunch break and a short siesta.'

'Sounds like a great routine.' Lisa grinned.

Cassie didn't reply. A long lunch and a snooze wasn't her idea of an efficient business model.

'Luciano's worked so hard to build up the gallery,' Jane said.

'It will be great to see it,' Lisa said. Her wrist full of bangles jangled as she raised her glass to her lips.

Cassie sighed. Lisa looked so relaxed and happy. She didn't seem worried about Aunt Jane at all. Didn't she notice that Jane's conversation was all: 'Luciano this, Luciano that'? Wasn't she concerned that their aunt's eyes lit up at the mention of her fiancé's name like a silly teenager? Lisa had agreed to join Cassie on her mercy mission to rescue Aunt Jane but it was becoming clear that she wasn't going to be much help. There was only one person who could save Jane – and that was Cassie.

Lisa chatted on about their journey over. Jane talked about her new life, throwing Luciano's name into the conversation at every opportunity. Cassie clinked the cocktail stirrer against the ice cubes in her drink. It was lovely to see her aunt after such a long time, but it was hard to keep her feelings to herself. Aunt Jane would eventually see sense, Cassie was sure of it. Slowly, slowly, she would gather the evidence against her aunt's ill-thought-out marriage and confront her when the time was right.

'Well, I'll see you later, girls.' Jane got to her feet. Cassie kissed her aunt's soft cheek. Jane's scent was different: warm and spicy, nothing like the fresh lily of the valley she had always favoured before.

Jane walked into the lobby, pushed open the revolving door and stepped into the street.

'Didn't she look happy?' Lisa said.

'That's what worries me.' Cassie stabbed a piece of ice with her cocktail stirrer and drained the last of her drink.

'Let's not be hasty. Let's meet him first,' Lisa said. 'Come on, we may as well go up. Can I hop in the shower first? You know I'll be quicker.'

'Of course.' Cassie wanted to hang her clothes up. She couldn't relax until everything was organised.

Cassie carefully counted the hangers and took her half. Everything seemed to be creased despite her careful packing. She arranged her tops and underwear in one of the drawers. By the time everything was to her satisfaction, Lisa had vacated the shower.

Cassie inhaled deeply. The pink grapefruit shower gel perfumed the air pleasantly and it was good to wash off the grime of travel. She wrapped her hair in a towel, slipped on one of the hotel's white dressing gowns and stepped out of the steamy bathroom. Lisa was sitting in the armchair in the corner of their twin bedroom flicking through the *Lucca Attractions* booklet that had been lying on top of the leather-bound *Guest Directory*; her clothes were strewn across her bed. Cassie was surprised to see that Lisa had changed into a striped cotton dress; it was nice that she'd bothered to make an effort for once. If only Lisa wore flattering clothes and make-up every day, she would give herself a chance of meeting someone half decent.

'Won't be long,' Cassie said. She started to run a travel iron over her white linen trousers.

'No rush. We've got plenty of time. I've checked the map again; the Piazza Anfiteatro is only a few minutes' walk away.'

'Good,' Cassie said. She was pleased they were going to meet Luciano at his gallery; the pictures on the wall would distract them from the inevitably awkward conversation. She unplugged the iron and pulled on her white trousers. She'd come to Lucca for a serious purpose, but it was nice to wear something that gave her that holiday feeling. She reapplied her eyeliner and spritzed some scent behind her ears.

Lisa was right; they didn't have to walk far before they found an archway that led to the Piazza Anfiteatro. They were greeted by a substantial oval *piazza* ringed by tall, yellow-toned buildings housing restaurants, cafés and shops.

'What a beautiful place,' Lisa said. 'I'm so glad we came.'

Cassie had to agree. Despite the commercial nature of the establishments, nothing looked brash or jarring. Cassie smiled approvingly at the elegant cream umbrellas shading the patrons of Café Europa. And she couldn't help noticing that a group of half a dozen men sitting outside were casting admiring glances in their direction. She flicked her hair self-consciously, feeling rather flattered. Then she realised they were looking at Lisa; her dress was virtually see-through in the early evening sunlight.

Cassie felt a surge of irritation. Ever since they were teenagers, Lisa had always caught the boys' eyes. No matter how much effort Cassie made, choosing her pretty dresses carefully and brushing her hair until it shone, scruffy Lisa with her unpolished shoes and unravelling hems had always been the centre of attention. Cassie didn't want men fighting over her; after all, she had Paul. But she couldn't help wishing that just for once the admiring glances would come her way.

'There it is, over there – Galleria Guinigi,' Lisa said.

Cassie made a concerted effort to wipe the scowl off her face. 'Oh, yes, you're right. And there's Aunt Jane, but who's she with?'

The man talking to their aunt was no more than thirty – rather good-looking, Cassie thought, although his wavy hair, which reached past the top of his collar, was slightly too long for her taste.

'That certainly can't be Luciano,' Lisa quipped.

Cassie couldn't help laughing. Even with her freshly dyed hair, Jane was unlikely to have picked up a toy boy.

Jane spotted them and waved. 'You didn't have any trouble finding your way, then,' she said.

'Oh, not at all – it was very easy,' Lisa said.

'Luciano has had to pop out to via Fillungo for some varnish. He'll be back in a few minutes. But let me introduce you to Alonzo.'

Alonzo pushed his sunglasses up into his thick, dark hair. He smiled, flashing a set of straight, white teeth. There was a small mole just above the top corner of his soft, full lips. 'I have heard so much about you both,' he said.

'Pleased to meet you,' Lisa said.

'Pleased to meet you, too,' Cassie said. Alonzo's gold-flecked green eyes gazed back at her from under his high, tanned forehead. Lisa was saying something to Aunt Jane but Cassie had no idea what it was. She felt unusually distracted.

'Do come in.' Alonzo held open the gallery's door.

A striking young woman dressed all in black with no make-up apart from a slash of red lipstick stood behind the small counter near the door.

'Viviana runs the gallery and organises our sales and marketing,' Alonzo said.

'Great to meet you.' Viviana smiled broadly.

'The girls were admiring my ring,' Jane said. The three diamonds in the star-shaped setting sparkled even more brightly under the shop lights.

'I'm so glad you approve,' Alonzo said.

'Alonzo's an amazing jeweller,' Viviana said.

'Viviana is a good saleswoman,' Alonzo joked.

'We'd love to see some more of your jewellery, wouldn't we, Cassie,' Lisa said.

Cassie nodded.

'These were all designed by me.' Alonzo gestured towards the contents of three perspex display cases.

'That's lovely. White gold is my favourite.' Cassie pointed out a fine diamond-shape pendant and matching earrings.

'And mine. But I think with your colouring you would suit something like this rose-gold choker.'

'Rose gold. I don't think so . . .'

'I am not trying to sell you anything, I assure you. But I would like to see it on you. Why don't you try it on, just for fun?'

'Oh, go on, Cassie,' Lisa said.

'I've never worn rose gold,' Cassie said.

'There's a first time for everything, don't you agree,' Alonzo said. He lifted the lid of the perspex box and unhooked the choker from its velvet stand. He passed Cassie the necklace.

'It's heavier than I expected.' Cassie had assumed the links would be hollow.

'Gold vermeil. The pink gold is electroplated onto a base of sterling silver. I learnt the technique when I was studying in London. It means I can keep the prices lower. I don't want only wealthy people to enjoy my work.'

Cassie struggled to fasten the clasp.

'Here, let me,' Alonzo said. Cassie opened her mouth to protest but Alonzo had already taken the choker. 'If you move over there, you will be able to see yourself in the full-length mirror.'

Alonzo stood close behind her, their bodies almost touching. She caught the scent of some subtle, oriental cologne. His firm, warm fingers brushed against her skin as he expertly fastened the choker; she could feel his breath on the back of her neck. Cassie bit her lip; she surreptitiously wiped her damp hands on her linen trousers.

Alonzo stood back. '*Perfetto!*'

'It's perfect,' Lisa said. 'That pink gold has really lit up your complexion; you're glowing.'

'Very pretty,' Jane added.

'But do *you* like it?' Alonzo's green eyes scanned Cassie's face.

'I love it,' she murmured.

'Allow me,' he said.

She held her breath as he unclipped the clasp.

'If you could excuse me, I shall say goodbye now; I can hear the phone ringing in the back room,' Alonzo said. He flashed them another dazzling smile and disappeared through the beaded curtain. He was still holding the rose-gold necklace.

'Aah! Here's Luciano,' Aunt Jane said.

The large man in baggy pink shorts and a bright red linen shirt seemed to fill the gallery's narrow doorway. He threw both arms up in the air.

'Welcome! Welcome!' His voice boomed out.

Cassie tried not to stare. She hadn't known what to

34

expect, but she hadn't been expecting *this*. Luciano's beard and unruly hair were familiar from the slightly blurred snapshot Jane had forwarded from her recently acquired smart phone but Luciano was so big! And those clothes! Whatever was Jane thinking?

Luciano pulled Aunt Jane towards him and pecked her on the cheek. Then he turned his attention to the two nieces, greeting each in turn.

Cassie forced a smile. 'Glad to meet you.' Luciano was obviously completely unsuitable but at least he didn't look like a conman. In Cassie's imagination that type of man was a slick, snappy dresser.

'Congratulations on your engagement,' Lisa added.

'I am the luckiest man in Lucca!' His eyes twinkled.

Aunt Jane was beaming. Luciano gave her another kiss. 'Now I must introduce you both to my favourite café.'

'We should show them your paintings before we go,' Jane said.

'Another time.' Luciano waved his hand dismissively. 'I am sure they would much rather go for an aperitif. Alonzo and Viviana will look after the shop.'

'I'd love one,' Lisa said.

'Good, that's settled. As long as it's okay with you, my darling.'

'Of course it is. They do a delicious Aperol Spritz at Café Europa,' Jane said.

'*Ciao*, Alonzo!' Luciano shouted.

'*Ciao!*' Alonzo's voice echoed from the back room of the shop.

'*Ciao*, Viviana! Café Europa, here we come!' Luciano held open the door.

Cassie glanced behind her at the window of Galleria Guinigi. Alonzo was putting the choker back out on display.

She turned and followed the others towards the cream umbrellas of Café Europa. Luciano was whistling. Lisa was chatting away. Aunt Jane just looked happy.

The waiter and Luciano greeted each other loudly with guffaws, a handshake and a back-slapping hug. Aunt Jane was kissed on the cheek. Chairs were pulled back and cocktail menus distributed. Cassie was glad to sit down. She was feeling a little peculiar. Perhaps she had caught a touch of the sun.

Chapter Five

The aroma of freshly baked bread mingled with sweet, ripe melon and freshly made coffee; it was worth flying to Italy for this alone, Lisa thought. She hesitated for a millisecond before picking up the metal tongs and helping herself to a flaky *cornetto*. Maybe it was a little unhealthy to add a slice of *crostata* as well, but the glossy peach tart criss-crossed with bands of golden pastry looked irresistible. Cassie was probably limiting herself to a bowl of fresh fruit and a yogurt.

Lisa added a token apple to her plate and walked out through the glass doors onto the Hotel Tosca's sweet little terrace, which was shielded from the pavement by a wooden trellis. Heavenly smelling white jasmine blended with the scents from the terracotta pots filled with pink flowering thyme and a deep green herb called *nepitella* that looked a lot like mint. Lisa had been tempted by a hotel just outside the city walls, which offered guests a spacious dining room with folding doors that led onto a large sunny garden dotted with loungers shaded by striped parasols, but she was glad that Cassie's husband had booked them into this cheaper little hotel in the centre of the town.

'Hi,' Cassie said. She was nibbling on a slice of fragrant melon but the smattering of golden flakes on the yellow tablecloth was evidence that she, too, had succumbed to the temptation of the basket of pastries.

Lisa sat down, hooked up one of the spaghetti straps on her faded vest top and tore off a piece of *cornetto* with her fingers. 'Delicious, aren't they.' She glanced meaningfully at the crumbs on Cassie's side of the table.

'We're going to be doing a lot of walking.' Cassie gave her sister a rueful grin.

'I'm not sure these will hold up much longer.' Lisa stuck out a foot. One of the straps on her well-loved flip flops had broken and was held together with a small gold safety pin.

Cassie pursed her lips; Lisa knew she was struggling not to comment on her worse-for-wear footwear and slightly chipped purple toenail polish.

'Coffee, ladies?' A young man with an ankle-length apron tied around his waist hovered attentively.

'A latte and a cappuccino please,' Cassie said. She looked relieved by the waiter's interruption.

'I'm only joking about wearing these flip flops today. I'm going to change into my trainers – the new ones.'

Cassie's face softened. 'Would you mind watching my handbag whilst I go back to the buffet?'

Lisa wondered who Cassie thought would rifle through her things if she didn't keep an eye on them. The old couple on the next table, who had greeted them with a cheerful *buongiorno*, or the harassed mother in the corner, who had more than enough to contend with as she tried to control two toddlers whilst her husband scrolled down his mobile, oblivious to the chaos?

Cassie reappeared with a solitary peach on a clean plate. She glanced at her dainty watch. 'We'll have to leave in twenty minutes.'

'What's the rush? It's only nine o'clock. I thought we weren't meeting them until eleven,' Lisa said. She was looking forward to doing absolutely nothing for at least an hour after breakfast.

'I didn't think you were listening properly. We're meeting Aunt Jane at half past nine even though Luciano won't be joining us 'til eleven.'

'Oh, why's that?'

'Apparently he's not an early riser. Aunt Jane says he sometimes stays up painting until three in the morning.' Cassie tutted.

'Perhaps he gets inspired and can't stop,' Lisa said. She couldn't help smiling at the image of the great bear of a man flinging paint at a canvas in the middle of the night.

'It just shows how unsuitable he is,' Cassie continued. 'Aunt Jane has always gone to bed early. The last thing she needs is some man crashing around in the small hours and lying in bed until lunchtime.'

'Eleven o'clock is hardly lunchtime,' Lisa said. She picked up a teaspoon and scraped up the last remnants of froth from her cappuccino.

'That's beside the point.' Cassie drained her latte, folded her napkin neatly and pushed back her chair. 'May I use the bathroom first?'

'Be my guest,' Lisa said.

Cassie disappeared back inside the hotel. Lisa took a deep breath and leant back in her chair, soaking up her surroundings. How much more relaxed she felt now Cassie had gone back upstairs. Immediately, she felt guilty. It would have pleased Mum so much to see her daughters on this holiday together. Mum had always longed for the two of them to recapture their childhood closeness. Lisa had tried, she honestly had, but Cassie could be so irritating. Lisa didn't begrudge Cassie her so-called perfect life, but she did object to the unspoken assumption that Lisa should try to emulate her success.

Lisa had been proud of her bright little sister until Cassie started devouring the schoolbooks that Lisa was struggling to understand. It was easier to slope off to the park with her mates or play the class clown than force herself to study when it was clear that Cassie was the clever one. What did it matter? Lisa didn't want to climb some dull corporate ladder. She was happy with her life.

She fiddled idly with her empty coffee cup. A skinny tortoiseshell cat lay at the base of a potted lemon tree, soaking up the sun that was already burning through the cloudless blue sky. It was going to be another glorious day. Snatches of rapid Italian came from the other side of the terrace as the citizens of Lucca walked or cycled past. Ten minutes ticked by. Lisa stood up reluctantly; she could have sat on the terrace all morning but it seemed Cassie and Aunt Jane had other plans.

'Where is she?' Cassie's head swivelled from side to side. 'Aunt Jane is never late. It must be that Luciano's fault.'

'Won't he still be in bed?' Lisa said.

'Exactly. That sort of lolling around is catching.' Cassie scuffed the tip of her shoe on the ground. She'd done that with her Start-Rite sandals when she was an impatient toddler. Lisa suppressed a smile.

'So sorry, girls.' Aunt Jane was panting slightly.

'I do hope you didn't rush on our account,' Cassie said. Lisa was pleased that her sister sounded genuinely concerned rather than sarcastic.

'Oh no, I had to return a recipe book to Livia, Viviana's mother. I never thought I'd be cooking with ingredients like chestnut flour but it's such fun to learn new things. Are you both okay to set straight off?'

'Definitely,' Cassie said.

'Good. I thought we might take a short stroll around this part of town and get our bearings before we meet Luciano. If we head this way, we'll come to the Guinigi Tower.'

'Guinigi – isn't that the same name as the gallery?' Lisa said.

'Yes, the gallery is named after one of Lucca's famous merchant families,' Jane explained as they walked along. 'Those wealthy families competed to build the highest, most prestigious towers. Apparently, there were around two hundred and fifty towers here, but there's only a handful left standing. Look, you can see the Guinigi Tower now, just ahead of us.'

'Are those trees growing out of the top? Surely not?' Cassie stepped back and shielded her eyes with one hand.

'Holm oaks,' Jane said. 'There's a viewing platform on the top.'

'Are there good views?' Lisa said. She longed to climb up and look over the town.

'Marvellous, I believe, though there are two hundred and thirty-two steps to reach them. I haven't been up yet, so when I found out you were both coming, I thought it was something we could do together.'

Cassie bit her lip and shook her head.

'The clock tower is even taller, but there are plenty of wonderful things we can see without climbing any steps.' Aunt Jane smiled at Cassie. 'The Basilica of San Frediano has a stunning byzantine mosaic on the façade. We should have time to squeeze that in.'

'Great,' Lisa said. She wasn't particularly interested in old churches but she was already falling in love with Lucca. There was something so special about the atmosphere in the old town. Perhaps it was the soft light and the wonderful colours everywhere: the yellow and peach-coloured houses;

the bright mopeds that leant against pink and toffee-coloured walls and the deep green of the shutters and leafy trees that contrasted so beautifully with the cream awnings on the cafés.

Lisa followed Jane along the pavement-less streets. She propped her sunglasses on top of her head, the tall buildings either side providing plenty of shade.

'Here we are,' Jane said.

Lisa had never seen a church quite like this. The lower part was an unremarkable plain white marble that provided an effective foil to the shimmering golden mosaic above.

'It's beautiful,' Cassie said.

'The church dates back to the twelfth century but I believe the mosaic was added in the thirteenth,' Jane said.

'More than eight hundred years old; I can hardly get my head around it,' Lisa said.

'There's so much history here.'

Lisa looked at Jane's beaming face; her aunt sounded so proud of the wonderful old buildings and ancient churches that enlivened every corner of the Italian town where she and her new fiancé lived. How brave and adventurous Jane was, leaving behind everything and everybody she knew so well to start a new life at seventy. Lisa hoped that if she were ever in Jane's situation that she, too, would have the courage to do the same and not fear the consequences.

Jane smiled at her as if she could read Lisa's thoughts. Lisa felt a surge of affection for the older lady. Before she knew it, she was giving Jane a spontaneous hug. Jane gave a little shriek of surprise then hugged Lisa back.

'You too, Cassie.' Jane reached out one arm and pulled Cassie towards them. The three of them stood for a few seconds in a slightly awkward group hug. Lisa's face was pressed against her sister's clean, shiny hair. She inhaled her sister's perfume. Miss Dior, the scent Cassie had worn ever since she had begged Mum for a bottle for her sixteenth birthday.

'*Atchoo!*' Lisa jumped backwards. 'Sorry, Cassie, your hair was tickling my nose.' She rummaged in the bottom of her tote bag for a tissue as another sneeze threatened to come.

'Would you like me to take a photo?' The man spoke English with just a faint trace of an Italian accent. He was holding the lead of a small brown terrier.

Lisa straightened up. She was about to reply but Aunt Jane spoke first.

'Matteo, *buongiorno!*' Aunt Jane exclaimed. '*Come stai?* How are you? How lovely to see you.'

'*Bene, bene, grazie.* You are well too, I hope. Are these the nieces I have been hearing so much about? No, Bella! Sorry, she likes to jump up.'

'Dear little thing.' Jane patted the dog's head. 'Yes, this is Lisa and this is Cassie. Girls, this is Matteo.'

Matteo wasn't particularly tall; he wasn't even conventionally handsome, but when he smiled his whole face lit up; his dark eyes glowed as soft and warm as two candle flames.

'My sister, Viviana, mentioned she had met you both,' he said.

'So, you're Viviana's brother?' Lisa said. Why had she come out with such a silly observation? Who else could he be? And she could see the resemblance; he had his sister's high forehead and slim physique.

'Yes, that is right,' Matteo said. He smiled again and Lisa's stomach flipped over. She glanced surreptitiously at his bare ring finger before she smiled back. A flirtation with an attractive Italian man would add an extra frisson to her holiday but she would never dally with a married man. Not after the way Dad had treated Mum.

'Do you live in Lucca?' Lisa asked.

'As much as I live anywhere . . . But yes, Lucca is the place I call home. My mother and sister are here, and of course, Bella.' He ruffled the dog's fur.

'Is she your mother's?' Lisa asked.

'Yes. I have always wanted one of my own but it is not practical. I travel too much. I like to be spontaneous, to see the world.'

'Same here,' Lisa said. She didn't like to dwell on the fact that she had been working at Rosie's Gift Emporium for nearly three years and during that time she hadn't dropped everything to go on a great adventure, or even woken up one morning and gone to Paris on a whim. But she could if she wanted to, couldn't she? She had options, possibilities, freedom. She wasn't tied down like Cassie with her semi-detached, her five-year career plan and dull husband.

'It is nice to meet someone who agrees, for a change.' He smiled.

Lisa was about to ask him what he meant; for some strange reason she wanted to know everything about this man, but Cassie interrupted, telling Matteo that they would love him to take a photograph of the three ladies.

Matteo held up Cassie's sparkly pink phone case. Lisa and Cassie moved either side of Aunt Jane. 'Say cheese,' he quipped. 'Now the two sisters together, I think. It will make a nice souvenir when you return home, yes?'

Lisa gamely put her arm around Cassie's waist. When had she last done *that*?

'Shall I take some on your phone now?' Matteo said.

Lisa handed Matteo her old smartphone. His fingers brushed against hers. She swallowed; her mouth felt dry. She was glad she had succumbed to Cassie's nagging and stashed a bottle of mineral water in her bag. Matteo gestured that they should stand nearer to each other. Cassie leant against Lisa so that their heads were touching.

Matteo handed the phone to Lisa for her inspection. She expanded the photograph until there were just two faces filling the screen. How close they looked; no one would guess how far apart they had grown.

'May I?' To her surprise, Matteo put out his hand to take her phone again.

'Sure.'

'Would you stand up there on the steps? I am going to stand right over there, I would like to get the mosaic in the shot . . . That's right, *perfetto!*'

Lisa stole a glance at Cassie and Jane, but Matteo gave an almost imperceptible shake of his head. Lisa fiddled with her shoulder strap, which was in danger of falling down again. She shifted slightly from foot to foot. Matteo raised the phone and looked straight at her. Lisa tried to smile naturally; she was certain she was grinning like an idiot.

Matteo lowered the phone. Lisa descended the steps.

'Here . . . take a look. I could not resist taking your photograph. Look at your golden-brown hair, that pale green top you wear – see how it picks out that colour in the mosaic.'

Matteo leant over her shoulder as she studied the photograph. She could feel the heat from his body. She felt her face burning and looked away. It was as though a magnet was pulling her towards him. Had she ever felt an attraction as strong as this?

'Oh, Jane, it's gone half ten!' Cassie's voice broke the spell. Trust her to check the time.

'You have to go?' Matteo said.

'We're meeting Luciano for a coffee at Café Europa,' Lisa said.

'He's joining us for a little sightseeing,' Jane added.

'Please give him my best. And I do hope you have a wonderful day.'

'Why don't you come with us?' Jane said.

Lisa felt her heart give a little skip.

'I wouldn't want to intrude . . .'

'We would be delighted,' Jane said.

'Thank you but I will only be able to join you for a short while. I have a rehearsal later on.'

Cassie visibly blanched. Lisa's heart sunk. Matteo was an actor. It was just her luck. Why couldn't he be a jeweller like Alonzo or an artist like Luciano or even a taxi driver or a postal worker or a chef? Anything but the profession that had blighted their childhood. She wouldn't, couldn't, flirt with an actor. Nothing could ever happen between them. Cassie would never forgive her. And she would never forgive herself.

'We wouldn't want to mess up your day,' Lisa said. Even to her own ears she sounded a little cold.

A shadow crossed Matteo's face. 'I am sorry, Jane. I have just realised that I confused the time. It's less than an hour 'til our rehearsal. I will look forward to meeting you all another day.'

'What a shame. We really must be going. See you soon, Matteo. Give my love to your mother.'

Lisa couldn't wait to leave the Piazza San Frediano and sit under one of Café Europa's big cream umbrellas, though she knew there was little chance that people watching in the bustling Piazza Anfiteatro would distract her from the intense disappointment that threatened to overshadow her day.

Chapter Six

Lisa gave Cassie a gentle nudge. Cassie lifted her handbag onto her lap. The flustered-looking couple squeezed into the space next to them.

'Sorry, we always seem to be late,' the woman said in her soft Scottish accent. She placed her shoulder bag on the floor between her feet.

Her husband made a show of looking at his watch. 'Nonsense. Plenty of time; the concert doesn't start for another three minutes.'

The woman raised her eyebrows. Lisa shot her a sympathetic smile.

'It probably won't start for another half an hour. This is Italy!' Luciano said.

Lisa shifted on her seat. It wasn't particularly comfortable but she was glad to sit down after their day spent sightseeing. She noticed the Scottish woman had brought a cushion.

'Isn't that Viviana over there, sitting near the front?' Cassie said.

The light was dim and the church was packed but Viviana's short haircut and black dress stood out amongst the pale linens and summery clothes that filled the rows.

'Oh, yes, she's bound to be here,' Jane said. 'Her brother is playing tonight.'

Lisa's body tensed.

'The guy we met this morning?' Cassie asked.

'Matteo,' Lisa said quietly.

'Oh yes, Matteo's a violinist. He travels all over the world so Viviana and her mother make sure they see him play whenever he comes back home.'

'Even if it's five nights in a row,' Luciano chuckled.

Lisa didn't know whether to be thrilled or dismayed. Matteo wasn't an actor after all. He wasn't off limits. There was no reason to keep her distance, but thanks to her foolish assumption, she had scuppered any chance of getting to know him. What a fool she was.

'Ssh . . .' the woman sitting in front of her hushed her two children. The small group of musicians was filing onto the makeshift stage. Lisa picked Matteo out at once. This morning she would have described him as nice-looking rather than conventionally handsome, but what a difference his crisp white shirt and black jacket made. Lisa couldn't take her eyes off him.

Matteo picked up his violin; the concentration on his face gave him an endearing look of vulnerability.

A statuesque woman dressed in a long-sleeved sequinned gown began to sing. Her voice was pure and full of emotion, holding the highest of notes. The woman was blocking Lisa's view of Matteo, but even though Lisa could no longer see him, she couldn't get his face out of her mind. She had thought about him all day. She couldn't forget the look of confusion and disappointment on his face that morning.

The woman sang on. Lisa couldn't understand the words, but the sound was heart-rending. The last notes died away. The woman accepted the rapturous applause with a modest gesture to the musicians accompanying her.

'*Brava, brava!*' Luciano boomed. The Scottish woman looked rather startled.

A short, bearded man joined the previous singer for the Love Duet from Puccini's *Madame Butterfly*. Their voices portrayed the story with such emotion that Jane had a tear in her eye.

Song after song filled the packed church; some duets, some solos. Most were new to Lisa though she recognised 'Nessun Dorma' straight away. She forgot the discomfort of her seat and let the music wash over her.

The two singers took a bow. Lisa clapped so hard that her hands stung. Matteo dropped his head, his violin in one hand and the bow in the other.

Aunt Jane's party were one of the first out of the church thanks to their seats near the back.

'I was going to tell Matteo how much we enjoyed it.' Jane hovered by the porch. Cassie peered doubtfully back inside. 'It's still a bit crowded in there.'

Lisa fiddled with the strap of her handbag. She wanted to see Matteo again, but did she want to see him *right now*?

'I imagine the performers will stay behind chatting for a while yet,' Luciano said. 'We should hurry along. Our table at Umberto's won't wait for ever, and I'm looking forward to a plate of *osso buco*.' He patted his large stomach at the point where his shirt buttons were struggling to cope.

'Oh dear, we should have been there twenty minutes ago,' Jane said.

'No matter.' Luciano took Jane's arm and set off humming.

Lisa felt Cassie's fingers digging into her lower arm. 'What?' Lisa said.

Cassie shot her a *we've-got-to-talk* look. Lisa slowed her stride so that the two of them lagged a little way behind.

'Did you see that woman?' Cassie hissed.

'Which woman?' Lisa looked around the piazza.

'Not here. In the church. Sitting a few rows behind Viviana, next to the pillar.'

Lisa frowned. She had no idea what her sister was talking about. 'No . . . sorry.'

'You must have seen her – really flamboyant, black hair swept up in chignon with a white streak in the front. She had a purple dress and a bright pink stole over her shoulders. She kept looking over at us.'

'Sounds like you were the one looking at her,' Lisa laughed.

'It's not funny, Lisa. It was really weird.'

'Churches can be a bit creepy sometimes . . . Come on, we're going to lose Luciano and Jane – we need to catch up.' Lisa's thong sandals made a slapping sound as they hurried across the Piazza del Giglio. It was a beautiful, still evening.

Cassie grabbed Lisa's arm. 'Look, look. There she is!'

A woman in a purple dress was just emerging from the church. Her bearing was proud and upright. A bright pink stole was knotted around the handle of the emerald-green bag swinging from the crook of her arm. She turned into a side street. Luciano and Jane carried straight on, through the row of trees that marked the entrance to Piazza Napoleone.

'Are you sure she was looking at us? Why would she do that?' Lisa said.

'It's not us I'm worried about,' Cassie said. 'She wasn't looking at you or me. She kept looking at Aunt Jane.'

Chapter Seven

Lisa's thighs were protesting, but she didn't care. Ninety-eight, ninety-nine, one hundred . . . only another one hundred and thirty steps to go. She rested a hand on the rough brick; a pigeon poked its nose out from a hole in the wall and eyed her curiously. A family were clattering up the metal steps below her.

'How many more steps, Jack?' a woman's voice said.

Lisa redoubled her efforts. She no longer envied Cassie, lingering over a second latte on the terrace of the Hotel Tosca. She was nearly there, nearly at the top of the Guinigi Tower and she knew, even before she stepped out onto the rooftop viewing platform, that it would be worth the climb.

There was something special about looking down on a town or village, and wherever Lisa went, she never felt she had got to know the place until she had climbed to its highest point and experienced a bird's-eye view of the streets below. Being up high had a magic of its own that had captivated her since she was a small child.

One of Lisa's earliest childhood memory was a cold winter's afternoon. She was with her dad walking along the high street. They had been down to the butcher to order the Christmas turkey. The pavement was crowded; Lisa was intimidated by the forest of people's legs and pushchairs surrounding her. As they neared the ironmonger's at the top of the high street, the street became even busier. Lisa squeezed her dad's hand tightly though she could not feel it very well through her thick mitten. 'Dad!' Her voice was a little squeak.

The next moment she was up on his shoulders, his big hands gripping her woolly tights. For a split second she was scared, then she was elated. She was no longer eye level with people's knees and car number plates. She could see for miles. There was a tall tower block in the distance – it looked just like the streets in the old black-and-white movies that Mum liked to watch in the afternoon if she managed to get all the housework done. Lisa told her dad she could see America. He just laughed but she knew she could see New York.

Her dad hadn't carried her on his shoulders again. He said she was too heavy but he didn't carry Cassie either, even though she was a tiny little thing. Lisa didn't mind too much; she would walk along the top of her neighbours' brick walls singing *I'm the king of the castle and you're the dirty rascal* feeling daring and free whilst Cassie trotted along timidly at ground level holding onto Dad with one hand and clutching Ele-pants by one of his grey velour ears with the other.

Lisa had adored her tall, dark, handsome father with his thick brown hair and sparkling eyes. And she wasn't the only one; women looked at him wherever he went. He was an actor, starring in TV commercials and regional theatre, always waiting for the big break that never came. Lisa remembered the day he left as clearly as though it was yesterday: the raised voices quickly hushed; the front door slamming; her mum's tears. Aunt Jane arrived the next day bringing her red tartan suitcase and two big bars of milk chocolate. She stayed for a month.

The next time Lisa saw her dad was at a local shopping centre; Mum had taken them there on the bus to choose party dresses as a special treat. Lisa saw them first: Dad and the young woman with the bouncy ponytail. The woman's stomach was huge; it looked as though she had a beach ball stuck up the front of her dress. Lisa stood rooted to the shiny grey floor tiles and stared at this strange woman who was holding her dad's hand. Cassie hadn't seen Dad; she was busy telling Ele-pants off for doing something naughty. Lisa wasn't quite five years old but some instinct told her it was a day they would never speak of again.

Lisa felt Mum's hand tighten on her shoulder as she steered them away. They went to the park and Mum sat on the bench looking tired and sad. She didn't even look up when Lisa started to clamber up the biggest climbing frame, even though it was supposed to be for much older children. When Lisa reached the top all by herself and looked across the park she felt very alone, but she wasn't scared. She realised she could do anything. She didn't need her dad. She didn't need anyone. And she knew that if there were fewer clouds around, she would be able to see all the way to America.

Lisa still had that wonderful sense of freedom whenever she climbed to the top of a tall building, and that thrill of knowing there was a whole world out there to explore was as strong as ever. From the top of the Guinigi Tower there were views in all directions. The terracotta rooftiles, towers and churches were laid out before her and beyond these, the hills met the perfect blue sky. She walked slowly around the perimeter, stopping every few strides to lean on the railings to take in the view and to wonder about the eccentric Guinigi family who had crowned their tower with the famous holm oak trees that were now synonymous with the city.

The *Lucca Attractions* leaflet was in her pocket. She unfolded it and tried to identify the different churches she could see. But she didn't need the little guide's help to spot the Basilica of San Frediano where she had met Matteo less than twenty-four hours before. If only she had asked him straight away what type of rehearsal he was attending, she would have known he was a musician, not an actor like Dad. Instead, her defences had gone up and she had missed her chance to get to know him.

She picked up her phone to take a couple of selfies against the jaw-dropping views but her heart was not in it. Her finger hovered over the 'photos' icon. It was too tempting to look at the ones Matteo had taken. She shoved the phone back into her bag and began to climb back down the stairs. She didn't want to keep Jane, Luciano and Cassie waiting. They were going to visit the gardens of the Palazzo Pfanner; she would concentrate on enjoying the day. It was stupid to think about Matteo; she and Cassie were only visiting Lucca for a few days, the most she could have hoped for was a holiday fling. Another short-term failed relationship to add to a long list. She pushed away the nagging feeling that had been troubling her ever since he walked away.

Lisa bent over the rose bush until her nose was almost touching the fragrant red petals.

'Watch out for bees!' Cassie exclaimed.

Lisa bit her bottom lip to stop herself laughing. Her younger sister was so cautious, she found imaginary dangers lurking everywhere, even here in the tranquil gardens of the Palazzo Pfanner. Lisa closed her eyes and inhaled the sweet scent.

'*Buongiorno*,' Cassie said.

Lisa opened her eyes and turned around. Her breath caught in her throat. It was Matteo. 'Hi . . . err . . . *buongiorno*,' she managed to mumble.

'*Buongiorno*.' He smiled but his eyes no longer sparkled flirtatiously.

'How lucky we've bumped into you again,' Jane said. 'We wanted to tell you how much we enjoyed the music last night.'

'*Stupendo!*' Luciano said. '*O mio babbino caro*, my favourite by far.'

'Lisa and I thought it was great,' Cassie said.

'You play the violin very well,' Lisa muttered.

'Thank you,' he said. He looked relieved when Luciano interrupted them and steered him away from the rose bushes, talking in Italian.

'*The gardens were designed in the eighteenth century by Filippo Juvarra, who designed the gardens of many houses in the surrounding countryside*,' Cassie read aloud as they strolled down a gravel path lined with lemon trees in heavy terracotta pots.

The path led to a hexagonal pond. A fountain in the centre was sending a plume of water skywards. Two ordinary grey pigeons swooped behind the spray; they looked as romantic as doves in the fairy-tale setting.

'This is so beautiful, don't you think?' Jane said.

Lisa usually preferred messy cottage gardens with tangles of overgrown blooms and meadows of self-seeding wild-flowers but on this occasion, she had to agree with her aunt. The gardens were perfect. Weathered statues stood amongst deep red roses. A woman in a floral smock was clipping a laurel hedge. It would be so relaxing if only Matteo wasn't there. She felt so awkward.

'*There are statues representing each season and the gods of Olympia*,' Cassie continued. 'Oh look, Lisa. That must be autumn holding the sheaf of wheat. I'm going to try and find Diana, she's my favourite.'

'Mmm . . .' Lisa murmured. Since when did her sister have a favourite goddess?

Cassie wandered off. Lisa didn't move from her spot by the fountain. She was watching Matteo and Luciano out of the corner of her eye.

'I've found her.' Cassie had reappeared and was tugging on Lisa's arm.

'Found who?'

'Diana, of course. Come on, let's take some photos beside her.'

'Sure.' Lisa followed her and faked a smile for the camera. Cassie took a couple of shots and handed over her phone. Lisa nodded approvingly. They weren't bad photos of her but neither was half as good as the picture Matteo had taken outside the Basilica of San Frediano.

'I'll take one of you both,' Aunt Jane said. 'Then shall we take a look inside the palazzo?'

'You ladies go ahead. I have seen it a hundred times. Matteo and I will stay out here,' Luciano said.

Lisa followed Cassie and Jane from room to room as they exclaimed over frescoed ceilings, great chandeliers draped with chains of sparkling crystals, a heavily embroidered bed canopy and the copper pots on the walls of the old kitchen. She wished she could share their enthusiasm, but she was distracted by the view from the windows of the figures of Luciano and Matteo in the gardens below.

The two men abruptly broke off their conversation as the three women descended the wide stone staircase.

'What a place to live!' Cassie sighed.

'I am so glad you liked it, but now perhaps it is time for a coffee, I think,' Luciano said. 'Matteo is going to join us – I've absolutely insisted. We'll go to Café Orto. It's a favourite of mine; I can't believe Jane hasn't taken you there yet.'

'That's because you have so many favourite places,' Jane laughed.

'Most of them involving good food and drink, I am embarrassed to say,' Luciano said, but he didn't look a bit embarrassed.

'Eat, drink and be merry,' Jane said. Her eyes were sparkling.

'I'd love a latte,' said Cassie.

'That's all settled then,' Luciano said. He took Jane's hand. 'This way!' He strode out through the gates. Matteo and Cassie followed close behind.

Lisa hung back slightly on the pretext of removing a piece of gravel from her sandal. Ahead of them, the sound of Luciano humming the tune of *O mio babbino caro* drowned out whatever her sister was saying to Matteo.

Café Orto was situated down a narrow side street. The tall buildings on either side blocked out the sun but Luciano, who was rather red in the face, and Jane seemed glad of the shade.

Lisa quickly took the seat next to Luciano. She wasn't sure whether to be disappointed or relieved when Matteo chose the seat furthest away from her and carried on talking to Cassie in a low voice.

'You are enjoying your visit to our beautiful town?' Luciano asked. He tore a chunk of pastry off his custard-filled *cornetto* and crammed it in his mouth. He closed his eyes for a second in a parody of ecstasy. He didn't seem to care that he was the only one who had ordered something to eat.

'Yes, very much, but I'm feeling rather guilty.'

Luciano raised his eyebrows. 'Why is that?' He took another bite; little flakes of pastry scattered over the front of his bright orange shirt.

'We've been here nearly two days and we haven't asked you about your wedding plans.'

'No matter. What is one wedding compared to hundreds of years of history?' Luciano laughed. He placed his big hairy hand over Aunt Jane's and smiled at her. 'How much have you told them?'

'Nothing yet, only what's printed on the invitation.'

'Ristorante Donna Carlotta,' Lisa remembered.

'A lovely, covered terrace and a big function room. I spotted it when I was out birdwatching,' Jane said.

'That sounds perfect. Have you found your wedding outfit yet?'

Jane looked at Luciano. 'It's a secret.'

Luciano clamped his hands over his ears. 'I'm not listening!' He hummed a snatch from 'Nessun Dorma.'

'Pale pink,' Jane whispered. 'A silk jacket with a scalloped edge and a tiered chiffon skirt.'

'Lovely!' Cassie and Lisa chorused.

'But I didn't realise how difficult it would be to find matching shoes, though I suppose cream or white would do . . . It's okay, Luciano, you can listen now,' Jane said.

'Hmm, hmm-di, hmm,' he carried on, oblivious. Lisa inadvertently caught Matteo's eye. He smiled, then he turned his attention back to chatting to Cassie.

'Luciano!' Jane said loudly. She lifted his hands away from his ears.

'Oh, that was quick. When women start discussing outfits it usually takes a long time.'

Jane made a little noise of disapproval.

'What are you doing for the rest of the day?' Matteo asked her.

'We haven't made any plans yet, but Luciano mentioned an art exhibition this evening.'

'Chiara Marinetti has produced a new series of landscapes. She's hosting a private view tonight. She's an old friend of mine, so we're all invited,' Luciano said.

'How kind,' Jane said.

'Is she going to show some of her work at Gallery Guinigi?' Cassie asked.

'It would be a great honour to represent her but as soon as you see Chiara's work, you will realise that it would be impossible. She paints on – how do you say? – a different scale. Her landscapes are vast.' Luciano flung his arms wide apart. Aunt Jane had to duck.

'Her work is impressive,' Matteo added. 'Great, colourful pieces. Her views of the Tuscan countryside are instantly recognisable. She paints scenes that other artists have captured time and time again, yet she conveys the feeling of the places in a way I have never seen before.'

'Sometimes when I look at her work, I want to go back to my studio and burn it to the ground,' Luciano declared.

Cassie gasped.

Jane touched his arm. 'But your paintings are beautiful.'

'I am good. I will never be great.' He shrugged. 'But I am lucky to make a living doing something I love and that has given me a wonderful life.'

'You will enjoy the exhibition, I'm sure,' Matteo said. 'I would go myself if I weren't playing in the concert tonight. If you have no plans for this afternoon, I would suggest a visit to the cathedral if you have not been already.'

'I'm afraid we haven't got around to that yet. I thought I would leave some places for the girls to explore on their own. I could do with putting my feet up for a few hours to be fresh for this evening.'

'Of course!' Lisa said. She was amazed by Jane's energy. She wasn't surprised her elderly aunt needed a rest.

'Well, if you have no objections, I would be delighted to show your nieces around the cathedral,' Matteo said.

'That's a great idea. We'd love that, wouldn't we, Lisa?' There was genuine delight in Cassie's voice.

'Yes, of course.' Lisa felt uneasy. She couldn't help suspecting that Cassie was the reason behind Matteo's change of heart. The pair of them had been chatting so intently. Lisa wasn't worried about Cassie; she knew her happily married sister would never look at another man, but the thought that Matteo might be interested in Cassie made her heart sink.

Chapter Eight

Pia placed a fresh glass of water on the embroidered cloth that covered the bedside table. Her mother stirred gently but she did not wake; she looked so vulnerable with her dark eyes closed. Her eyelashes were still ever so sparse, but her hair was growing back now; it was short and fluffy like the downy feathers on a baby bird.

Pia crept back into the kitchen. She selected a knife and pressed the blade against her thumb – nice and sharp. She sliced into the first artichoke. Although the galley kitchen was situated at the back of their apartment, she could still hear every word coming from the balconies at the front of their block. Elena from the flat below and Mariella who lived in the flat next door conducted all their conversations at top volume. They didn't have much choice if they wanted to hear each other above the noise of crying babies, blaring televisions sets and scooters roaring along the narrow street below. Pia was used to the noise, as were her neighbours; it provided the soundtrack to the lives of all those living in this old part of Naples.

Every afternoon, without fail, Elena and Mariella stood on their balconies discussing what they were cooking for supper and arguing about which stallholder in the market had the tastiest, ripest tomatoes and the biggest and best bunches of basil. Food was a conversational topic they never tired of, even though they cooked the same old dishes time and time again.

'Mario's peppers are the best today – I never saw such beauties,' Elena shouted.

'No, no, no! It is Marco who has the best. He had some today that I swear were as big as my head,' Mariella bellowed back.

Pia knew their discussion was likely to last for quite some time. The two women had no trouble spending half an hour arguing over the best way to chop an onion, a debate that had yet to be settled after more than a decade. Pia was glad her mother was able to sleep through the noise. If they shut the balcony door to their second-floor apartment, the rooms quickly became stiflingly hot and airless.

Pia finished slicing the artichokes. She chopped some garlic whilst the oil sizzled in the large aluminium skillet. Her mind wandered back to the examination she had sat that morning.

'Pia . . .'

She swung around at the sound of her mother's voice. 'Mamma. What are you doing out of bed? The consultant said you should be resting.'

'She said to rest, not sleep all day.' Rosetta reached over and took a wooden spoon from the earthenware pot of utensils.

'I don't need any help,' Pia said. She had been making artichoke risotto since she was seven years old; she could do it with her eyes closed.

'Okay,' Rosetta said. 'But you won't object if I sit on the stool whilst you cook?'

'Of course not.'

Rosetta carefully pulled herself up onto the three-legged wooden stool. She readjusted her floral cotton dressing gown — it was now at least two sizes too big for her — and fastened the belt in a double bow. Pia turned towards the stove; she didn't want her mother to see the fear in her eyes. She tipped some arborio rice into the pan and mixed it around until all the grains were coated. She added the vegetable stock a ladle at a time.

'How good that smells,' Rosetta said.

Steam rose from the pot of risotto. Pia carried it over to the gate-leg table that was wedged into the corner of the living room.

Rosetta perched on a wooden chair. 'Just a little, please . . . Now, tell me how your exam went.'

'Okay, I think. It's so hard to be sure. I know the first-year exams don't count for much but I still want to do well.'

Rosetta touched Pia's arm. 'Of course you do. You worked hard to get to university and one day you'll be a doctor. I can hardly believe it; your papa would be so proud of you if he was here.'

Pia nodded. She didn't risk saying anything.

'Come on, tell me more. Did you get the questions you wanted?'

'More or less.'

'Then I'm sure you did well. I can see it in your face,' Rosetta said. But it wasn't her performance in the examination that was making Pia smile, it was the sight of her mother eating every last grain of rice on her plate.

Pia picked up the plates to carry them through to the kitchen. 'Would you open the bottom door of the dresser,' Rosetta said.

'Why?'

'You'll see.' Rosetta smiled.

Pia bent down. She lifted out a white cardboard box tied with curly, red metallic ribbons. It was sealed with a gold oval sticker. '*Da Frederica!*' Pia said. It was the name of the fancy *pasticceria* by Piazza del Plebiscito. She carried it over to the table.

'Open it,' Rosetta said.

Pia untied the ribbon. She lifted the lid and breathed in the sweet scent of vanilla. The sides of the cake were decorated with crushed hazelnuts, and the words *Buon Compleanno* had been piped across the top in dark chocolate. She looked up at her mother.

'You didn't think I would forget your birthday.'

'But how . . .'

'Mariella collected it for me; she dropped it in whilst you were at the university. I'm sorry I couldn't make one myself this year.'

Pia swallowed the lump in her throat. 'It's beautiful.'

'Shall we have a slice straight away?'

'I'll get two plates.' Pia felt herself grinning from ear to ear. Mamma was definitely getting her appetite back – that was such good news, even though a triple-layered sugar-laden sponge didn't feature on the doctor's diet sheet.

Rosetta ate her piece of cake very, very slowly as Pia chatted on. By the time she laid down her fork she seemed to have a little colour in her cheeks.

'I've got you a present as well,' Rosetta said.

'Mamma!' Pia exclaimed.

'You'll find it wrapped in pink paper in the bottom of my wardrobe. And there's a wooden box on the top shelf – could you bring that in too?'

'Of course. Go and sit on the couch, Mamma. I'll clear the table later.'

Pia found the parcel straight away, resting on a jumble of shoes. It felt soft; perhaps it was a silk scarf, she liked to knot them around the strap of her shoulder bag. The

64

wooden box was on the top shelf, just where her mother had said it would be. It was about a foot wide with an inlaid wooden lid and a key with a faded yellow tassel. Pia hesitated. There had been something strange about her mother's tone of voice; she couldn't quite put her finger on it.

'It's right at the back!' Rosetta called.

'I've found it, Mamma!' Pia carried the box and present into the living room and sat down next to her mother.

Rosetta pushed the pink parcel towards her daughter. 'Go on, unwrap it,' she said.

Pia held the moss-green sweater up against her chest; it was gossamer light and oh, so soft. 'This is so pretty! I can't believe you knitted this for me.'

'I had to find something to pass the time between all those appointments. I'm so glad you like it. But now there's something I need to tell you.'

Rosetta carefully rearranged the cushions. She blinked several times. Her hand was trembling slightly and she was biting her bottom lip. Pia felt slightly sick. Mamma had bad news, she could feel it. She leant forward.

'What is it, Mamma? What has the doctor said?'

'Oh, *carina*! I didn't mean to scare you; this is nothing to do with the hospital. The doctors say I'm making good progress. Nothing has changed.'

'Then what is it, Mamma?'

Rosetta glanced towards the wooden box by Pia's feet. 'There's something that I have been meaning to tell you. I was going to tell you soon after Nonna died . . . but then your papa . . .'

Pia squeezed her mother's bony hand.

'You remember that last day in the hospital with Nonna,' Rosetta said.

Pia nodded. She would never forget it.

'She asked you to go and fetch her a copy of *Oggi* and a can of lemon soda.'

'I had to walk down all those long corridors, and take that slow, old lift. The magazine kiosk was only a couple of streets away but it seemed to take for ever. And by the time I got back . . .' Pia blinked away a tear; it upset Mamma to see her cry. 'I always suspected she sent me away deliberately, that she wanted to spare me.'

'She did. She said you were too young.' Rosetta paused, swallowed. She took a sip of water. 'But there was another reason. She had a secret she needed to share.'

'A secret?' It seemed inconceivable that Pia's plump, homely grandmother had any secrets. Nonna Concetta had lived the simplest, most straightforward of lives.

Rosetta nodded. 'It was something that happened a long, long time ago, something that she had buried away and sworn she would keep to herself. But in the last few days it had been troubling her. I think she needed to unburden herself before she could die peacefully.'

Rosetta hesitated. Pia shifted along the brown couch so that her knees were nearly touching her mother's. Rosetta looked down; she twisted the end of her dressing gown belt around her fingers. Pia waited. Outside, Elena and Mariella were passionately discussing the price of zucchini.

At last, Pia's mother spoke: 'Nonna told me that Nonno Domenico wasn't my real father.'

Pia gasped. 'I can't believe it! Do you think that Nonno knew?'

'That was the first question I asked her; I couldn't bear the thought of my dear papa being deceived for all those years.'

'Surely Nonna wouldn't have kept something so

important from him,' Pia said indignantly. She had loved Nonno Domenico; he had always made time for her.

'Yes, he knew. And he thought I ought to know, but Nonna said that he kept putting it off, and every year that passed it got harder and harder to tell me the truth. He was so fearful of losing me. My poor papa – fancy thinking that way. I could never stop loving him.'

'I can't believe that Nonna Concetta was unfaithful.' Pia shook her head.

'Oh no, it was nothing like that. Nonna was just sixteen when she fell pregnant with me. She was so naive she barely knew what she was doing. When she realised, she was scared out of her wits. She thought her parents would make her give me away. Things were so different in those days; there was so much guilt and shame. But thankfully she confided in someone. You remember your great aunty Maria-Luisa? She was Nonna's best friend.'

'The one with the exotic perfume and the strange felt hats?' Pia smiled at the memory.

'That's right. Nonno Domenico was her older brother. He had always been sweet on my mother, so he saw his chance and asked her to marry him. She was five months gone when they wed. There were a few disapproving looks but no one questioned my parentage; they assumed that he and Nonna had been courting all along.'

'So, who was your father?'

'Nonna didn't tell me. It took so much out of her to tell me as much as she did. Her voice got weaker and weaker. She was struggling to go on. I waited for her, then the sound of her breathing changed. I rang for the nurse but it was too late. She was gone.'

'That's when I came back with Nonna's lemon soda and magazine. But why didn't you tell me all this?'

'It had barely sunk in. It was such a shock – finding out about my real father, and Nonna dying, all at the same time. And your own papa wasn't well.'

'But I could have helped you through it.' Pia did not mean to sound exasperated. She thought of Mamma having to deal with the news all alone. It wasn't right.

'I know that, *carina*, but you were only seventeen. You had just lost your nonna. I couldn't put all that on your shoulders. But now you're nineteen. I didn't want to wait any longer. Each year your studies will keep you busier and busier.'

'I'll always make time for you, Mamma.'

'But soon you won't be able to spare the time to go and search for your real nonno.'

Pia stared at her mother. 'But we don't know who he is. We don't even know if he's . . .' She quickly stopped herself from saying any more.

'Alive. You're right, we don't know for sure, but I've got the strangest feeling my biological father is out there somewhere. After Nonna Concetta and your papa died I was too wrapped up in grief to give much thought to the past. But lately I've become curious. This illness has made me think differently. I don't know how much time I've got left.'

'Mamma! Don't say that! The doctor said you were doing well.'

'I expect I'll be around to bother you for a while yet,' Rosetta laughed.

Pia gave her mother a weak smile. She hated it when her mother made light of her illness. But she could see how Rosetta's eyes were shining; the prospect of finding her real father seemed to have given her mother a new lease of life. Pia couldn't help feeling they would be searching in vain, but if this project helped Mamma, Pia would do whatever she could.

'Of course, I'll help look for your papa,' she said. 'But where on earth do we start?'

'When Nonna passed away, I thought I'd lost my one chance to find out who my real papa was,' Rosetta said. 'I resolved to put it out of my mind; there was no point dwelling on Nonna's words. The past can't be altered and besides, no one could replace your Nonno Domenico. He was my true father; he loved me all those years as if I was his own.

'It was a long time before I could face going through Nonna's things. But then I found that wooden box stashed away in the back of her wardrobe. I knew at once it must contain something important. When I opened it, I found all Nonna's precious keepsakes.'

'A photograph!' Pia gasped. She hadn't realised that she had been holding her breath.

'No, that was too much to hope for. There were photographs, of course: of Nonna's wedding, and of me and your uncle Giorgio when we were small, but that was all.'

'So, we still don't have a clue,' Pia sighed. The discovery of the wooden box had promised so much but it seemed as though they were no further forward.

'There wasn't a photograph of my father but I found something else in the box. Would you open it?'

Pia didn't need to be asked twice. She undid the lock, laid the key with its plump yellow tassel aside and lifted the lid. There was a faint scent of musty old papers and sandalwood.

'Old Valentine's cards,' Pia said.

'So pretty, aren't they? All from Papa.'

Pia opened a scallop-edged card decorated with red roses. She recognised Nonno Domenico's beautiful, curvy handwriting at once. 'He's written a poem inside.'

69

'He wrote one every year. Your grandparents were married in haste, but it's obvious that they were very much in love,' Rosetta said.

Pia hesitated. She wanted to read her grandfather's poems but she was itching to hear what else her mother had discovered.

Rosetta seemed to read her mind. 'Why don't you put them aside to read later.'

Pia turned her attention back to the box. She lifted out a dozen black-and-white photographs and a small pile of letters tied up in pink ribbon. She looked up at her mother.

Rosetta shook her head. 'I read them all but none of them mention him.'

No pictures, no letters. Finding Mamma's real father was looking less and less likely.

'Look at that drawing,' Rosetta said.

Pia carefully took out a sheet of white paper. The blue pastel drawing depicted nearly the same image that she saw in the mirror every morning.

'Didn't Nonna always say she looked exactly like you when she was young.'

'I could see a resemblance in some of her old photographs, but this – this is something else!' The drawing was a wonderful find, but Pia could not imagine how an old sketch of her grandmother was going to help them.

Rosetta's eyes were shining. 'Look at the writing in the bottom corner.'

'*La ragazza più bella - Firenze. Bacci, L.* The most beautiful girl – Florence. With kisses, L. It's a beautiful drawing but I still don't get it.'

'Look at the date – right there in the bottom corner: 11ᵗʰ June 1965. That portrait of Nonna Concetta was drawn exactly nine months before I was born.'

Chapter Nine

'There are so many cathedrals in Italy, all beautiful in their own way, but Lucca's is special. At least I like to think so.' Matteo flashed that wonderful smile of his as he, Lisa and Cassie crossed the Piazza Bernardini.

'Everything about this place is special,' Lisa said. The glorious piazzas, the quirky churches, the mighty city walls . . . she loved it all. A bicycle bell pinged. Lisa stepped aside as an elderly woman with gold sandals sailed past. The woman raised one hand in acknowledgement, the other held the long lead of a chihuahua that was scampering along behind her.

'So dangerous . . .' Cassie murmured.

'Good thing I didn't have headphones in!' Lisa joked.

'The bicycles in Lucca are almost as bad as the scooters in Naples.' Matteo had a straight face but she knew he was teasing them.

They carried on down the via Santa Croce; the cathedral was ahead of them now. Cassie slowed down.

'I know this sounds really rude, but I've done so much sightseeing I'd rather sit down at that café over there and have a coffee and write my postcards. Would you mind terribly if I didn't come to the cathedral with you?'

'Of course . . . if you prefer,' Matteo said. 'You will let me show you the cathedral, Lisa, won't you?'

'Yes, that would be great.' Lisa gave Cassie a quizzical look. Cassie carefully limited the amount of caffeine she drank. And who on earth still wrote postcards? If Cassie did, she had certainly never sent Lisa one. Cassie's expression revealed nothing; her face was as blank and innocent as a choirboy's.

As soon as she was out of earshot, Lisa turned to Matteo. 'How strange.'

Matteo laughed. 'I think your sister is kindly giving us the opportunity to spend a little time together.'

'But . . . I . . .'

Matteo touched Lisa's arm. 'It is okay. When I saw how uncomfortable you looked this morning, I realised there must be a reason why you seemed to snub me yesterday. I did not want to embarrass you by asking so I quizzed your sister. You thought I was an actor, that is right? And that brings back bad memories for both of you, I understand.'

Lisa glanced down. 'I shouldn't have jumped to conclusions. I'm sorry.'

'No, it is I who should be sorry. I went off and sulked like a child. I decided to forget I had met you. Then I saw you at the concert . . .'

'You saw us in the audience?'

'I had to look away; it was affecting my playing. Every time I caught sight of you, I could hardly concentrate on the notes.'

Lisa smiled. Matteo's lines were corny, but his dark eyes were sincere.

'Besides, how could I miss you? You were sitting next to a huge hairy artist in a bright red shirt.'

'Luciano is rather flamboyant, isn't he?' Lisa laughed.

'And your aunt is so sweet and quiet. They make an unusual couple, but sometimes opposites attract, I guess.'

'Try telling my sister that. She's very protective of Aunt Jane.'

'And of you, too.'

'Of me? I don't think so.' Lisa shook her head. Why would Cassie be protective of *her*? It had always been the other way around.

'Here we are.' Matteo gestured to the three-arched portico that framed the entrance to the cathedral. 'I would like to share with you my favourite part: the tomb of Ilaria del Carretto.'

'Sure,' Lisa said, though she couldn't imagine how a tomb could be anyone's favourite feature.

'But first, this.' He took a fine cotton scarf from his pocket.

'Oh, thanks.' She felt herself blush. She hadn't thought about the necessity of covering up in the holy building but a notice in the entrance made it clear that a strappy vest top wasn't suitable attire. He draped the soft striped fabric around her shoulders. She felt his strong warm hands through the flimsy material. He was so near to her. She held her breath.

'Perfect. Now we go inside.'

Lisa blinked as her eyes became accustomed to the dim light after the brightness of the piazza. It was pleasantly cool inside. Huge pale columns stretched skywards. The interior was vast; even her clumpy sandals looked tiny against the inlaid marble floor. She tipped her head back to look at the gold stars on the vaulted ceiling.

'And now I will take you to meet Ilaria del Carretto. Come this way.'

The sculptor had depicted Ilaria in a high-necked draped dress. She lay atop a carved tomb decorated with cherubs. Her eyes were closed, her head rested on a carved tasselled cushion.

'She looks so peaceful,' Lisa said. It was hard to resist the urge to reach out and touch the figure's smooth marble cheek.

'It's called *The Eternal Sleep*. She was the second wife of Paolo Guinigi, Lord of Lucca. She was terribly young when she died in childbirth.'

Lisa's hand flew to her mouth. 'How awful.'

'Her husband commissioned Jacopo della Quercia, one of Italy's greatest sculptors, to build this monument to commemorate her. Look, here at her feet is her little dog, a symbol of her faithfulness. Such tenderness, such devotion preserved for eternity . . .' Matteo's voice trailed away. He was silent, seemingly lost in thought.

'It's one of the most beautiful things I have ever seen,' Lisa said. To her surprise she realised she was close to tears.

Matteo touched her cheek. 'You are not the first or last person to be moved by this. It is tragic when somebody dies so young.'

'I don't know how people can move on from something like that,' Lisa said.

'But they do,' Matteo said. 'Though it is hard. Look at Luciano.'

'Jane told me he'd been widowed but I didn't realise his wife had been so young,' Lisa said. The cathedral was glorious, but she was glad they were making their way back out into the sunshine.

Matteo held open the heavy wooden door. 'I wasn't thinking of Luciano's wife; she was in her late sixties, though of course that's no age at all. No, it was his brother who was taken early.'

'Jane has never mentioned that.'

'Frankie passed away when he was just a teenager. It was a real shock. One moment he was playing football in the street. The next he was gone. An undiagnosed heart condition, they said. Luciano doesn't mention him often. He still finds it hard to talk about, even with your aunt, I imagine.'

'No wonder. How dreadful.'

'I think that is one of the reasons Luciano is so keen to enjoy life. He knows how easily everything can change. But that is enough sadness. Let us go somewhere less poignant.'

'Where do you have in mind?'

'Gelateria Gabriele. The best ice-cream in Lucca.' He gave her a boyish grin.

Lisa laughed.

'See, you are happy again and we haven't even got there!' He took her arm and they walked in the direction of the city wall. She still had his cotton scarf wrapped around her shoulders; she began to unravel it.

'No, keep it. It suits you and it will stop your shoulders getting burnt.'

'Thanks,' Lisa said. She knotted the scarf's two ends together to stop it sliding off. Whenever she tilted her head, she caught a waft of Matteo's citrus cologne.

Cassie watched Lisa and Matteo walk away. She headed up the side street and took a seat outside the tiny café she had spotted.

An elderly woman with a white pinafore appeared unusually quickly.

'A latte please.' Cassie surprised herself; she didn't normally drink coffee past lunchtime.

'*Mi dispiace . . .*'

Cassie smiled blandly. 'I'm sorry, I don't speak Italian.'

'Please, one minute.' The waitress disappeared back inside the dark interior. Cassie waited. A young boy sitting at the next table slurped noisily on a raspberry-coloured drink. His mother toyed with her phone. Cassie studied her fingernails critically; one had a slight snag. She took out her nail file.

'Excuse me . . .'

Cassie looked up. It was a much younger waitress this time. 'I am so sorry, *signora*, our coffee machine – it is broken. My brother, he will fix it today but when, I do not know . . .'

'Never mind.' Cassie slipped her nail file into the inside pocket of her bag. She stood up.

'You will find several cafés in Piazza Napoleone, that way, just the other side of Piazza del Giglio. Do you want me to show you on the map?'

'No, it's okay, I will find it, but thank you, *grazie*.'

Cassie recognised the Piazza Napoleone immediately; it was where they had dined at Umberto's the previous night. Three sides of the large rectangular piazza were edged with huge leafy plane trees. The fourth was completely dominated by a sandy-coloured building.

The piazza was clearly a popular place by day, too. Every eating establishment was buzzing with people, some of whom had parked their mopeds and bicycles in the racks under the trees. She scanned the seating areas to no avail.

She was about to give up when she noticed some white tables and chairs in a shady spot situated just off the piazza. A waiter wearing an apron down to his ankles was moving between the packed tables with a round tray crammed with drinks balanced on one shoulder. Seeing Cassie hovering, he inclined his head towards a tiny table awkwardly positioned right in the middle of the rows of seating.

'Please, take a seat,' he said.

Cassie shuffled sideways past a table of three women all talking at once in rapid Italian, pulled out a white metal chair just far enough to enable her to squeeze in and placed her handbag on the adjacent seat. She breathed in through her nose, held her breath for the count of three and slowly exhaled. It was such a relief to be alone. She didn't regret coming to Italy with Lisa; she knew how happy their late mother would be to know her daughters were spending quality time together, but a week with Lisa was already starting to feel like a long, long time.

It was now hard to believe how close they had been as children. Cassie had adored her big sister, but by the time they were teenagers they had started to drift apart. Once they were older, they had tentatively tried to rebuild their friendship but it was never the same. And when Cassie announced her engagement to Paul, the thin crack between them became an unbreachable chasm. Lisa's attitude to Cassie changed. Cassie was sure Lisa looked down on her for settling for someone as safe and sensible as Paul. Cassie felt judged and she did not like it one bit.

'You are ready, *signora*?' The waiter tilted his head towards her, careful not to unbalance his tray which was now loaded with empty glassware.

'Just a latte, please.'

Cassie used her fingerprint to open her phone. The screen sprang to life, Paul's face appearing on the screen saver. Her husband might well be dull by Lisa's standards, but he was certainly handsome. She ran her forefinger over the smooth gold curve of her wedding ring. Paul was a good man and they shared the same goals and aspirations. That mattered more than the times when he buried himself in his spreadsheets in preparation for yet another terribly important meeting and Cassie wanted to rip them out of his hands and shout 'Look at me! Speak to me!' Cassie was determined to focus on the positives. She knew that deep down, every woman wanted a stable marriage like hers. No one really wanted to drift from partner to partner and end up alone. Everyone needed someone. Just look at poor Aunt Jane, so lonely since Eddie died that she had thrown away her life in England to move in with a man she hardly knew.

Cassie checked her emails. Several from Paul, all concerning their new kitchen extension, no doubt. She felt a little frisson of excitement mixed with nerves. It was such a big project; so many things could go wrong. And the cost – she hardly dared think about that, but the bank had agreed in principle to extend their mortgage and it *was* an investment, wasn't it?

She clicked on the first email; a local firm had supplied an alternative quote. Cassie skimmed quickly to the estimate. It was still an awful lot of money but the computer-generated drawings were everything she had dreamt of. She could imagine it all so clearly: standing at the central island with her sleeves rolled up chopping fresh, green herbs; the aroma from a huge copper casserole simmering on the stove; and one day two children (a girl and a boy she hoped) playing in the corner of the room. It would all be worth it.

If only Lisa would settle down too, one day their children might play there together. If they both became mothers, they might have something in common again. Maybe Cassie had been wrong to encourage Lisa's interest in Matteo – he was never going to be husband material – but she had seen the way they looked at each other. And what harm could a trip to the cathedral do? A brief flirtation might cheer Lisa up; she had been a little down since her break-up with Max the poet, no matter how much she insisted to the contrary.

Matteo wasn't an actor after all, thank goodness, but he was a musician and men like that – with flaky jobs and unsettled lifestyles – weren't long-term prospects. Nor were artists, Cassie thought grimly. Luciano seemed nice enough and Cassie had to admit he had done nothing to arouse her suspicions, but she knew enough about men to know that artistic types, particularly *Italian* artistic types, didn't fall for unworldly, quiet, seventy-year-old ladies. It couldn't, wouldn't work. But how was she going to convince Aunt Jane? She picked up the cup of coffee that had appeared silently by her elbow and sipped it, lost in thought.

'*Ciao*! Hello again.'

Cassie felt Alonzo's presence almost before he spoke. Her nostrils filled with the intoxicating scent of his oriental cologne. Her body tensed, all her senses switched to high alert like a gazelle facing a lion in one of Paul's favourite wildlife documentaries. Heat rose to her cheeks as her memory flashed back to her first evening in Italy, the visit to the Guinigi Gallery and the moment when he had fastened the rose-gold choker around her neck.

'Hi . . . err . . . *ciao*!'

'May I?'

Cassie glanced around. Her handbag was taking up the café's only spare seat. She slipped her phone back inside.

'Of course.'

Alonzo tried to suppress a smile as Cassie perched her new bag on the edge of the table. What did he think she was going to do with it? It was white leather; she certainly wasn't going to plonk it on the floor.

'Another coffee?'

'No, thank you . . . I mean yes . . . yes please.' Cassie didn't want another coffee; she wanted to grab her bag and go, but she knew it would look rude – and odd. She desperately wanted to act as normally as possible. And to *feel* as normal as possible, instead of experiencing this strange mixture of elation and panic.

'*Due caffè per favore*,' Alonzo said. The waiter nodded. 'I ordered you an espresso. I couldn't order you another latte, all that milk in the afternoon will play havoc with your digestion.'

'Thank you,' Cassie said. She didn't care what he ordered as long as she had a cup and saucer in front of her. It would give her something to do with her hands.

Alonzo stretched back in his seat clasping his hands behind his head. She couldn't help noticing the bulging muscles under the fabric of his white shirt. He tilted his face towards the sun.

Cassie shifted in her seat. If only she could feel half as comfortable as Alonzo looked. Five minutes ago she had been perfectly relaxed; now she could feel a trickle of nervous sweat running down her neck. Alonzo's eyes were half closed. She wished he would fall asleep so she could slip away quietly.

He opened his eyes and smiled lazily. 'I hope I am not interrupting you, but there was nowhere else to sit.'

'Not at all. I was just catching up on some emails; my husband has been updating me on our kitchen extension.' The words *my husband* suddenly sounded so unreal.

'That sounds like a big project.'

'Yes.'

'And it is going well?'

Cassie didn't believe Alonzo was remotely interested, but she was glad they had found a neutral subject of conversation. Talking about practical matters might distract her from Alonzo's limpid green eyes and the little mole placed tantalisingly above his full lips.

'Yes. Paul, my husband, even managed to track down the floor tiles I wanted the other day. I found them in an old copy of *House and Garden*, they were discontinued, you see.' How boring she sounded.

'I know that magazine. I could introduce you to the Italian version, but I feel it could be dangerous.' He laughed. He had a lovely, genuine laugh. It was so hard to think about kitchen tiles.

'Shall I show you?' Cassie busied herself rummaging for her phone in her bag. She couldn't understand why she found Alonzo's presence so disturbing. She was a happily married woman. Very happily married.

'Of course . . . let me see . . .' She handed him the phone. Its pink, sparkly case looked ridiculously feminine in his large hand. 'These are beautiful. The design is so subtle yet exotic at the same time.'

'They're called "Shades of Egypt". I've been fascinated with Egypt ever since I first watched *Death on the Nile*.'

'"Shades of Egypt"? Yes, yes, of course. I see it now. You have chosen well – and to tile your floor for three hundred pounds you have found quite a bargain.'

'Per metre.' Cassie spoke before she could stop herself.

Alonzo's eyes widened. 'That's going to add up to thousands of pounds unless your kitchen is very small.'

'Just under five thousand – but we're getting basic units from Ikea.' Cassie knew she sounded rather defensive.

'Of course. Forgive me. It was rude of me to comment on the cost of your plans. This project is important to you, I can tell.'

'Yes, it is.' Cassie swallowed half a mouthful of espresso. She and Paul had spent hours scrolling through websites and flicking through kitchen brochures. Her dreams and plans had dominated her life for months. Why should she feel embarrassed about that? Alonzo's expression was neutral but she was sure he was judging her. She felt a surge of irritation. 'So, what would you do with the money?'

He leant forward, his forearms resting on the table. 'That's a very good question . . . I would rather like a new car. But if I already owned a smart car and I loved the idea of Egypt, like you, I would take a trip there and sail down the Nile on a wooden gulet.'

'All that money – on a holiday?'

'Perhaps you are right. A holiday only lasts a week but with your new tiles you will experience a little bit of Egypt every day.'

There was no hint of sarcasm in Alonzo's voice. Her eyes met his, but they betrayed nothing but warmth and friendship. Even so, Cassie felt herself bristling. She pushed back her chair and stood up.

'Thank you for the coffee, but I must be going.'

The lobby of the Hotel Tosca was cool and quiet. Cassie and Lisa's room key was still hanging on the little hook behind the reception desk. Cassie climbed the stairs and unlocked the door. The beds were freshly made and someone had folded her yellow cotton nightdress and put it under her pillow. She propped a couple of quilted cushions against the painted headboard and tucked her legs up under her.

Cassie reopened the first email from Paul and enlarged the image of the floor tiles. They *were* beautiful. She *would* experience a little bit of Egypt every day. She turned her attention to the other two messages that she hadn't had chance to peruse thanks to Alonzo's unexpected appearance. They were both quotes forwarded from local painters and decorators. She and Paul had chosen a warm, sandy colour for the dining area and off-white for the kitchen with a feature wall in golden-yellow. Or rather Cassie had chosen the colours and Paul had made a grunt that she had taken as approval. The extension had seemed so important.

Now she couldn't be bothered to click on the attachments. Maybe Alonzo was right. Perhaps there was something more exciting that she and Paul could spend the money on. Something that would help bring back the closeness she'd felt before Paul started working late all the time.

She lay back on the bed staring at the ceiling fan turning slowly. Images from *Death on the Nile* drifted through her mind. She imagined herself in a long, wafty dress sailing through a land of camels and pyramids under a fierce, high sun. But try as she might, she couldn't picture Paul there. She could only see Alonzo in a white linen shirt gazing at her with his mesmerising green eyes.

A rap on the door shook her out of her reverie.

'Cassie!'

'Uh, hold on.'

'Thanks.' Lisa tossed her shoulder bag on her bed.

'New scarf?'

Lisa touched the striped fabric self-consciously. 'It's Matteo's.'

'So, you had a good time?' Cassie did not need to ask. Lisa's glow obviously wasn't just caused by the sun.

'Yes. The cathedral was beautiful, really worth visiting. Then we went for an ice-cream at Gelateria Gabriele. I had the most amazing caramel and *stracciatella* – that's vanilla with shards of dark chocolate. And Matteo, he's lovely, he really is. Thank you.'

'What for?'

'For smoothing over our misunderstanding then leaving us alone together. But I'm surprised. An Italian musician . . . I didn't think he was the sort of man you approved of.'

'I don't.' Cassie shrugged. 'But I saw the way you looked at each other. At least he's got nice manners and he's clean and smartly dressed for a change, but I don't suppose it really matters what he's like.'

'Because it won't last?'

Cassie bit her bottom lip and glanced down. 'You don't have the best track record.'

'Maybe I don't want to settle for Mr Boring,' Lisa snapped.

Cassie's head jerked up. 'So, you admit it at last. You think Paul's boring. You think I'm boring.'

'Hey!' Lisa put her hands up. 'Wait a minute. I never said that.'

'No, but you think it. Ever since Paul and I got engaged, you've looked down on me because I've got an office job and married the first man who asked me. Being a free spirit doesn't make you superior. All you've got is a dead-end job and a series of short-term flings.'

'Superior!' Lisa spluttered. 'You're joking! I wouldn't want your life but has it ever occurred to you that maybe I couldn't get a job like yours?'

'You could have tried harder at school instead of skiving off to lie around in the park sharing cheap bottles of cider with your mates.'

'At least I had friends!'

'See! You always make me feel bad. How do you think I felt studying alone in my room whilst you were always Little Miss Popular?' Cassie said.

'What about me? How do you think *I* felt watching you race through the books I was struggling with before Mum took them back to the library, knowing my little sister was smarter than me?' Tears sprang to Lisa's eyes. She bit her lip. She looked as though she was going to cry. Cassie's big sister never cried.

'I'm sorry, Lisa. I never thought . . .'

'No, you never do. You never think before wading in and telling me how I should live my life.'

'And you never think before you judge me,' Cassie sniffed.

They faced each other across the room. Glaring. Voices rose from the street below.

'Maybe you're right, maybe I have been judging you,' Lisa said. She sounded tired.

'I'm sorry,' Cassie muttered. She wasn't that sorry, but she couldn't bear raised voices and arguments. She had heard enough of those as a child.

'I'm sorry too,' Lisa said. 'Let's forget it. We'd better hurry up and get ready. We don't want to keep Jane and Luciano waiting.'

'Don't mind if I use the shower first? You know it takes me ages to blow dry my hair and redo this French pleat.'

'Sure.' Lisa flopped on the bed and picked up her dog-eared paperback. Cassie suppressed the urge to tut; she hated the way her sister turned down the pages to mark her place.

Cassie stood under the hot shower. She took a deep breath, her nostrils filling with the scent of the pink grapefruit shower gel. She exhaled slowly. Gradually she felt the tension in her body begin to ebb away. She hated arguing with Lisa, but in a way it was a relief to finally articulate some of the resentments she had harboured for so long. At least their fight had distracted Lisa from asking Cassie how she had spent the rest of the afternoon. She wasn't sure she would be able to mention Alonzo without betraying a hint of the strange tangle of emotions he aroused in her.

She stared at her reflection in the misty shower screen, watching the frothy soap suds run down her legs. She looked no different on the outside but something within her had shifted. Back in England she had been so content with her life, so confident about everything. Meeting Alonzo had shaken her out of her complacency. Her calm existence had been turned inside out by a man she had only just met. Now she no longer knew what she wanted. Her house, her husband, her plans for the future – they all seemed to belong to someone else's life. She couldn't allow this to happen. She had to get her life back on track. She would avoid Alonzo for the rest of the holiday. She would forget they had ever met.

Chapter Ten

Concetta wanted to skip and run and jump for joy but she forced herself to walk slowly down the steep street that led to via Toledo. Mamma was watching her from the balcony whilst she pegged out the sheets. Concetta tucked her bobbed hair behind her ears and swept her long fringe out of her eyes. She wished she was wearing her new pink dress with the big white buttons but she couldn't risk arousing Mamma's suspicions. Her old check skirt and yellow blouse would have to do.

She did feel a bit bad telling Mamma that she was spending the day with Maria-Luisa (the only girl with a mother stricter than her own) but she couldn't take the chance that she could be prevented from leaving the house.

Once she hit the main shopping street she quickened her pace, swinging her arms and singing to herself: long, long live love! *The English singer, Sandie Shaw, was her new favourite. London was so cool; 'swinging London' they called it. She had seen the photographs of the Kings Road and Carnaby Street. It was a world away from the backstreets of Naples. Maybe she'd go there someday. Maybe* they'd *go there.*

Concetta turned into Spaccanapoli, the old Greek thoroughfare that crossed the city. It had rained in the night; water was trickling across the dark paving slabs and the gutters were overflowing. The sun had come out now, but Concetta didn't care if it carried on raining until Christmas. Today was the most exciting day of her life. She was off to meet the boy she was going to marry.

Maria-Luisa was so excited to share Concetta's secret. Neither of them could believe how lucky she was. Fate had smiled on Concetta the day she met the boy from Lucca as he sketched by the side of the River Arno. Mamma's sister, Aunt Zita, allowed Concetta to wander the streets of Florence at will on her twice-yearly visits. Concetta could go wherever she pleased whilst Zita lolled on the couch reading her beloved movie star magazines. It was their little secret.

Concetta had fallen in love with him straight away. He was so funny and kind and handsome – even cuter than George Harrison, her favourite Beatle. She would never forget their first kiss. Then on their last evening together, he had taken her to the small hotel where he was staying. She had felt a mixture of excitement and nerves as he gently undressed her. He had stopped and asked her if she was okay. She nodded; she knew she did not want him to stop. She wasn't sure exactly what had happened, but after discussing it with Maria-Luisa, Concetta's suspicions were confirmed. She had done 'it'. She knew it was wrong because she wasn't married, but she didn't regret it one bit.

When she had finally got back to Aunt Zita's apartment that evening, her aunt had given her an appraising look. Concetta thought Zita was going to ask her some awkward questions, but her aunt was more interested in showing her the new pictures of Gina Lollobrigida in Bolero Film.

Concetta passed the Capone fountain; she was nearly at the railway station. She was still a few minutes early. She smoothed down her check skirt, took out her compact and lipstick – she would need to remember to wipe it off before she got home – and carefully applied her make-up.

She waited by the station entrance, hopping from foot to foot. It was impossible to keep still. Would he kiss her in public? She hoped he would. There was nowhere in Naples where they could be alone.

The passengers pouring off the train slowed to a trickle. He was not amongst them. She tried to tell herself she must have got the day or time wrong, although she knew she hadn't. They had written it on the backs of their hands.

Train after train arrived. She waited there all morning. Still, he did not come. Morning turned to afternoon, afternoon to evening. Men in business suits began to exit the station, some hugging waiting wives and children.

Tears ran down Concetta's face as she walked away. He hadn't loved her. He didn't care. It was all a lie.

She would have to keep their brief relationship a secret from everyone, apart from Maria-Luisa. If people knew what she'd done she would be shunned, labelled as 'damaged goods'. Mamma would be so ashamed. She thanked God there couldn't be any consequences. Maria-Luisa had told her you couldn't get pregnant the first time.

Concetta walked down Corso Garibaldi in a daze and made her way through the Porta Nolana to the marina. There was less chance of meeting anyone she knew this way. She trudged along slowly, dragging her heels. She dreaded going back to their apartment and fielding Mamma's cheerful enquiries about how she and her best friend had spent their day.

She stopped partway home and sat on a rock overlooking the harbour. The sun was beating down. Two girls sunbathed nearby, oblivious to her pain. Eventually the darkening sky forced her to make her way back home.

The aroma of her mother's meatballs lingered in the hallway, but Mamma and Papa weren't there. A note leaning against the coffee pot told her that they were visiting their downstairs neighbours who had recently acquired their own television. Relieved, she threw herself on the bed and sobbed into her pillow.

When she didn't think she had any tears left, she leant down and yanked open the bottom drawer of the bedside chest. She unfurled the blue pastel sketch and stared at the portrait he had drawn. Her face smiled mockingly back at her. How happy she looked. What a fool she'd been.

She gripped the sketch by opposing corners, about to rip it in half. A key turned in the lock. Papa's voice: 'We're back!'

She quickly rolled up the picture and hid it at the very bottom of the drawer. She wouldn't destroy it, but she vowed she would never look at it again as long as she lived.

Chapter Eleven

Chiara Marinetti's exhibition was packed. Luciano was busy talking to an earnest young man in oversized glasses and an air-force-blue boiler suit. Lisa and Cassie were on the other side of the room. Jane hoped the two girls had not fallen out; there was a strange atmosphere between them.

Jane held her glass of sparkling wine close to her chest. She squeezed into a gap in the crowd. She studied the giant painting in front of her: an avenue of cypress trees leading to a lone villa set amongst rolling hills. The classic view of the Tuscan countryside had been painted a thousand times before, but Chiara had made it her own. The canvas pulsated with vibrant colour. The scene was so strange, yet so real. Jane felt that if she ran straight through the canvas she would find herself in the hills above Lucca instead of knocked out cold on the gallery floor. She swayed forward slightly. The painting seemed to be calling her like a siren luring a fishing boat onto the rocks. Chiara's work was incredible, but she wasn't sure she liked it very much. Jane stepped away, feeling slightly disturbed.

A hand touched her arm. Jane felt the hairs on the back of her neck stand up.

'Buonasera.' Viviana was smiling at her. As usual, the younger woman was dressed all in black except for an extraordinary necklace that looked as though it had been fashioned from shards of green glass.

'*Buonasera*. This is quite a turnout. You must be pleased.'

'Chiara's shows are always popular.' Viviana turned her beaming smile on a passing waiter. 'This lady would like another drink.'

'Oh, thank you.' Jane was surprised to find she had drained her glass. The waiter held the bottle at an exaggerated height and poured out a stream of wine. Tiny bubbles fizzed on the surface of Jane's glass.

'Her work is extraordinary, isn't it?' Viviana's eyes were shining.

'I've never seen anything like it,' Jane said truthfully.

'I'm terribly sorry, I have to go.' The boy in the boiler suit was tugging on Viviana's sleeve. Jane was left standing all alone.

She turned her attention to the painting on the opposite wall: an ancient olive grove of gnarled old trees in shades of purple; a small tower on the horizon; a vineyard of shocking pink grapes. Jane remembered snippets from the History of Art night classes she had attended long ago. What would her classmates have thought of this? Hints of Van Gogh, Hockney perhaps. But it was hard to analyse Chiara's techniques when Jane's hand itched to reach out and pluck a grape from the dense paint.

'Excuse me!'

Jane realised she was standing in the way. She moved aside to allow an elderly woman in a turquoise turban and floor-length kaftan to take a better look. The woman had at least six strings of amber beads strung around her crepey neck. Everyone in the room looked so cool and arty; Jane's classic pleated skirt felt all wrong.

Jane squeezed between two people to look at the next painting. She could just about get near enough to read the small print on the little card on the wall. *Olive Grove 3*.

She stepped out of the way. A waiter was wending his way through the crowd, holding out an oval platter.

'Would you care for a *vol-au-vent col cacio*?'

'*Grazie.*' The cheesy filling oozed out as Jane bit into the pastry case. She quickly crammed in the rest before it fell on her skirt. A flake of pastry caught in her throat and made her cough. A man with frameless spectacles and his willowy partner shot her sympathetic glances.

All around her, fashionable people talked nineteen to the dozen in rapid Italian. Jokes were laughed at; opinions shared. Everyone looked so confident. This was nothing like the art exhibitions she had attended in her village hall. Everywhere she looked, the kaleidoscope of colours made her head spin. It felt as though Chiara's paintings were closing in on her.

Jane undid the button at the throat of her silk blouse. Someone knocked into her from behind. She clamped her hand over the top of her glass just in time. She looked around the crowded room but Lisa, Cassie and Luciano were nowhere to be seen. Suddenly she longed to be back in Sundial Cottage with a small glass of sherry, a shepherd's pie in the oven and Hercule Poirot on the television. She didn't belong in this world.

'Excuse me! Excuse me!' Jane picked her way through the throng, not caring if she elbowed one or two people. She desperately wanted to get outside. She sighed with relief when she felt the soft breeze. She gulped in a lungful of cool air.

A streetlight glowed softly against the dark sky. The strains of Puccini's '*E lucevan le stelle*' from a nearby window carried on the still night air. Jane realised she was still holding her wine glass. A feeling of calm came over her as she slowly sipped her drink. She watched a ginger cat rubbing its head against the base of the lamppost.

Jane felt a hand on her arm. She let out a small cry.

'Jane, darling! I didn't mean to startle you,' Luciano said. 'Are you okay? I was looking everywhere for you.' He wrapped his arm around her waist. She leant her head against his shoulder, breathing in his familiar, comforting scent. She looked up into his kind eyes. How she loved this man. She would brave a hundred opening parties to be with him. She couldn't imagine why she had felt so despondent just a few minutes before. She loved her life here, but everything was new. She should have known it wasn't always going to be easy.

'I'm fine,' Jane said. 'But it was a little warm in there and rather crowded.'

'But it is wonderful to see so many people supporting such a talented artist,' Luciano said.

'It seems to be a great success. I noticed there were some of the red *sold* stickers on the name cards already.'

'I predict a sell-out. I truly believe she is the best colourist since Matisse. Such a marvellous exhibition and later there is an after-party at a nightclub off Piazza Napoleone. I believe Viviana has invited Lisa and Cassie, so I think that's best left to the young people. I am happy to leave now and go home for something to eat, are you?'

Jane nodded, relieved.

'Good, but before we go, I must introduce you to Chiara herself. We'll just say hello quickly. She is an old friend of mine; I should have introduced you before.'

'Of course.' Jane braced herself to renegotiate the throng but the crowd parted for Luciano as they made their way to the far side of the room. Everyone seemed to know who he was.

'There she is.'

Luciano pointed out a tall woman in a peacock-blue dress with her back to them standing next to a small wooden table piled with greetings cards and postcards featuring vignettes from the paintings. Her jet-black hair was piled up on the top of her head and secured with a large silver barrette.

'Chiara . . .' Luciano said.

The artist turned around.

Jane did a double-take; she had seen the woman somewhere before.

'Chiara, may I introduce my fiancée, Jane? Jane, this is Chiara,' Luciano said.

Chiara patted the white streak at the front of her hair. She gave Jane an appraising look. There was a pause. '*Piacere*, pleased to meet you,' Chiara said.

'Pleased to meet you, too.' Now Jane remembered – Chiara was the stylish woman she'd spotted in the café the other day.

'I have heard so much about you,' Chiara said pleasantly.

Luciano cleared his throat.

'Your paintings are so . . . stunning,' Jane said.

'It is kind of you to say so.'

Jane hovered awkwardly. Was she expected to conjure up some meaningful insight?

'We have greetings cards and postcards of Chiara's work for sale,' the boy in the blue boiler suit said. Jane hadn't even noticed him sitting there with his metal cash tin and card reader.

'I must take a look.' She was glad to escape Chiara's searching gaze. She selected a couple of designs quickly; she liked to keep her supply of greetings cards replenished.

'Put these in a paper bag for the lady,' Chiara said.

She plucked the ten-euro note from Jane's hand before the boy had a chance to take it. Chiara's hands were laden with heavy rings on every finger. Her long, midnight-blue nails were studded with tiny gemstones that sparkled in the artificial light.

The boy put the cards into a paper bag. His stubby nails were discoloured and there was oil paint under his cuticles. Jane slipped her purchase into her handbag. Chiara tipped a five-euro note and a handful of change into Jane's hand.

'Thank you.' Jane felt Chiara's eyes on her as she turned away. She opened her hand, totted up the coins and frowned. 'Excuse me, I think you've given me too much change.'

'That should be twelve fifty.'

'But I only gave you ten euros.'

'How silly of me, I gave you change for twenty.' Chiara gave a little tinkling laugh. She gave the boy the additional change to put in his tin.

'Nice to have met you,' Jane said.

'You too,' Chiara said. There was more warmth in her voice. She looked as though she were about to say something else, but Luciano had already slipped his arm through Jane's and was pulling her away.

'Let's go,' Luciano said. '*Ciao*, Chiara.'

They walked home through the quiet dark streets. Luciano was humming to himself. Jane was glad she didn't need to talk. She was still trying to process the events of the evening. She was certain that Chiara hadn't made an innocent mistake; she had deliberately given Jane too much change. It was almost as though Chiara was testing her. But why would she do that?

Chapter Twelve

'This was such a great idea,' Lisa said. She shuffled along the wooden bench to make room for Cassie in the pizzeria's cosy booth.

'It'll be a bit of a squash once my two friends get here but they do the best pizzas,' Viviana said. 'I'm starving. I didn't get the chance to try any of the food earlier and I don't suppose there will be anything at the after-party.'

'Same here,' Cassie said. She hadn't touched Chiara's canapes. It was tricky eating standing up and she hadn't wanted to risk getting grease on her white broderie anglaise dress. She unfolded a couple of paper napkins and spread them out on her lap.

'Wow! Those look delicious,' Lisa said, swivelling around to look at the young waitress emerging from the kitchen door with a bicycle wheel-sized pizza in each hand.

'They smell fantastic,' Cassie added. After the afternoon's bust-up, it was good to find something they could agree on.

Lisa smiled. 'Can't wait!' Whatever her sister's faults, Cassie had to concede that sulking after a row wasn't one of them.

'They'll take our order in a minute,' Viviana said. 'Have you chosen yet? It's very traditional here, just *marinara*, *margherita* and a handful of others. None of those terrible American toppings like chicken or pineapple.'

Cassie gave a weak smile. She was rather fond of a Hawaiian and it was Paul's favourite. But at least you couldn't go wrong with a *margherita*.

'Aren't we going to wait for your friends?' Lisa asked.

'No need, they're here now.' Viviana waved in the direction of the doorway.

An incredibly chic, willowy blonde in her twenties wearing what looked like a vintage Pucci tunic was picking her way between the tables. Her companion's skin-tight jeans were artfully distressed; he had a ring through his eyebrow. Cassie exchanged glances with Lisa; she was pretty sure they were going to look rather out of place at Chiara's after-party.

'*Ciao*, Viv!'

'*Ciao*!' Viviana made the introductions. The two newcomers squeezed into Viviana's side of the booth. Cassie didn't catch their names and she didn't like to ask them to repeat them; she felt a little intimidated by their confident manners and the ease with which they switched to English as soon as the waitress had jotted down their orders.

Lisa touched her arm. 'Are you sure you still want to go?' she whispered.

'Of course I do.'

'Just thought it might not be your scene.'

'Why? Because I'm boring?' Cassie snapped. She'd promised herself she would not let their argument affect the rest of their trip but that was easier said than done.

'Whatever . . .' Lisa shrugged.

Cassie fiddled with the edge of the check tablecloth and sipped her Diet Coke in silence as Lisa, Viviana and her friends laughed and joked. No one seemed to notice that she wasn't joining in. She felt like going back to the Hotel Tosca but she was determined to join the party. She wasn't going to prove Lisa right.

'Are you looking forward to *Casa della Nonna*, Cassie?' the cool blonde asked.

'*Nonna*? Isn't that Italian for granny?' Cassie frowned. She'd picked up the odd word from watching *Inspector Montalbano*.

'Yeah, the bar's called Granny's House. It's done up like an old lady's front room, all lacy cushions and fringed lampshades. It's so cool and retro. Great dress, by the way. I love that ironic Fifties housewife look.'

'Umm, thanks,' Cassie mumbled. Housewife – did she really look that dull? She wasn't sure how to respond.

'Who's having the *margheritas*?' The waitress hovering at the end of the booth rescued Cassie from the need for further conversation.

Viviana's friend was right. *Casa della Nonna* was well named. The wooden clock on the mantelpiece was just like the one in Aunt Jane's spare bedroom, the room she'd never got round to redecorating – and probably never would now that Sundial Cottage was on the market. Cassie sighed. Tonight she didn't want to think about Jane's predicament. She was determined to show her older sister that Lisa wasn't the only one who knew how to have a good time.

'I'll go and get us some drinks,' the boy with the skin-tight jeans said.

Cassie unzipped her handbag.

'No need. I'm paying, I insist.' He smiled.

'Thanks,' Cassie said. She tried not to stare at the ring in his eyebrow.

'*Soramara* all round?'

'It's a local beer, I hope that's okay,' Viviana said. She and the boy disappeared in the direction of the bar before Cassie had the chance to ask for a glass of wine instead.

Lisa was right – the party wasn't really Cassie's scene; it was too arty for that, but the event had attracted people of all ages. Cassie wasn't sure why she had expected a much younger crowd; after all, Chiara looked as though she was in her sixties. It was strange that Jane and Luciano weren't in attendance. Luciano would surely know most of the people in the room, but perhaps he and Jane wanted the rest of the evening to themselves after spending so much time with their visitors.

Viviana and the boy with the piercing returned with the beers then drifted away to talk to some friends. Lisa and Viviana's blonde friend were now deep in conversation. Cassie felt a pang of envy. Lisa's ancient, crumpled maxi dress wasn't particularly fashionable but it gave her an air of cool nonchalance and she didn't care that she knew nothing about art; she chatted easily sure in the knowledge that people would be interested in what she said. Cassie couldn't think of anything to say.

Cassie slipped away, clutching her glass of *soramara*. She wandered around the perimeter of the room wondering why on earth someone would decorate a bar with porcelain chilli peppers, giant rolling pins and embroidered antimacassars. Purple stools lined the bar area where Chiara was holding court surrounded by a small coterie of admirers. Her golden orb necklace glistened in the light cast by the gaudy crystal lamps that threw strange shadows across the white marble countertop. There was something familiar about the artist. Cassie could swear she had seen her somewhere before but she couldn't remember where.

Cassie took a sip of her beer and made a face. She looked around for Lisa. Her sister was standing nearby, beaming. Matteo had arrived. He had his arm around Lisa's waist. Their heads were close together. Matteo said something. Lisa threw back her head and laughed.

'They've hung some of Chiara's smaller works on that wall just for tonight.' A girl's voice made Cassie jump.

She looked in the direction the girl was indicating. Cassie wasn't sure she liked Chiara's orange houses and yellow trees and there was something slightly creepy about the way the paintings seemed to draw her in. But she couldn't help noticing that the colours would tone beautifully with the paint samples she and Paul had chosen for their new kitchen. Not that she was in the market for original art; the granite worktops she'd set her heart on had already blown their budget.

'What do you think of them?' the girl asked. Her brown eyes were big and earnest.

Cassie hesitated. She was pretty sure 'they match my kitchen accessories' wasn't going to be an acceptable answer. 'Umm, er, great . . .' she mumbled.

The girl began expounding on Chiara's genius, but Cassie was no longer listening. She was staring at the figure in the doorway. It was him. The man she couldn't stop thinking about. Alonzo was here.

Alonzo made his way across the room, stopping every few feet to greet someone with a hug, a slap on the back or a kiss. His thick dark hair was styled into a quiff and his black linen shirt was unbuttoned to reveal a slim gold chain with a star-shaped charm. His metal belt buckle gleamed. Cassie dared not let her eyes drop below the waistband of his dark denim jeans. She unzipped her bag and fanned herself with her exhibition programme. She turned away and forced herself to study a painting of blue and yellow trees.

'*Ciao*, Cassie! I did not know you would all be here.' He was standing so close she was surprised he couldn't hear her heart hammering. She took a sip of *soramara* to moisten her dry lips.

'Us all?'

'Yes – you, Lisa, your aunt and Luciano.'

'Oh, Luciano and Jane aren't here. Lisa and I came with Viviana.'

'After the *pizzeria*? She did mention she'd be going there first.'

'It was great. You should have come.' Cassie was glad he hadn't turned up there. She wouldn't have been capable of swallowing a morsel.

'Cassie, I . . .' Alonzo began but Cassie didn't get the chance to hear what he was about to say. Chiara had stepped onto a packing crate. She held out her arms and looked around the room. Everyone fell silent.

Chiara spoke quickly and passionately, her breasts quivering as her hand gestures grew more animated. Cassie hoped she wouldn't go on for too long; she felt a bit of a fraud standing there pretending to look interested when she couldn't understand a word the woman was saying.

Chiara clapped her hand to her heart. She flung her arms wide apart. The applause was loud and heartfelt.

'*Grazie, grazie mille.*' Chiara acknowledged her fans. The applause continued. The artist cast her eyes down modestly.

A rotund man with a luxuriant head of black hair and a bushy moustache stepped forward with an enormous bunch of sunflowers finished off with a huge red bow. Chiara bowed slightly, accepted the bouquet and clasped it to her bosom. She stepped down from the crate. The boiler-suited assistant Cassie had seen at the exhibition hurried to remove it. Chiara stepped into the throng. The young man disappeared through a door behind the bar clutching Chiara's flowers.

To Cassie's surprise, the place began to empty out. She stole a glance at Alonzo. He hadn't moved. 'Has the party finished? It's not very late.'

'People aren't heading home. They're going downstairs for the music. There's a dance floor in the basement. Can you see those stairs in the corner?'

'Oh,' Cassie said. 'Are you staying?'

'Of course. I've only just arrived.'

Alonzo put his hand under her elbow and guided her in the direction of the stairs. The touch of his skin on hers sent shivers through her body.

'Oh look, there's your sister and Matteo,' he said.

'Hi, Alonzo,' Matteo said. Lisa was clutching his arm.

'Coming downstairs?' Alonzo asked. He dropped Cassie's arm and walked ahead talking to Matteo in Italian.

'Fun, isn't it?' Lisa said. She looked flushed and happy.

Cassie forced a smile. Talk about bad timing. Or perhaps it was good timing that Lisa and Matteo had interrupted them. Cassie had been determined to forget about Alonzo, but after a few minutes in his company all her resolve had vanished. And she knew deep down that the possibility that Alonzo might be at the after-party had been one of the reasons she had been so keen to attend.

'So, how's it going with Matteo?' Cassie asked. She needed to focus on something other than the sight of Alonzo's pert behind going down the stairs ahead of her.

'Well . . .' Lisa gave an uncharacteristically girly giggle. By the time she had finished telling Cassie how wonderful Matteo was, Alonzo was embroiled in talking to a group of Italians. *It's for the best*, Cassie told herself but she couldn't resist glancing over in his direction whenever she thought Lisa wasn't looking.

'I really am sorry about earlier,' Lisa said quietly.

'I'm sorry too.' Cassie knew it would be difficult to forget the things they'd said. She was relieved when the DJ cranked up the music and conversation became nearly impossible.

'Are those old singles he's playing?' Lisa shouted over the thumping rhythm.

'Yep, all vinyl. I guess it's part of the retro vibe.' Matteo grinned.

Cassie was glad. She didn't really rate much modern music. The old disco classics were much more her style. She felt her foot tapping.

'Let's dance!' Lisa said. She was always the first on the dance floor. The DJ put on *Dancing Queen*, Matteo grabbed Cassie's hand and led her and Lisa into the middle of the room.

'I'm the luckiest man here – dancing with two gorgeous girls,' Matteo shouted over the music but Cassie could see by the way he looked at Lisa, shimmying in her floaty dress, that he only had eyes for one sister. But Cassie didn't mind as she twirled and spun to ABBA, Sister Sledge and Boney M interspersed with the odd Italian disco beat. Every so often she glanced around, checking Alonzo was still there.

The DJ switched to *Yes Sir, I Can Boogie*. Matteo slipped away to fetch some more drinks. Lisa grabbed Cassie's hands and they danced together, singing along to the words and spinning each other around. The skirt of Cassie's white broderie anglaise dress flew up, almost revealing her big sensible knickers. But she didn't care; she was glad she and Lisa had made up – for now. She hadn't had this much fun for a long time.

'Cassie!' Matteo had reappeared. He was holding out a glass of wine. She was glad it wasn't another beer.

'Thanks.' Cassie stopped dancing. She took a large swig of wine, conscious that she really should switch to water. She was beginning to feel a little light-headed despite the huge pizza and her feet were killing her.

No one else appeared to be flagging. She was surrounded by people of all ages dancing with abandon to the Seventies beats. Chiara looked as though she had travelled even further back in time, swaying from side to side and waving her arms in the air like an acid-tripping hippy at Woodstock.

The young man in the boiler suit danced beside her with his eyes closed as if the music and Chiara's presence had sent him into a trance. Gradually he disappeared into the haze of purple clouds emanating from the DJ's smoke machine. Cassie caught Lisa's eye and they both started laughing.

The smoke clouds thickened, enveloping the dance floor. Cassie could hardly see; she started to cough. Just when she thought she might need to go and find a glass of water, the air cleared. The fog lifted to reveal Viviana dancing right in front of them, shaking her hips, her spiky green glass necklace lit up by the glittering disco ball.

Alonzo emerged from the crowd. The DJ switched to the dulcet sounds of *Sexual Healing*. Cassie's fingers tightened around her glass of wine. Alonzo put his hand on Viviana's arm, leant in close and said something. Viviana nodded. They began to sway together, moving in harmony to the music, no more than an inch of space between their bodies.

'They look good together, don't they,' Lisa said.

Cassie couldn't answer, she could only stand and stare. Alonzo ran a hand through his dark hair as his hips gyrated in time to Marvin Gaye's crooning. His eyes never left his partner's face. A smile played on Viviana's perfect red lips. The blonde girl in the Pucci dress and the boy with the pierced eyebrow were dancing beside them but all eyes in the room were focused on the sensuous dark-haired duo. They danced as if no one else was there.

Cassie felt the bile rise in her throat. Viviana and Alonzo were together. No one could deny they made a perfect couple – their dark good looks, their stylish clothes, their shared love of the arts. Love must have blossomed in the gallery whilst they worked. Why hadn't she guessed?

'I need the bathroom,' Cassie said.

She brushed past Matteo and Lisa and headed towards the sign above the double glass doors at the far end of the room. She slammed the cubicle door shut, slid the bolt across and plonked herself down on the wooden seat. Her reflection stared back at her from the mirror on the back of the door. She studied it for a long time. There was nothing about it that pleased her. Her carefully applied blue eyeliner and mascara had smudged under her eyes, giving them a hollow look, her nose was shiny, her cheeks too chubby and pink and her favourite white dress and pearlescent beads looked gauche and unsophisticated compared to Viviana's chic shift dress and edgy glass necklace.

Cassie wiped at her smeared eye make-up and blew her nose. The door to the cloakroom banged open. Two female voices were whispering in Italian. There were only two cubicles, Cassie couldn't hog this one all night. She pulled back the bolt, opened the door and turned on the tap. The girl in the Pucci dress was leaning against the wall. Someone's hands were running up and down the back of her dress, caressing her. Female hands with dark red nails. She was kissing someone. It was Viviana.

Viviana opened her eyes. They met Cassie's.

'What are you looking at?' Viviana said.

Cassie froze, her hand on the soap dispenser. 'Um . . . er . . . nothing.'

'Then why are you staring at me and Annika? Haven't you met anyone gay before?' Viviana's voice was cold.

'Oh, no, it's not that . . .' Cassie wished the ground would swallow her up. 'It's just, well . . . what about Alonzo?'

'Alonzo?' Viviana said. 'What's he got to do with anything?'

The blonde girl smirked. She said something in Italian.

Viviana's expression softened. 'Oh, I see. You thought Alonzo was my boyfriend because of the way we were dancing.'

'Well, you looked so good together,' Cassie admitted. She squirted out a blob of pink soap and lathered her hands.

'Thanks, I'm flattered. I love dancing with Alonzo, he's a wonderful dancer, but we've known each other since we were children. He's like a brother to me.'

'And I don't mind,' the blonde said. 'I like to see her dancing so wild and free.'

'But why would you care about Alonzo's feelings? You don't even know him,' Viviana said. Her dark eyes met Cassie's.

Cassie couldn't think of an answer. She busied herself drying her hands very carefully with a paper towel from the dispenser on the wall.

'Perhaps you're interested in him yourself.' Viviana laughed.

Cassie twisted her engagement and wedding rings. 'Of course not. I'm married. Very happily married.'

'Of course, I forgot,' Viviana said. She gave Cassie a knowing look.

Cassie pushed her way back through the double doors to the bar; her face burning. The theme tune from *Saturday Night Fever* was blasting from the speakers. She remembered her next-door neighbour's twenty-first birthday party, Paul leaping about pointing his finger in the air like John Travolta. She couldn't imagine Alonzo doing something so embarrassing, he was far too cool. She felt a stab of guilt. She forced herself to think of the times she and Paul had slow-danced together. How safe she felt in his arms and how handsome he looked in a tuxedo, just like the first time they met.

Cassie crossed the dance floor. Lisa and Matteo were exactly where she had left them. They were so wrapped up in each other they'd barely noticed she'd gone. Cassie felt a pang of envy. She knew she was being daft; Lisa's relationship was only a short-lived holiday fling. Cassie was the lucky one, she and Paul would be together for ever. She checked her watch. It was one in the morning. It was time to call it a night. She would leave Lisa and Matteo together. She could find her way back to the hotel, it wasn't far. It was too late to call Paul tonight but she would message him first thing in the morning.

She tapped Lisa on the arm. 'I'm off now. Stay as late as you like. Don't worry about waking me up when you get in.'

'Don't go, Cassie.' Lisa grabbed her arm. 'We're having so much fun.'

'What's another hour? The party will be over by two,' Matteo said.

'And you always dance to this song,' Lisa added.

Cassie couldn't deny it; she loved a bit of *I Will Survive* and right now the lyrics seemed more apt than ever. 'Maybe after this one then,' she said.

'Like to dance?' It was the boy in the boiler suit.

'Okay,' she said. Chiara's gawky assistant only looked about eighteen but accepting his invitation was better than hanging around like a gooseberry whilst Matteo and Lisa gyrated against each other in the semi-darkness.

The boy bopped in front of her, gazing earnestly through his owl-like glasses; he had an excruciating lack of rhythm. Cassie plastered a smile on her face and forced herself to concentrate on her partner, if only to distract her from Alonzo who was standing nearby. She sang along to the words inside her head, trying to lose herself in the music.

The DJ switched records. The boy smiled at her, expectantly. Cassie stepped away; one dance was more than enough. She opened her mouth to excuse herself but she didn't have chance to speak. Alonzo had stepped between them. Cassie caught her breath. The boy took one look at his older rival and backed away.

'I thought you might need rescuing.' Alonzo grinned.

'Yes, um . . . thanks.'

'You like to dance?' Alonzo said.

Cassie nodded dumbly.

Alonzo took her hand. Under the strobe lights, his face looked more handsome than ever. Those cheekbones, those long eyelashes, the little mole above those soft lips . . . She tried to switch her focus to Barry White's rumbling voice. 'My First, My Last, My Everything'.

Cassie had never danced like this, her body absorbing the rhythm, lost in the music. She was as light as a feather; her feet no longer hurt. Her shoulder strap slipped down, revealing a glimpse of white bra; she didn't bother to hoik it up.

The DJ switched to a slower number. Alonzo pulled her close. Someone must have switched on the heating because the temperature in the room soared several notches. Cassie's whole body was melting and moulding itself to Alonzo's. She knew she shouldn't be doing this. She should have made her excuses and left. She shouldn't have let it happen. *It meant nothing when Alonzo danced with Viviana. It means nothing now.* She repeated it like a mantra. But when she looked into Alonzo's green eyes she knew she was lost. Like a sailor helplessly following a mermaid into the depths.

The route back to the Hotel Tosca was dark and silent. Lisa held Matteo's hand, their arms swinging as they walked along. Neither of them spoke much. She sneaked a look at his handsome profile; his hair was all mussed up but she resisted the urge to smooth it down.

'Okay?' Matteo asked.

'Yep, all okay.' Lisa smiled. She couldn't remember when she'd last felt so happy.

They were taking a long time to get to the hotel. Matteo's progress was hampered by Cassie. He kept one arm tightly wrapped around Cassie's waist; she'd already stumbled twice. It was surprising she could walk at all in her white strappy sandals. Lisa had never understood heels. And she didn't understand her sister these days. Cassie had never been a party animal; she'd always been the sort of girl who bopped shyly on the sidelines but tonight she'd transformed into a disco diva.

Whenever Lisa looked round, Cassie was dancing with a different partner: first there was Chiara's boiler-suited assistant with his strange jerky movements, then the wild, uninhibited dancing with Alonzo (Lisa's jaw had dropped, she had to admit) then the slow dance where it looked as though Cassie was leaning against Alonzo in an effort to keep herself upright. And after that, when Alonzo was dancing with Viviana again, Cassie had put on quite an extraordinary display of eyebrow-raising hip-bumping boogying with the blonde in the Pucci dress. Just when Lisa thought that Cassie would go on dancing all night, she'd suddenly insisted on going back to the hotel and Matteo, quite rightly, wouldn't let her walk back alone.

The Hotel Tosca was in darkness save for the soft glow of the lantern hanging from an iron bracket by the front door; the desk clerk had closed up for the night. Lisa was thankful she'd had the foresight to bring her key.

A small mouse scuttled away as they approached.

Matteo paused in the doorway. 'Here we are.'

'Thanks for walking us back,' Lisa said.

Matteo dropped the lightest kiss on her lips. Their eyes met. She wanted to kiss him so much, to wrap her arms around him and hold him all night, but his arms were otherwise engaged, holding onto Cassie.

'I'll text you tomorrow. You're sure you'll be all right getting your sister upstairs?'

'What are you talking about, I'm fine,' Cassie muttered.

Matteo smiled. 'Goodnight then.'

The light in the lobby turned on automatically as Lisa and Cassie entered. Cassie sat down heavily on the wooden bench in the corner and struggled with the straps on her sandals insisting she didn't need Lisa's help. They climbed the stairs with less trouble than Lisa anticipated; Cassie clutched her shoes in one hand and gripped the banister with the other, taking the steps very carefully.

The door key worked first time. By the time Lisa had finished brushing her teeth, Cassie was fast asleep on top of her bed in her lacy bra and sensible big knickers. How sweet she looked. However annoying Cassie was, she'd always be Lisa's little sister. Maybe this afternoon's row hadn't been such a disaster; perhaps they had begun to understand each other a little better. Lisa gently eased the bedspread over her sister. Cassie gave a little snuffling sound but didn't wake.

Lisa crept into her own bed as quietly as she could. She lay back staring at the pale blue ceiling. She didn't want to go to sleep straight away; she wanted to lie there and think of Matteo. His smile, his voice, the touch of his hand, the sensations that flooded through her body when they kissed – she'd never felt like this before.

Meeting Matteo had knocked her sideways. She'd been sure that everlasting love was a myth – she'd believed that ever since Dad had left Mum. She'd dismissed the idea of finding 'The One' as a load of old nonsense. But the more she saw of Matteo, the more she found herself believing that she could never be truly happy without him. Why was she being so foolish? Matteo was a travelling musician who moved from place to place. Wherever he laid his violin was his home. He was a free spirit, the sort she'd imagined herself to be. She had to accept that. She'd gone into this relationship (if she could even call it that) with her eyes open. She was a grown-up and she knew the score. She didn't know what had got into her. She'd be fine once she got back home. It was only the holiday vibe – and too many drinks – that was making her feel this way.

Chapter Thirteen

Pia traced her finger over the sheet of slightly musty-smelling paper and studied the blue pastel sketch of her grandmother for what felt like the hundredth time. *The most beautiful girl – Florence. With kisses, L.* It wasn't much to go on. Florence was a big city. She wouldn't have known where to start but Mamma suggested she head to the streets around the Uffizi Gallery where the city's artists touted for business. Someone might recognise the artist's style and remember 'L'. He would be an old man by now; he might not even be alive. But there was still a tiny chance that 'L' could still be living there sketching tourists to help eke out his pension.

She slipped the portrait back into its envelope, stashed it in her striped canvas tote bag and made her way down the staircase and out into the narrow street below. It was early but the Florentine streets were already buzzing with locals and backpack-carrying tourists. Everyone seemed to be swarming in the same direction – towards the iconic, brick-domed cathedral. Pia ducked and dived her way through the crowds that thankfully began to thin out as she headed towards the River Arno.

She stopped outside a tiny church. An old lady was perched on the steps trying to induce passers-by to part with some cash in exchange for small pictures of saints. Nearby an old fellow with a baker-boy cap sat sketching.

Pinned to his easel was an ink sketch that succeeded in making three beautiful Oscar-winning actresses look as plain as a trio of washerwomen.

The old man caught Pia's eye. He motioned for her to join him with a nod of his head. She smiled and walked over. She had to start somewhere, didn't she? At least she wouldn't be tempted to buy one of his pictures.

'You like this?' He gestured with an ink-stained thumb.

'It's lovely.' Pia hated lying but what else could she do? It was far better than insulting the man.

'*Grazie*.' He cracked a genuine smile. His teeth were stained and misshapen, but his grey eyes were soft and friendly. 'I will make a beautiful picture of you too. Thirty euros but for you twenty.'

'I'm not looking to have my portrait done. I'm sorry.'

'Don't apologise, young people so rarely do. It's all selfies these days. But a real picture is different, it is something to keep for a long, long time.' He gave a little shrug, as though he had said the same thing to many people.

'You are right,' Pia said. She reached into her tote bag and carefully extracted the buff-coloured envelope.

'Aah, you already have a picture? Let me see.'

Pia handed him the envelope. He slid out the drawing and examined it with great care.

'This is you . . . but, no, this date . . . it cannot be.'

'My Nonna Concetta.'

'Of course. *La ragazza più bella* – the most beautiful girl.' He flashed a toothy grin. 'You have a story to tell, I am sure of it. Please sit down.'

'I don't want to keep you from your customers.'

'Customers . . . pah! I have so few. I will enjoy talking to you. It will help pass the time. Please sit. I insist.'

The artist listened as Pia's tale unravelled. Every so often passers-by stopped to look at the two of them, waiting for the old man to pick up his ink pen and get to work. They soon moved on, some tutting in disgust as though they were being deprived of their rightful entertainment.

'And this drawing is your only clue?'

Pia nodded. It was nice of the man to listen to her story even though there was little chance he could help. He was silent for a while, lost in thought.

At last he spoke: 'I have an idea who drew this.'

'Really?' Pia gasped. She could hardly believe it; it seemed too good to be true.

The man sighed and bit his lip. He seemed to be weighing something up.

'I can tell you who to look for, but . . .'

'Please tell me. It's so important.'

'This blue pastel crayon – it is an odd choice; most artists would use a neutral shade. But there was one artist here who liked to use unusual colours like this: Luigi Vasari. He retired several years ago. I do not even know if he is still alive but his grandson is an artist too. He works down by the Uffizi Gallery where most of the portrait artists work. Ask for Young Luigi – everybody knows him.'

Pia hesitated. There was something in the man's voice that told her she might not like what she found. 'But . . .'

The man sighed. 'Young Luigi is exceptionally talented, no one can dispute that. He can capture someone's looks and personality in just a few deft strokes. He is one of the best I have seen, and I've been around a long time. But he is not someone a nice girl like you should get involved with. He has a bad reputation around here.'

Pia leant forward. 'Why, what has he done?'

The old artist patted Pia's arm. 'Don't look so alarmed. He hasn't murdered anyone or anything like that.' He allowed himself a little chuckle. Then his face darkened. 'He's as charming as a sunbeam when he wants to be but then he can turn on you, just like that. He's the sort that rips off tourists and cheats at cards. He's not to be trusted.'

'I'll be careful, I promise,' Pia said. She stood up. 'Thank you so much for all your help.'

Clutching her tote bag close, she crossed the road into the Piazza Della Signoria. The square was like no other that Pia had ever seen. One end was dominated by the bulk of the Palazzo Vecchio topped by a dramatic clock tower. Nearby, a triumphal naked Neptune presided over a fountain decorated with water nymphs.

She turned and took the pedestrianised street that ran down the side of the Uffizi. The queue to enter snaked right around its austere exterior. The gallery was Italy's finest, packed with works by its greatest artists: Titian, Michelangelo, Botticelli. Part of her wanted to join the queue and finally see *The Birth of Venus* – she had missed their school trip when Mamma was ill – and browsing in the gallery would delay the moment she commenced her daunting task. Pia dismissed the temptation. She had a job to do.

A dozen artists had erected their easels at intervals around the gallery's forecourt. She looked at the portraits of celebrities they displayed on the side of their easels to show off their talents. The old man was right – the first artist she spoke to was able to point Young Luigi out to her. Pia stood quietly for a while, watching him from a discreet distance. He was rather scruffy with two-days stubble on his wan, pinched face.

Luigi was putting the finishing touches to a charcoal drawing of a plump, pink-faced tourist who was perched awkwardly on a stool that wasn't quite large enough to accommodate her girth. She was an ordinary-looking woman but Luigi had brought out the beauty in her features. He turned her to face the finished work. She clapped her hands in delight.

Luigi wrapped the portrait with a sheet of brown paper and string. The happy tourist departed. Pia wiped her palms on the front of her jeans and walked over.

Luigi looked up and smiled but his eyes were cold. 'Take a seat. Charcoal or pastel?' he said in English.

'*Buongiorno*! I have not come to have my portrait drawn but I am hoping you may be able to help me.'

'*Sei italiana*?' He sounded surprised.

'Yes, from Naples.'

'Naples . . . I see.' He didn't bother to hide his distaste. He fixed his green eyes on her; they were cold and murky, like pond water.

'So, what do you want from me?'

Pia took the envelope from her bag and repeated the story she had told a few minutes before. 'So, you see,' she concluded, 'your grandfather may be my real grandfather too.'

Luigi's face betrayed no emotion. 'You'd better open that envelope and show me this picture.' He placed the drawing on his lap, lit a cigarette and studied it for a few minutes. It felt like an hour. Pia realised she was biting her fingernails, a habit she thought she had finally cracked.

'This is good, but it's not one of my grandfather's best.' He picked up a bulldog clip and added the picture of Nonna Concetta to his display. Pia was about to protest but thought better of it. She wasn't going to antagonise this man until she had extracted all the information she needed.

'Are you sure he was the artist?'

'I don't believe any of the others around here drew their portraits in blues and greens like Nonno sometimes did. And this dedication – it is typical of him.' He gave a nasty little laugh.

'What do you mean?' Pia had a strange feeling of dread. She suddenly felt vulnerable, perched on the wooden stool, her legs dangling in the air.

'*La ragazza più bella* – that's what Nonno said to all the girls. How foolish women are. They like the idea of being in love with an artist. A few well-rehearsed words and they fall into bed with you. My grandfather was like me; he seduced many cheap women. And if one or two of them ended up in your grandmother's predicament . . . well, there are ways of dealing with that. Of course he would deny having touched them. Who knows how many other men had been there too.'

'My nonna was nothing like the women you describe,' Pia said quietly. She could feel her eyes pricking with tears.

'So you think,' Luigi sneered.

Pia had heard enough. She jumped to her feet and reached for her drawing but she wasn't quick enough. Luigi grabbed her wrist with his bony fingers. His signet ring dug into her flesh. He was leaning over her, his face inches away from hers.

'I will keep this picture. I will add it to my nonno's collection.'

Pia wasn't very big and she wasn't very strong but a rush of adrenaline made her feel superhuman. She raised one knee and caught Luigi in the crotch. He staggered backwards. His easel crashed to the ground. Charcoal sticks and coloured pastels scattered across the forecourt. Pia grabbed Nonna's picture from the display and ran.

'Bitch!' Luigi shouted. Then: 'Stop, thief!'

She ran along the *lungarno* by the side of the river half blinded by tears. She did not stop and look behind her until she came to the Ponte Vecchio. No one was following her. She leant on the bridge's low wall looking over the river. Her breath was coming out in loud gasps. Her chest hurt but it was nothing compared to the anger and pain she felt. She couldn't, wouldn't, tell Mamma about her discovery. It would break her heart to learn that Nonna had been seduced by a man like Old Luigi. She would have to tell Mamma her search had been in vain. It was a secret she would carry for ever.

She wept loudly, letting the tears run down her cheeks without wiping them away. People were turning and staring but she didn't care. How she wished she hadn't come to Florence on this fool's errand. She longed to be back home in Naples with the scooters roaring up and down their narrow street and Mariella and Elena arguing about how much liqueur to put in a tiramisu.

She trudged back to her hotel. The man behind the reception desk handed over her key with a smile.

She smiled back weakly. 'I'd like to check out.'

The man frowned. 'It is too late – I will have to charge you for today. Will you not stay until the morning? Is the hotel not to your liking? It cannot be Florence that disappoints.'

'The city is beautiful and your hotel is perfect.'

'That I am glad to hear. But please – I hope I am not intruding – but I cannot help sensing that you came to Florence for a reason, something that has nothing to do with Titian and Michelangelo and all our marvellous masterpieces.'

'You're right. I brought a picture with me.'

Pia slid the drawing out of its envelope. One corner was now missing, caught in the bulldog clip on young Luigi's easel; she didn't know how she was going to explain that to Mamma. 'This is my nonna.'

The man took the picture and laid it on the reception desk. He stroked the rough surface of the paper with his thumb. 'This "L" – who is he?'

'I was told that "L" was an artist who used to work by the Uffizi, Old Luigi.'

'And this morning you have been looking for him?'

'I was until I found out that he had passed away. But I met his grandson.' Pia tried to keep her voice neutral.

'Young Luigi? I suppose he told you this was drawn by his grandfather.'

Pia bit her lip and nodded.

'In that case I am sure he was lying. It is true Old Luigi liked to draw using these coloured pastels, sometimes blues, sometimes greens. It gave a lovely soft quality to his work. But I have seen many, many of his drawings and this is not his style. Besides, maybe I am sentimental, but I can tell this portrait was drawn by a man in love. It's not just the inscription, it's there in every line. Old Luigi wouldn't recognise love if Cupid walked up and smacked him in the face. I'm sure this "L", whoever he is, loved your nonna. I can feel it.'

'Oh, I do hope you're right.'

'If only he had signed his full name. I don't suppose there is anything on the back?'

'If only. There's nothing there apart from some tiny pencil doodles: a dog, a funny little building and a cloud.'

'May I?' He carefully turned the picture over. 'These are very faint. I will need my reading glasses.' He reached into his shirt pocket and pulled out a slim case. 'That's better. Now I can see more clearly. Yes, a little dog. Perhaps he belonged to the artist but that does not help us much; there are thousands of little dogs in Florence. But this . . . oh yes . . . this could be something . . .'

'What is it?' Pia could not mistake the excitement in his voice.

'We have a clue, a real clue. This tiny drawing – you think it is a tower with a cloud on top. But this is not a cloud, it is a tree – a holm oak, to be precise.'

Pia leant forward and squinted at the tiny scribbles. 'How can you tell that? And why would anyone draw a tree growing out of the top of a tower?'

'Because such a thing exists. You have one of those smartphones? Type in *Guinigi Tower* and take a look.'

'What an extraordinary building. It's in the middle of Lucca. That can't be too far from here.'

'Those little doodles are so personal I wouldn't be surprised if your artist lived there. There's an art gallery in the Piazza Anfiteatro. They might know something about this "L". Of course, it is just a guess, but you can easily reach Lucca by train. My cousin is the general manager of a small hotel there, the Hotel Tosca. I could ring and see if he has a room, he will give you a good rate. It's a beautiful town. You'll enjoy looking around even if you don't find your artist.'

'Thank you. It's got to be worth a try.'

The man picked up the phone. He talked for several minutes about family matters. Pia realised she was biting her nails again. At last he got down to business. He put down the phone with a smile.

'You have a room booked at the Hotel Tosca; my cousin will charge you a little less than you are paying here.'

'Thank you so much.'

Pia wanted to throw her arms round him. The search for Rosetta's father – her own biological grandfather – was back on. She felt a rush of excitement.

Chapter Fourteen

'Aunt Jane should be here in a moment.' Cassie checked the time on her watch and looked around the Piazza Anfiteatro.

'I'm glad we arranged to have a coffee here before we do any more sightseeing. I'm still half asleep,' Lisa said. 'Are you sure you're okay?'

'Of course I am.' Cassie couldn't help snapping.

Lisa raised her eyebrows and grinned. 'If you say so. At least you fell asleep straight away.'

Cassie wished she hadn't. She still had an ugly pink mark under one arm where her bra had been digging in all night and she hated knowing she'd gone to bed without taking off her make-up or brushing her teeth.

'It was a great night, wasn't it.' Lisa grinned.

'The music was brilliant. That DJ played all my favourite songs.' Cassie smiled at the memory.

'I don't think I've ever seen you dance like that,' Lisa laughed.

Cassie wasn't sure she'd ever danced the way she'd danced last night. She'd never felt so alive. She'd been twirling and spinning like a sexy goddess but she'd probably just looked like a fool. 'I suppose I looked really stupid,' she muttered.

'No, not at all. That's not what I meant. You looked great . . . maybe just a little wild.'

'Wild?' Cassie cringed. 'I'm not sure that's such a good look.'

'Who cares, if you were enjoying yourself.'

That was easy for Lisa to say, she'd never been self-conscious.

'You were having a lot of fun with Alonzo . . .'

Cassie tipped an extra sachet of sugar into her coffee, glad that her sunglasses were hiding her eyes. 'He's a good dancer.'

Her face burned and her hand shook slightly as she picked her cup up by its ludicrously tiny handle. She knew it wasn't the effects of the caffeine or the alcohol last night. She waited for Lisa to say something else but she'd lost interest in the subject and was thumbing through the *Lucca Attractions* booklet.

Cassie leant her elbows on the table, even though she tutted when other people did that, and studied her sister. How did Lisa look so perky and healthy in those unflattering cut-off jeans and lime-green strappy top? If Cassie wore that colour, she'd look positively bilious.

Maybe it was love that was making Lisa glow like that. She and Matteo had looked so happy last night. Cassie felt bad that she'd insisted on going home before the party ended. Lisa had looked at her the way she looked at her so many times in the past when Mum had taken them home because Cassie had whined that the sea was too cold or the sand pit too sandy or a big dog had jumped up and made her cry.

Last night, Cassie had no choice. Watching Alonzo dancing with Viviana and those other girls had aroused such violent emotions within her that she feared she would grab one by the hair, knock her aside and pull Alonzo into her arms so that she and she alone would hold her body against his for the rest of the night. It was crazy. She couldn't understand where those feelings had come from. She and

Paul were perfect together; she couldn't let anything ruin that. She would be polite to Alonzo if she saw him again, no more than that. And for the rest of the trip she'd do her best to keep out of his way.

She shifted her chair very slightly so that she could no longer see Gallery Guinigi from out of the corner of her eye. That was better. She would be all set to face the day if only she could get rid of the cotton wool feeling in her head. And the memories of last night.

She took a sip of her latte. A memory came out of nowhere. 'I know who Chiara is,' she said.

'What do you mean? Of course you do. She's the artist whose exhibition we went to,' Lisa said.

'No, not that. I've just remembered where I'd seen her before. She was that woman in the church?'

'Which church?'

'The one we went to for the concert. Chiara was that woman I saw, the one I pointed out to you in the street.'

'The one you thought was staring at Aunt Jane?'

'Exactly. Don't you think that's strange?'

'You were probably mistaken – why would she be staring at Jane, she seemed quite normal last night.' Lisa picked up a teaspoon and started scraping the remnants of cappuccino foam from around her cup.

'Maybe she's jealous of Jane's relationship with Luciano.'

Lisa raised an eyebrow. 'You think she's a spurned lover?'

'Or a mistress. It could be why he didn't want to go to the after-party last night.'

'You think Luciano's got two women on the go? He seems like an unlikely lothario.'

'Mmm . . . maybe you're right.' Cassie sighed and picked up her latte. There was no point trying to get Lisa to accept that Luciano might not be all that he seemed.

124

'There's Jane,' Lisa said.

Cassie put down her coffee cup and swivelled her head. 'Where? I can't see her.'

'Just coming through the archway – on the green bicycle.'

'On a *bicycle*? Oh, yes, you're right. I can't believe she's riding a bike.'

'Do you think she's spotted us?' Lisa stood up and waved.

Jane took one hand off the handlebars to wave back. The front wheel of her bicycle wobbled alarmingly causing her to almost collide with Viviana, who was wheeling two bikes across the piazza.

Jane propped her bicycle against the wall of Café Europa, near to the table where Cassie and Lisa were sitting. Viviana parked her two bicycles next to Jane's.

'What a lovely morning! You'll have a coffee with us, won't you, Viviana,' Jane said. 'Girls, I was just saying how much we all enjoyed Chiara's exhibition.'

'Thank you, Jane. If I'm not intruding . . .'

'Of course not,' Lisa said.

Cassie rested her hand on top of her white leather handbag, which was perched on one of the spare chairs; she didn't want to put it on the floor. Luckily Lisa had already chucked her tote bag onto the ground and was pulling out two empty seats for Jane and Viviana.

'I should really be at the gallery,' Viviana said, 'but fortunately, Alonzo has also come in this morning so there is someone to cover for me.'

Cassie felt herself flush at the mention of the jewellery designer's name. She unfolded the menu lying on the table and ran a finger down the list of drinks.

'Would you like another coffee, girls? Cappuccinos all round?' Jane said.

'Just an espresso for me,' Viviana said. She flashed a smile at one of the loitering waiters who scurried over.

'Still water for me, please,' Cassie said.

'Are you feeling all right, Cassie?' Viviana said.

'Why shouldn't I be?'

'Oh, you know, late night and all that.'

'Oh, I slept very well.'

'Good for you.' Viviana's smile was genuine.

Cassie braced herself for the inevitable comment about Alonzo but none came.

'Looking forward to today?' Viviana said.

'Yes, it's such a shame that Luciano can't be with us. He's in Florence for most of the day, but it will be nice for the girls and me to spend the day together,' Jane said.

'Yes, it'll be lovely,' Cassie said. She wouldn't be able to dissuade Aunt Jane from her crazy plan to get married without gathering as much information as she could about Luciano, but it would be nice to spend a full day exploring the town without the stress of sizing up her aunt's unlikely suitor.

'I'm really looking forward to seeing some more of the town,' Lisa said.

'You'll be able to see so much more now you've got the bicycles,' Viviana said.

'The bicycles?' Cassie said. Surely Aunt Jane wouldn't expect them to go cycling around the town. Cassie hadn't been on a bike since she was too old to ride on the pavement. She'd been far too nervous to ride on the road.

'I thought it would be a fun way to get around, and Viviana has kindly lent us these.' Jane inclined her head towards the pair of bicycles that Viviana had leant up against the wall.

'I'm not sure . . .' Cassie said. Dodging mopeds and mad Italian drivers wasn't her idea of a relaxing day.

'You used to love cycling when you were little,' Lisa said.

All Cassie could remember about her cycling days was the fear of being left behind as she frantically pedalled for dear life as Lisa fearlessly rode on ahead. Cassie looked at Lisa but there was no sign that she was deliberately being sarcastic.

Cassie fiddled with an unopened sachet of sugar. 'I'm not used to riding on the roads. The traffic . . .'

'Your aunt has chosen a good day,' Viviana interrupted. 'Today is Ecological Sunday; there are no cars allowed into the city. But on any normal day only bicycles and police cars are allowed on the walls. You'll be able to ride an unbroken circuit of the whole town.'

'The path on the top was created when Lucca was ruled by Maria Luisa of Bourbon,' Jane added. 'It's flanked by two rows of plane, chestnut and ilex trees. It's the perfect place to cycle or stroll – so beautiful.' She looked almost misty-eyed.

'I noticed people cycling up there yesterday,' Lisa said. 'I'm so glad we'll get the chance.'

Cassie smiled weakly. She was outnumbered.

Viviana stood up and smoothed down her black capri pants. 'I'm afraid I have to go. The gallery will be starting to get busy. But I'll meet you later, on the bench that over-looks Palazzo Pfanner. I do hope you enjoy your morning.' She turned and walked briskly across Piazza Anfiteatro.

'Viviana has insisted on bringing us a picnic at lunch-time,' Jane explained.

'How kind,' Lisa said.

'We'll find a nice, cool spot under the trees,' Jane added.

Cassie nodded. The sun had started to strengthen, and she was glad of the shade afforded by the large cream umbrellas of Café Europa. She scrabbled in her handbag to retrieve her purse as the waiter headed for a table nearby.

'No, I insist.' Jane fished the bill out from under the sugar bowl and handed it to the waiter along with two notes.

Lisa wheeled Viviana's two bicycles away from the café. 'Here, let me hold that steady.'

Cassie was relieved that Lisa handed her the smaller of the two bikes and took the cumbersome larger model with the wicker basket for herself. Cassie let out the strap on her handbag by a couple of notches so that she could wear it cross-body style and swung her leg over the bike's old-fashioned brown leather saddle. It was surprisingly comfortable.

She set off tentatively; fortunately, the bicycle was the right height so she could reach the handlebars without leaning forward and obscuring her view of the road ahead.

'Chiesa San Michele,' Jane called over her shoulder. She stopped her bicycle in front of a substantial church that dominated the square. Cassie squeaked to a halt.

'What an extraordinary façade,' Lisa said.

'It was built over several centuries, that's why it's such a mish-mash of styles,' Jane said. 'Luciano has painted this church time and time again, but he's never entirely satisfied with the result.'

'It's very intricate. I love that inlaid work on the arches.' Cassie pointed to the tiers of twisted columns of white and green marble.

'There are some beautiful churches here; in some ways it's a shame that Luciano and I are planning a civil ceremony,' Jane said.

'I'm sure your wedding will be beautiful,' Lisa said.

Cassie didn't respond. She found it easier to talk about the architecture than her aunt's fiancé.

'Ready? We'll turn left down via Vittorio Veneto into Piazza Napoleone.' Jane made a hand signal and her two nieces followed her. Cassie was glad there were no cars around as she veered off a straight line for the third or fourth time.

'Let's stop!' Jane called. 'Look, there's Umberto's where we ate the other night. And there's a statue of Maria Luisa.' She nodded her head towards a marble statue of a woman in a toga holding a lily-staff and a scroll.

Cassie wasn't paying attention. Her eyes were drawn to the small café where she and Alonzo had sat whilst Lisa had been off exploring the cathedral with Matteo.

'Now we'll head across town,' Jane said. 'We can take a slope that leads up to the walls; we won't want to haul these bikes up the stairs.'

Cassie's legs ached as she cycled the gentle slope up onto the medieval walls. She really was unfit; she must get around to fitting a gym session into her weekly schedule.

'Isn't this wonderful?' Jane said. Cassie was too puffed out to reply but when she looked around, she couldn't help smiling. From the top of the wall, she had a clear view across the terracotta rooftops. She could even make out a trace of snow on the mountains in the distance. There wasn't a cloud in the bright blue sky.

'What a great view,' she said.

They set off again. Cassie was now riding with much more confidence, but she was still rather slow. Even though the atmosphere was remarkably tranquil, the walls were teeming with life. Cassie had to concentrate hard on avoiding the people and the bicycles and the dogs – many on long extendable leads that seemed deliberately designed to trip up the unwary. A thin jogger in snakeskin-patterned leggings and a racer-back vest jogged effortlessly past her, the shiny dark ponytail sticking out through her pink baseball cap bouncing up and down. Two old men looked up from their bench as the jogger ran past and murmured something approvingly.

A woman in her sixties with rows of costume jewellery and stiff lacquered hair stopped in the middle of the road to answer her mobile phone. Cassie dodged around her, almost colliding with a bicycle coming in the other direction. The other cyclist was the epitome of elegance, dressed in a honey-coloured linen trouser suit accessorised with a carefully tied silk scarf in shades of brown and cream. The small golden-brown terrier poking his head above the rim of the woman's wicker basket looked as though he had been carefully chosen to match his owner's attire.

'Sorry!' Cassie called out as she swerved again. The woman shrugged and smiled.

Cassie finally caught up with Lisa and Jane; their progress had been slowed by a group of tourists ambling along behind a tall young woman holding up an orange flag on a stick and talking rapidly in French. Cassie could only understand a few snatches of her breathless commentary. She hadn't heard anyone talk that fast since Madame Saxifrage, their formidable old French teacher. She caught Lisa's eye. Lisa raised her eyebrows and laughed.

Cassie felt a small stab of nostalgia for the days when she and Lisa had communicated without the need for words – though that didn't stop them chattering for hours when they could. But those days were gone. Now they had nothing in common. After this mercy trip to rescue Aunt Jane was over, they would go back to living their separate lives.

Chapter Fifteen

They cycled along the walls, three abreast for a while.

'Let's wait here for a minute,' Jane said. 'This is where we're meeting Viviana for lunch later. It's not far from the gallery.'

They were looking down on the formal gardens of the Palazzo Pfanner, where a woman in a floral smock was deadheading the flowers in one of the large terracotta urns. Lisa put her hand up to shield her face from the sun.

'Oh yes, you get a really good view from here,' she said.

'Ready to carry on?' Jane said.

Cassie was surprised they hadn't stopped for longer. Since when had her aunt been so energetic? Cassie had always thought of Aunt Jane as old and frail, but with her flushed cheeks and auburn hair wafting in the light breeze, she looked almost girlish.

'Yes, let's go,' Lisa said.

Cassie turned her bicycle away from the view over the palazzo and followed Lisa. Her thighs were protesting even though they had scarcely begun their ride. Despite that, she was surprised how much she was enjoying pedalling along with the sun on her back. She had always considered cycling to be for children or grim-faced middle-aged men in Lycra. As they rode along, she began to enjoy the views as they continued to make a full circuit of the walls.

As they reapproached the lunch spot Jane had chosen, Cassie spotted Viviana coming towards them. Her all-black attire looked quite incongruous amongst the bright prints and light summery pastels that the other walkers and cyclists were wearing. Viviana was holding a round object bundled up in a check cloth and carried a rolled-up rug under one arm. Behind her, carrying a wicker basket in one hand and swinging the handle of a plastic ice box in the other, was a familiar dark-haired figure. Alonzo.

Cassie was suddenly conscious of the light film of perspiration on her face. Her nose must be glowing like Rudolph. She lifted her hand off the bike and wiped it across her forehead. A bicycle bell rang. Two teenage boys were riding straight at her. Cassie veered one way then the other as the boys headed first to her right then changed course and headed to her left. Cassie saw the young girl on a pink scooter just in time. She wrenched the handlebars to one side. The little girl scooted by unscathed. Cassie squeezed the brakes hard a moment too late. Her front wheel hit the trunk of a tree with a sickening thud. She jolted forward in the saddle. Aunt Jane screamed.

Lisa was by her side in an instant. Cassie let her sister take her by the elbow and gently lead her away from the tree. Alonzo turned and said something in rapid Italian to the small crowd that had gathered round them. The onlookers dispersed, some muttering as they went.

'Come and sit down,' Alonzo said. He had pushed his sunglasses onto the top of his head and was studying her carefully, his green eyes full of concern. Cassie didn't need any encouragement; she suddenly felt slightly faint. She sat down thankfully on the plaid picnic blanket that Viviana had spread under the shade of a chestnut tree.

'Are you okay?' Alonzo said.

Cassie nodded. The tears in her eyes were caused by shock, not pain. Her only injury was where the bark had grazed her hand after she had instinctively put it out to break her fall. It was only a scrape but tiny bubbles of blood patterned Cassie's palm.

'Here, let me see your hand . . . I'll rub a little antiseptic cream on it,' Viviana said. She fished a small red tin out of the basket on Lisa's bicycle. Cassie's bicycle was now leaning against the wall.

'Oh no, look at the bicycle!' Cassie gasped. The front wheel had buckled on impact. 'I'm so, so sorry.'

Viviana shrugged. 'You are okay – and that little girl too – that is all that matters.'

'But the wheel's bent . . .'

'It's really no problem. Our friend, Andrea, works in the repair shop. He will sort it out in no time.'

'You must let me pay for the damage.' Cassie reached for her handbag.

Viviana touched her lightly on the arm. 'No, there is no need. Andrea has been a friend for many years, he will not charge me.'

'I'll wheel it over to Andrea now before he closes up for lunch,' Alonzo said. He pushed his sunglasses back down over his eyes.

'You're not staying?' Cassie couldn't help feeling disappointed.

'I have some leftovers at home.' He took hold of the battered bicycle's handlebars. '*Ciao* everyone! Enjoy your picnic.'

'*Ciao*, Alonzo. Enjoy your afternoon off,' Viviana said.

'*Ciao!*' Cassie said. If Alonzo had the afternoon off, why hadn't he joined them? She was sure there was nothing in his fridge that could compare with the delicious-looking picnic that Viviana and Jane were laying out. He obviously didn't want to spend an hour in their company. She felt quite put out.

'Are you sure you're okay, Cassie?' Viviana was looking at her curiously as she unwrapped the check cloth to reveal an enormous golden pie.

Cassie put a big smile on her face. 'Yes, I'm fine now, honestly. Now, what's that? It looks amazing.'

'*Torta di erbe*. It's stuffed with beet leaves, herbs, salami and pecorino cheese.' Viviana wiped a knife on the check cloth and began cutting the thick pastry into generous slices. The smell of thyme made Cassie's mouth water.

'Mmm . . . this is still warm,' Lisa said.

'It's the best way to eat it. My mother made it for us; she dropped it round to the gallery just before I came out.'

'How kind,' Jane said. 'Your mother, Livia, is such a lovely woman. I've met so many wonderful people since I moved to Italy.'

Jane's eyes were shining. It obviously wasn't just Luciano's charms that were keeping her in Lucca; she had fallen in love with the beautiful town and the people in it too. Cassie was glad that her aunt wasn't lonely, but it was going to be a harder task to persuade Jane to come back to England than she had first imagined.

'Some bean salad?' Viviana interrupted Cassie's thoughts.

'Thanks.' Cassie helped herself to a scoopful. Viviana genuinely didn't seem bothered about the damage to her bicycle, but Cassie still felt awkward. She barely tasted the salad and delicious *torta di erbe* that Lisa and Aunt Jane were eating with such gusto. Although the other women insisted that she should not blame herself, Cassie knew it was all her fault. Once again she was the annoying little sister who ruined everybody's fun; the clumsy child who accidentally knocked over Lisa's carefully constructed doll's house, the wimpy cry-baby who was stung by a wasp and screamed and screamed until everyone had to roll up their beach towels, pack up the car and drive home.

Thanks to her, the afternoon's bicycle ride was ruined. And what made it worse was knowing that the accident would never have happened if she hadn't been distracted by Alonzo's unexpected appearance. She didn't know what had got into her. She had met plenty of good-looking men, she had even dated a few when she was single, and their personalities had rarely matched up to their looks. Her husband, Paul, was different; he didn't even seem aware of how handsome he was. Cassie was jolted by the sudden realisation that despite her good intentions that morning, she had barely given her husband a second thought. She pulled out her phone and sent him a quick message. He replied at once with three kisses and a pink heart emoji. As he always did.

'Have you thought about what you might do this after-noon?' Viviana asked. She was stacking the empty plastic food tubs inside each other and stashing them in her large wicker basket.

'There are plenty of places we can explore on foot,' Jane said brightly.

'Maybe we can go to Villa Bottini if it's open on a Sunday,' Lisa said.

Cassie would have been happy to sit with an ice-cream sundae outside Café Europa and watch the world go by, but she resolved to show some enthusiasm for whatever her sister and aunt decided to do. She owed them that, at least.

'It looks like you won't have to change your plans after all,' Viviana said.

Alonzo was cycling towards them, a great big grin on his face. Cassie felt her heart give a little skip. She looked away.

From now on she was determined to stay as far away from Alonzo as she could. And when meeting him was unavoidable, she would be polite and pleasant. Nothing more.

As Alonzo got nearer, Viviana started to laugh. '*Mamma mia*! I don't believe it.'

Jane gasped and clapped her hand over her mouth. Lisa gave a huge belly laugh.

Cassie looked at the other women in turn. What on earth was so funny? Then, reluctantly, she glanced at Alonzo. He was riding a most peculiar-looking bicycle. She looked again. He was riding a tandem.

'Where on earth did you get that from?' Jane said.

Alonzo pushed back his sunglasses. 'It used to belong to one of the companies that rents bicycles to tourists, but it got totally wrecked. Andrea took it off their hands; he thought it would be a fun project to restore it. He's just finished doing the repairs so he suggested I take it out for a spin. Your transport for the afternoon, Cassie; I thought you could ride on the back.'

'I really don't think so . . .' Cassie began.

'Oh, go on,' Lisa said.

Jane began to sing softly: *you'd look sweet upon the seat of a bicycle made for two* . . .

'It should suit you perfectly, you don't have to steer.' Alonzo gave Cassie a wink.

'I don't make a habit of riding into trees,' Cassie snapped.

Alonzo took a step back. 'I was only joking.'

'Cassie knows that.' Lisa gave her younger sister a hard stare.

'Yes, of course . . . sorry,' Cassie muttered. 'I'm just a bit nervous that's all . . .'

'Don't you trust me?' Alonzo's smile had come back.

'Of course she does,' Jane said.

'Come on, Cassie,' Lisa said.

They were all looking at her. Cassie swung her leg over the back of the tandem. So much for her plan to give Alonzo a wide berth; she couldn't be much closer if she tried.

'Have a great afternoon. *Ciao!*' Viviana said. She set off for Piazza Anfiteatro swinging the wicker basket in one hand and the empty cool box in the other.

People were staring as Alonzo and Cassie cycled along the walls; she had never felt so self-conscious in her life. Riding a tandem – it was just too ridiculous for words. Paul would never make her do something like this. And it was hard work, too.

Jane and Lisa sailed past. Alonzo turned his head. 'Did you see those two? We can't let them get away!' He began to pedal faster.

Cassie had to pedal with all her might to match Alonzo's longer legs. 'Slow down!' she screeched.

'No, we can't let them get away!' Alonzo shouted back. They almost caught up with Lisa and Jane as they drew level with Piazza Napoleone. Lisa turned around and made a *come and get us* hand signal. She and Jane sped up again. Cassie could hear Jane shrieking with delight.

If you can't beat them, join them. 'Come on, Alonzo!' Cassie yelled. They started pedalling like crazy. Alonzo veered around a group of teenagers some of whom held up their phones to film them as they went past. Finally, they caught the other two up.

'Enough!' gasped Jane, skidding to a halt.

The others stopped cycling too. Cassie was breathless but that didn't stop her laughing and laughing. She wiped the tears from her eyes.

'Let's sit on that bench and get our breath back,' Lisa said.

Alonzo steadied the tandem as Cassie dismounted. 'I hope you enjoyed that, after all.'

'Oh, yes.'

'I am glad,' he said. His face lit up as he smiled.

Cassie knelt down and adjusted the buckle on one of her white sandals. It didn't need altering but she wanted to avoid meeting Alonzo's eyes.

'That was wonderful,' Lisa said.

'I loved it,' Cassie said. She couldn't remember when she'd had so much fun in a long, long time. When had she and Paul last laughed like that?

Chapter Sixteen

Cassie made her way gingerly down the hotel corridor. Lisa tried not to laugh. Her sister was walking like a cowboy, a rather unlikely cowboy in pastel pink trousers.

'Are you okay?' she asked.

Cassie winced. 'That cycling used muscles I didn't know I had. How come you're not suffering? It's not as though you ever go to the gym and work out.'

Lisa shrugged. She took the stairs to the lobby two at a time.

'I'll have to slot a couple of weekly cycling sessions into my weekend's micro-schedule before I forget,' Cassie panted.

'Micro-schedule?' Lisa handed their key to the man behind the front desk.

'Haven't you heard of it? They've been micro-scheduling in Silicon Valley for years now. Paul's a great believer in it. Of course, he doesn't have a spare moment during the week, he's so busy at work, but it's so easy to let things slip at the weekend when you haven't got that structure.'

'So how does this micro-scheduling or whatever it is work?' Lisa wasn't at all interested but it gave her something different to talk about as she and Cassie made their way down the street.

'You divide the whole day into small intervals – ten or fifteen minutes; some people even do five – then you schedule in what you're going to do. It's a great way to focus, you don't waste any time at all.'

Lisa frowned. Wasn't wasting time what weekends were all about? 'When do you get to relax?'

'Oh, you schedule that in too. Some people even schedule five minutes to make a cup of tea.'

Lisa pressed her lips together firmly to stop herself laughing.

'Hi, girls, do come in.' Jane stood aside to let Lisa and Cassie through the narrow hallway to the stairs that led up to her and Luciano's apartment. 'Luciano has been busy in the kitchen, rustling up his signature *biscotti* for us to eat with our coffee.'

'I didn't know he baked,' Cassie said approvingly.

'Oh yes, but only once in a while.' Jane stopped herself adding *thank goodness*. The biscuits looked delicious but the mess in the kitchen had been something to behold. She'd spent the last half an hour trying to get the place into some sort of order before her nieces arrived. Clouds of icing sugar had dusted every surface. Luciano had used three mixing bowls. Three! She didn't even know they had that many.

'Where would you like me to put this?' Lisa asked. She was holding a potted geranium.

'Oh, you shouldn't have,' Jane said. 'But it's lovely. There's a perfect space for it out on the little sitting room balcony. Why don't you both go on through and chat to Luciano whilst I make the coffee.'

'I'll help you,' Cassie said.

'Honestly, there's no need. It'll only take me a minute.'

'If you're sure,' Lisa said.

'Quite.' Jane opened the fridge and reached for the milk jug.

She arranged some plates on a tray and added the scallop-edged napkins she had brought from Sundial Cottage. Laughter came from the sitting room. She was glad Luciano was keeping the girls amused. She'd worried that they might not get along, but it seemed her fears were groundless.

She tipped some sugar cubes into a small metal dish. Where were the tongs? Surely Luciano hadn't used those, but she wouldn't put it past him; he seemed to have made use of just about every other implement during the brief time he had spent in the kitchen.

Jane wiggled open the stiff drawer of the bureau. Perhaps the tongs had got buried in amongst the heap of old bits and bobs that were jammed in any old how. She rifled through the contents: kitchen scissors, corkscrews, spare weights for the old-fashioned kitchen scales, a fish slice . . . Aah, there were the sugar tongs, she could see them now, wedged right at the back, half hidden under a ball of twine and what looked like a couple of photographs.

Jane retrieved the tongs and the pictures. She studied the first image. Luciano was standing somewhere in the countryside, a row of cypress trees stretched into the distance. The photograph must have been taken a few years before as his hair was less grey and his waist a little slimmer. He was sporting the most extraordinary pair of custard-yellow dungarees. Jane suppressed a giggle.

Idly, she flicked the second picture over – Chiara's face beamed back at her. Standing next to her, in his crazy dungarees, was Luciano. His arm was around Chiara's waist.

The sugar tongs clattered onto the floor.

'Are you okay in there, my love?' Luciano called.

'Yes, just coming!' Jane shoved the pictures to the back of the drawer. She carried the coffee through to where her fiancé and nieces were sitting. Her knuckles were white where they gripped the tray.

'Let me take that.' Luciano was on his feet. He set the tray down and motioned for Jane to sit next to him. 'I'll pour the coffee.'

Jane was glad; she didn't want him to see her hand shaking.

'There you are, my darling, with a splash of milk, just how you like it.' Luciano handed her a cup. His eyes were warm and sincere. He took her hand in his and squeezed it. She loved him so much and he loved her. She knew he did. Chiara was just a friend. Why shouldn't he have a picture of the two of them together? Luciano had his arm around Chiara, but everyone knew how demonstrative Italians were. She resolved to put it out of her mind. It was an old picture. Something from the past. Today was what mattered.

Jane picked up the plate of *biscotti*. 'Now, who would like one of these?' she said.

Pia wheeled her suitcase along the path behind the cathedral. Lucca seemed so elegant and tranquil compared to the crowds in Florence and the colourful chaos of her hometown, Naples. It didn't take her long to find the Hotel Tosca. She checked in as quickly as she could, trying to hide her impatience as the desk clerk went through the formalities. As soon as she had stowed her case in the room, she returned downstairs and asked for directions to the Piazza Anfiteatro.

She found the place in no time at all. Tall yellow buildings all with small windows shaded by deep green shutters surrounded the oval piazza. Pia hesitated in the shade of an archway. Part of her was desperate to find the gallery but if no one there could identify 'L', she would be at a dead end. The prospect of going home with nothing to show for her trip was unbearable now she had heard the hope in her mother's voice that morning. The thought of finding her biological father had been like a tonic for Rosetta, and it was giving her something to focus on beyond her illness. Mamma had seemed so much brighter since Pia had agreed to the search.

Pia walked around slowly, past the restaurants serving clusters of tables that were grouped under their large cream umbrellas. There were a few boutiques too and a souvenir shop stacked with bottles of jewel-coloured liqueurs, olive-wood bowls and chopping boards, but there was no sign of the gallery. Perhaps it had closed down. She felt a stab of disappointment.

She was about to turn and go when her eye was caught by a curved lintel above a doorway. Italic letters on a creamy-white background spelt out Galleria Guinigi. Her breath caught in her throat. The gallery was still there. A young woman dressed in a black linen shift dress was moving around inside. Behind her, the back wall was chock-a-block with paintings. Even at a distance Pia could recognise some of the city's landmarks. One of the side walls held shelves dotted with rather arty-looking ceramics. Above the shelves was a large sun-drenched painting of the Ponte Vecchio in Florence, rendered in unusual tones of lavender and leaf green. Pia felt a rush of excitement. One of the gallery's artists had a connection to Florence. There was a chance, however small, that the artist could be connected to the grandfather she had never known.

Pia steeled herself to go inside. The woman she'd seen through the window was coming out of the gallery. They almost collided in the doorway.

'I'm sorry, we are just closing for lunch. We reopen at four.' The young woman smiled. She turned and pulled the dark green shutter down over the door.

Chapter Seventeen

Cassie stared at the dummy's fur-trimmed cashmere coat and tried to imagine Puccini wearing it more than a hundred years ago. She couldn't honestly claim to be particularly interested in Puccini's life but at least this visit to the house where he was born would give her something to talk to Luciano about. The more she spoke to him, the more likely he would let slip something that Cassie could use to dissuade Aunt Jane from her rash decision to up sticks and settle in Italy.

She moved from the small dressing room into the main bedroom, Puccini's parents' room. *The wedding chest dates back to the late fifteenth century*, she read.

'Fascinating,' a woman in a yellow dress said. 'It's amazing to think Puccini was born in this very room. I've come all the way from Chicago, you know.'

Cassie smiled politely. She continued through the rooms, quickly bypassing a rather strange plaster statue of the composer but lingering in the little study and the Turandot Room housing the glittering costumes from Puccini's opera of the same name. She exited into via di Poggio and paused by Puccini's statue in the Piazza Cittadella. The composer had one ankle resting on his opposing knee the way dear Uncle Eddie had always sat.

It was still only half past five. Aunt Jane and Lisa were bound to still be walking around the shops or sitting in one of the cafés on via Fillungo enjoying a cold drink. She wondered if they'd had any luck finding Jane's wedding shoes.

Cassie sighed. She would have enjoyed mooching around the shops, but she couldn't bring herself to join in. How could she *ooh* and *aah* over pointy toes and kitten heels when she had come to Italy in order to put a stop to the whole circus?

Persuading Aunt Jane to see sense was going to be much harder than Cassie ever imagined. She had anticipated a little gentle persuasion, a few choice words, the odd innocent comparison to Uncle Eddie – done ever so subtly, of course – and then comforting her aunt once Jane realised how ridiculous and unseemly the whole situation was.

The problem was things hadn't worked out quite like that. Before coming to Lucca, Cassie had assumed that Luciano was a manipulative gold-digger. Of course, Aunt Jane wasn't rich but she was comfortable enough with her teachers' pension and a little income from Uncle Eddie's sensible, low-risk investments. But Luciano didn't seem interested in money. He certainly hadn't persuaded Jane to fund an upgrade for his old car or the serviceable-but-basic kitchen in the apartment. He wore an ancient-looking watch with a worn leather strap, his mish-mash of baggy, colourful clothes looked as though they were sourced from the bargain box at the local market and he certainly didn't look as though he had troubled the barber's chair for many a long month.

His only extravagances were his oil paints and his food. Even with his gargantuan appetite, the bulk purchase of spaghetti was unlikely to bankrupt her aunt. Besides, when they ate out, Luciano was usually the first to reach for his wallet.

Comparisons with Uncle Eddie were dangerous; Luciano's work as an artist was undeniably more interesting than Uncle Eddie's position as Health and Safety officer at the local tyre factory. Luciano was fun to be with. He had a great sense of humour. He made Jane laugh and smile after all those sad years.

Cassie frowned. It was hard to find anything specifically wrong with Luciano. Perhaps his romance with her aunt really was a simple story of late-blossoming love? But Jane and Luciano's engagement was far too sudden. Spontaneous. Cassie shuddered. Marriage was a serious business; rushing into it was wrong. There were times when even she and Paul didn't get along even though she didn't like to admit it. How much harder would it be for Jane to cope where she barely spoke the language, far from her old friends and family. Cassie needed to help Jane realise she was making a big mistake. She wished she could count on Lisa's support but Lisa had been won over by Luciano's charms and she was too wrapped up in Matteo to worry about her aunt's future. Cassie had tried to seek Paul's advice when he had phoned that morning, but her husband didn't seem interested in her aunt's predicament.

Cassie's phone buzzed. Paul had forwarded her a video, a promotion for cooker hoods. She tutted in irritation. Her husband was supposed to be busy at work. Didn't he have anything better to do? She stowed the phone in the inside pocket of her white shoulder bag without replying and set off down via Vittoria Veneto in the direction of Piazza Napoleone. She could do with a cup of tea and she knew just the place.

She made her way to the little café just off the piazza. Two curly-haired women were sharing one of Da Giocomo's tables. Although one had a short bob and the other's hair cascaded over her shoulders, they shared the same high foreheads, narrow chins and wide smiles. They had to be sisters. They leant forward talking conspiratorially and laughing. They were so at ease in each other's company. Cassie felt a pang of envy. Why couldn't she and Lisa be like that?

Then she saw him. Alonzo. Sitting all alone. She felt a flutter of excitement. He was looking down at his phone; he hadn't spotted her yet. Cassie hesitated at the empty table by the two sisters. Alonzo looked up. She couldn't see his eyes behind his sunglasses but he must have seen her because he raised his hand and smiled.

Cassie pushed an empty chair aside and made her way over to his table. It was the exact same one they had both been sitting at two days before.

Alonzo pushed his sunglasses back up into his thick, dark hair. '*Ciao*, Cassie.'

His slow, lazy smile made her stomach flip over. She pulled her eyes away, with difficulty, from his soft full lips.

'May I?' She pulled out a chair before he had time to respond.

She caught a flicker of surprise as his gaze took in the half-empty café. 'If I'm not interrupting.'

'Not at all.' Alonzo put his phone away. 'What can I get you?'

He picked up his beer and took a long swallow. His fingers left prints on the cold glass. His tongue flicked away a fleck of foam just below the little mole at the corner of his mouth. The cup of tea she was about to order no longer seemed up to the task.

'A glass of white wine please.'

'Before six?' Alonzo whistled. 'I didn't think you did that.'

Cassie shifted on the metal chair. She never drank alcohol this early in the day but she hadn't remembered telling Alonzo that. He must think her terribly dull.

'Rules are made to be broken.' She laughed awkwardly.

'That sounds very Italian.' He smiled.

Cassie smiled back. It was difficult to speak when Alonzo's melting green eyes were on her. She hoped the table service would be quicker than the usual Italian dawdle. She really needed that relaxing glass of wine.

The waiter appeared with a huge glass, and two small pottery dishes, one filled with crisps, the other with green olives. Cassie was surprised Alonzo hadn't ordered another beer. She took a rather too large mouthful of wine. It was deliciously cold. She drank some more.

'No Lisa and Jane?'

'They've gone shopping. Aunt Jane is looking for her wedding shoes.'

'You didn't fancy joining them?'

'No. What about you, what are you up to today?' she said quickly.

'I've been hunched over my workbench all day. A good client has commissioned a rather intricate lariat. It's been a pleasure to work on but there comes a time when a man needs a break. I find that a stroll and a swift beer does the trick.' He ripped the paper wrapping from a wooden cocktail stick and speared one of the olives. He closed his eyes in pleasure. 'Mmm . . . so what have you been doing whilst your aunt and sister shop?'

'I went to Puccini's house.' She was glad to talk about something that would distract her from musing over his peculiarly long eyelashes.

'In via di Poggio? You liked it?' He took another olive. It was nearly the same green as his eyes.

'Yes, I loved the way they played his music as you walked from room to room. I liked everything apart from that creepy plaster statue.'

'That statue . . . yes, I tend to agree.' Alonzo grinned, showing his even, white teeth. 'Those costumes from *Turandot*. Aren't they great?' His eyes lit up. Was there anyone living in Lucca who wasn't in love with Puccini, Cassie wondered.

'I don't know much about opera,' she said.

'I only know a little. I am glad I'm a jeweller, not a musician. Music can take over your life. Take Puccini himself. When he was a teenager, he walked thirty kilometres from Lucca to Pisa to see Verdi's *Aida*. He was smitten. From that moment on he was determined to make his living from music.'

'Did he have time for anything else? Did he marry and have a family?'

'Yes, he married eventually. Elvira was his great love. He was just twenty-five when he met her, she was a couple of years younger. But nothing was straightforward. She was already the wife of a rich merchant. She gave up her life with her wealthy husband to be with Puccini. It was quite the scandal. They could not marry until many years later, after her husband's death.'

'How romantic . . .' Cassie murmured.

'Yes, romantic, but Elvira was difficult, as well as intelligent and beautiful. She could not control her jealous nature. Puccini admitted to several mistresses, but she believed he had more lovers that he was concealing, no matter how much he denied it. She was convinced he was involved with their young maid, Doria, and drove the poor girl to suicide with her accusations. Elvira was sentenced to five months in prison for defamation and instigating suicide, but she appealed and Puccini paid the family off.'

'Goodness.' Cassie swallowed a large mouthful of wine.

'Puccini and Elvira separated for a while but they were reunited. It seems he could not live without her.'

Alonzo leant towards her to reach for the dish of crisps. He was wearing the same aftershave he had been wearing the first time they met in the Galleria Guinigi when he fastened the rose-gold choker around her neck. The scent of his warm skin was intoxicating. She didn't doubt that a man like Alonzo could arouse the same level of passionate devotion as Puccini did. Cassie shivered with pleasure. She edged her chair a little closer.

Alonzo's green eyes sought hers. 'Love is not logical. A love like Elvira's can be destructive. But to live without love – that is intolerable.'

He smiled. Cassie smiled back. She leant forward, as if reaching for an olive and let her hand brush against his. This was the moment she had been fantasising about. He was going to kiss her. She was powerless to resist. She tilted her chin up towards his and closed her eyes.

Alonzo jumped backwards. 'Cassie, what are you doing!'

The metal table rocked; the little remaining wine sloshed up the side of Cassie's glass. Heat burned through her. What *was* she doing? She froze, unable to move or speak. People on the adjacent tables were looking around.

Alonzo sat back down. He seemed anxious not to make a scene.

'I'm sorry . . .' Cassie muttered.

'I thought you were happily married . . .' Alonzo's eyes were hidden behind his sunglasses once more.

'I was . . . I am . . . I mean . . .' Cassie couldn't sit there a moment longer. She grabbed her bag and scraped back her chair.

'Cassie . . .' Alonzo said.

She squeezed her way out through the gaps between the tables and walked away. She wanted to run but she was conscious of the stares of the other customers.

She marched across the piazza without looking back. What had come over her? How could she be so foolish? It was all Alonzo's fault. He had wormed his way into her brain with his dreamy eyes and his talk of passion and illicit affairs.

'Cassie! Cassie!'

Alonzo was running towards her. 'Please wait!'

She waited. There was no point in trying to outrun him. What did he want? Had he changed his mind? Was he going to tell her he'd made a mistake, that he had fallen for her too? What would she do then? She wasn't going to leave Paul for a foolish fantasy.

'You dropped this.' He held out a small booklet.

Lucca Attractions. She burst into tears.

'Cassie – no!' Now Alonzo did put his arms around her, comforting her like a child. She had never felt so humiliated.

She pushed him away and rooted in her bag for a tissue. She blew her nose loudly. What a sight she must look.

'Please. I do not understand. I do not mean to upset you.'

Cassie dabbed her nose with the soggy tissue. She looked at Alonzo's handsome face. His genuine look of bafflement told her all she needed to know.

'I'm sorry, Alonzo. I don't know what came over me. The heat, and the wine . . .' It was hard to blame the wine when she had only drunk one glass but Cassie was clutching at straws. 'When you told me the story of Puccini and Elvira, I thought . . .'

'That it was a clumsy way of telling you something?'

Cassie sniffed.

'But last time we spoke you were telling me about your kitchen extension, your husband, all your plans . . .'

'I know. I don't know . . . I'm sorry . . .' Cassie turned away.

Alonzo put one hand on each of her shoulders and twisted her back round to face him. 'There is no need to be sorry. Sometimes when we are on holiday, something strange happens. We try on a different life and think we have become someone else. Then when we go back home we realise that we are who we have always been.'

Cassie managed a quiet 'thank you'.

'Are you sure you're okay?'

Cassie nodded. 'Yes, I'm fine,' she lied. She was far from okay. Alonzo's kindness and understanding made it all so much worse.

Alonzo frowned. He looked as though he was about to say something but thought better of it. He turned and walked away.

Cassie trudged through the streets until she came to the ancient gate of San Pietro on the edge of the town. She took the main road that led out to the railway station. How tempting it was to hop on a train and escape somewhere. Anywhere.

She stopped in front of the station. A train must have just pulled in because a stream of people was exiting. Tourists dragged colourful cases behind them waving their paper maps; a group of six older ladies sporting baseball caps and carrying matching cloth bags emblazoned with a reproduction of Michelangelo's *David* were laughing and joking. Escaping wouldn't do Cassie any good. Wherever she went she would be surrounded by happy people.

She crossed back over the road and climbed the steps up to the old city wall. She sat on a bench and stared at the *campanile* of San Martino cathedral for a long time.

Her phone buzzed. Her body tensed. She didn't think she could bear to receive a kind, polite message from

Alonzo. But she couldn't resist reaching for it. There were two messages. Aunt Jane and Lisa were going to stop for a drink at Café Europa; she was welcome to join them. The second was from Paul. *What do you think of the cooker hoods? No rush. Hope you're having fun. I love you xxx.* She didn't send a reply.

She dragged herself back to the Hotel Tosca. The room key was still on the hook behind the front desk. Lisa must still be out with Aunt Jane. Cassie let out a sigh of relief. She couldn't bear to see her loved-up sister right now. She climbed the stairs, dropped her handbag on the floor and threw herself onto the bed.

Cassie buried her face in the pillow. Alonzo was wrong. When Cassie returned home she would be a very different person. All her old certainties were gone. She no longer knew what she wanted or who she was.

Chapter Eighteen

'Cheers!' Lisa said.

'*Saluti!*' Aunt Jane added. They clinked their glasses together.

The outdoor tables were filling up; Piazza Anfiteatro was going to be busy that evening. Lisa pushed her chair back from under the Café Europa's cream umbrella and turned her face to the afternoon sun.

Aunt Jane glanced at her watch again. 'Still nothing from Cassie?'

'No, nothing, but I'm sure she's fine. I'll check my phone, make sure I haven't turned it off accidentally,' Lisa said, though she knew that she hadn't.

'I do hope she's okay. It's very strange she didn't want to come shopping today; she normally loves giving advice.'

'Even if it's not always welcome!' Lisa joked. She hadn't been shopping with Cassie for a long, long time. Everything Lisa picked out was apparently 'too shapeless' or 'too scruffy,' or worse, 'a bit young'.

Aunt Jane smiled. 'She's not always terribly subtle. But it is rather strange . . .'

Lisa reached for her wine glass. She wasn't going to share her sister's reason for declining to join their afternoon shoe shopping party.

Jane fiddled with her engagement ring. 'I don't want to sound alarmist but don't you think she's been acting oddly the last couple of days? A bit distracted, don't you think?'

Lisa nodded. She'd been thinking the same herself. 'Sometimes I catch her staring into space with this strange smile on her face.'

'And she didn't mention that kitchen extension at all yesterday. When she first arrived it was all she could talk about.'

'Shades of Egypt via suburbia,' Lisa laughed. 'Perhaps I should have sounded more enthusiastic about it.'

Aunt Jane ran a finger around the rim of her wine glass. 'I think it's something more than that.'

'Maybe she's just missing Paul,' Lisa said. She took another sip of Prosecco.

'Or not . . .' Aunt Jane bit her lip.

'What do you mean?' Lisa said.

'Oh, nothing.' Jane reddened as if she had already said too much. 'I hope she enjoyed Puccini's house. It will give her something to talk to Luciano about this evening. She seems very keen to get to know him.'

'That's one of the reasons we came.' Lisa hoped her expression did not give too much away.

Jane put her empty glass on the table. 'Much though I'd love to stay for another, I'm going to have to go. I promised I'd hold the fort at the gallery for an hour. It will give Viviana a chance to catch up on the online orders whilst Luciano's still out painting.'

'Isn't that hard when you don't speak much of the language?'

'It can be a bit taxing but I never stay for more than an hour or two. I've got a list of useful phrases stuck to the side of the till so I can usually muddle through,' Jane laughed.

'Well, good luck.' Lisa leant and kissed Jane, her face brushing against her aunt's. 'It's been a wonderful afternoon but I'd better go too. I'm sure Cassie will be back at the hotel. She's probably forgotten to turn her phone on and wondering where we are.'

'I'm sure you're right,' Jane said.

Lisa walked through one of the archways of the Piazza Anfiteatro. Jane was right: Cassie had been acting oddly. She hadn't mentioned that kitchen extension for at least twenty-four hours and she hadn't even noticed when Lisa accidentally buttoned up her shirt skew-whiff. And what had Jane meant when she made that hasty remark about Cassie and Paul?

Lisa frowned. Maybe there was something amiss with her sister; she'd been too wrapped up in Matteo to notice. She felt a pang of guilt. She hurried through the door of the Hotel Tosca.

Their room key was missing from the rack. Lisa sighed with relief. Cassie was back. Lisa was too impatient to wait for the doll-sized lift. She climbed the stairs two at a time.

She raised her hand to knock on the door. It was very slightly ajar. A nasty trickle of fear crept down her spine. Cassie was always so careful about security. If she was in the room, that door would be closed. And locked. Tentatively, Lisa pushed open the door.

Cassie was face down on the bed. Her clothes were all rumpled and strands of hair had escaped from her fishtail plait. Her white bag was lying on the floor; the zip was undone, a lipstick had rolled across the tiles.

Lisa's stomach clenched. The slightly open door, the handbag tossed on the floor. For a split second she feared the room had been burgled and Cassie left for dead, but then heard the recognisable sounds of her sister snuffling in her sleep.

Lisa hadn't heard those noises since they were teenagers sharing a bedroom in the tiny flat Mum had rented after Dad had gone. She stifled a giggle. Cassie gave another small snort. She was definitely alive. Lisa's breathing slowed. She looked around the room. Cassie's purse was on the chest of drawers, her phone on a cushion on the bedroom chair. No burglar either.

Lisa quietly lifted her book from her bedside table. She would read in the corner of the hotel bar until it was time to wake her sister. As she crept back across the room and edged past Cassie's bed, Lisa spotted something poking out from the bedspread that lay crumpled by her sister's feet. A familiar grey, triangular shape. Lisa very gently loosened one of the bedcover's folds. She was right – it was a soft, velour ear.

Dear old Ele-pants. He only had one tusk now, and his stuffing had redistributed itself so that his bottom was round and lumpy and his head was nearly flat. Lisa had assumed her serious, unsentimental sister had dispatched him to landfill many years ago. What else lay hidden behind Cassie's grown-up façade?

She rearranged the cover to conceal the toy elephant. Lisa looked at her sister's round, pink cheeks, her unravelling plait. She looked so vulnerable. And so young. Lisa felt like the big sister once more. She would find out what was on Cassie's mind. She would be a better sister. She would be a better friend.

She closed the door quietly and took the stairs to the lobby. The sound of Puccini's *Un bel di, vedremo* was coming from the small speaker in the corner. A cosy winged chair in the corner of the bar awaited her. She snuggled back against a soft velvet cushion and luxuriated in the pleasure of thinking about Matteo, uninterrupted. She wondered what he was doing right now. Might he be thinking of her? She couldn't wait to see him tomorrow but she knew it was foolish to dream. They were going home in a couple of days and there wasn't much likelihood that they would keep in touch after she returned to England – though she supposed she'd see him again at Jane's wedding, if by chance he was back in Lucca.

Both she and Cassie had learnt early on that there were only two types of men: the exciting charismatic types like their father, who led you a merry dance then walked away, and the kind but rather dull, sensible sort like Paul and Uncle Eddie, who came home on time and never strayed. Lisa finally understood why Cassie had chosen the latter. It saved so much pain. Lisa's cherished freedom no longer seemed so appealing. Loving and leaving Matteo wasn't going to be easy.

She closed her eyes and let Puccini's music wash over her. She could imagine Luciano singing away whilst he painted. Jane had found a steady, kind man who was never likely to stray but who also set her heart racing. Luciano was her soul mate. There was a chance Lisa could find someone too. But first she'd have to rescue her heart from Matteo. They would spend tomorrow together. Then she would steel herself to walk away.

Pia scrolled through her photographs. It was a shame that Mamma insisted on using an old-style flip-top phone; she would have liked to send her some pictures. Rosetta would love the statues and rose bushes in the garden of the Palazzo Pfanner and the shimmering mosaic on the façade of the church of San Frediano. Pia had managed to see a few of the places listed in her *Lucca Attractions* leaflet after walking the whole circumference of the old city walls.

Now it was gone half six. If she didn't sum up her courage and go straight to the gallery, she would likely find it closed for the night. She'd dithered for too long. She hurried back to the Piazza Anfiteatro. Wiping her damp hands on her jeans she pushed open the gallery door. A bell jangled. The young woman in the severe black dress was no longer there, her place had been taken by a much older lady in a mauve blouse and a soft pink cardigan.

Pia made a show of looking at the ceramics and the intricate jewellery displayed in perspex boxes near the front of the shop. The gallery was cool but despite the elderly shop assistant's friendly demeanour, she felt hot and flustered. This wasn't the sort of place she was used to. She felt all at sea and out of place. She was tempted to turn and leave. She fiddled with the corner of the envelope holding Nonna Concetta's portrait that was safely stowed in her striped bag.

Pia pointed to the painting of the Ponte Vecchio; she had to start the conversation somewhere. 'That's a beautiful painting. The colours are so unusual.'

'Yes, isn't it,' the woman replied. Her Italian had a foreign accent, her voice hesitant. 'That's by Chiara Marinetti, a local artist. She usually works on much larger canvases. There's an exhibition of her work on nearby. You may like to see it.' She handed Pia a small square card.

'*Grazie.*' Pia tucked the card in her back pocket.

'If you like Florence, we have some small unframed works by another artist. Let me see . . .' She reached beneath the counter, brought out a green folder and fanned out some pencil sketches on the wooden surface.

Pia nodded politely. She felt such a fraud, knowing she wouldn't be buying anything. Why couldn't she pluck up the courage to say what she'd come for?

'And we have this.' The woman laid a small sketch of Florence Cathedral on the counter. 'The blue pastel is pretty, don't you think?'

Pia took a sharp intake of breath.

'Are you okay?' The woman studied her with kind blue eyes.

'Yes . . . I . . . yes, of course. I just wondered: who is the artist? Does he live in Florence?'

'No, Luciano lives here in Lucca.'

'Luciano?' Pia held her breath. Luciano began with an 'L'. Could she really have found her nonno already?

'Luciano Zingaretti. He sometimes makes trips into Florence but most of his subjects are here in Lucca. That large painting of Chiesa San Michele is one of his.'

'And portraits?' Pia could hear her voice tremble.

'I'm afraid not. Luciano concentrates on the wonderful architecture of Tuscany. Perhaps when he was young . . .'

'Is he an old man?'

The woman seemed startled.

'I'm sorry, I don't mean to be rude. I . . .'

'Don't look so worried. To you he would seem very old. But not to me.' Her eyes strayed to her unusual star-shaped ring that sparkled under the gallery's artificial light.

'That's pretty,' Pia said.

'It was made by a local jeweller, Alonzo. We stock some of his work here but Luciano had this made specially.'

'The same Luciano who drew this?'

'Yes.' The woman smiled shyly. Her hand smoothed her light auburn hair. 'I never imagined I would be marrying again.'

'Congratulations,' Pia said.

'Thank you.' A slight pinkness suffused the lady's cheeks. She seemed so sweet.

'If you want to ask Luciano about his work, he'll be here tomorrow. We should open at nine but on Luciano's days sometimes it's nearer to ten.' She laughed. 'It's a shame he isn't here now but he's busy completing a painting, and we have some family – my nieces from England – visiting so he needs to snatch the time when he can. Come tomorrow, say you spoke to me today. I'm Jane.'

'Pia. Thank you. I may come back.' Pia turned towards the door. A man who was probably in his seventies, who drew with a blue pastel and whose name began with an 'L'. It had to be Rosetta's papa. Tomorrow she would meet her nonno Luciano.

She walked across the Piazza Anfiteatro in a bit of a daze.

'Watch out!' a man shouted. Pia ducked out of the way of his horse and trap just in time.

'Sorry!' she called over her shoulder. Her heart was pounding. The last thing she needed right now was to get knocked down in the street.

The seductive sound of 'Musetta's Waltz' from Puccini's *La Boheme* drifted over from one of the cafés. She sat down at one of the outside tables and ordered a glass of white wine. She didn't often drink but she needed something to calm her down. She had found 'L', the father that her mamma Rosetta had never known. She should have been over the moon, instead she was filled with doubt.

The waiter put down her glass of wine, along with a small glass bowl of green olives and a saucer of chicken liver *crostini*. Pia took a long draught of the cold liquid. Throughout her quest she had only thought of finding her nonno; she hadn't given a moment's thought to the family he might have. A sweet, softly spoken elderly English fiancée, at least two nieces, perhaps children from a previous marriage, siblings, other grandchildren, who knew how wide Rosetta's family was? All those people probably knew nothing of Rosetta and Pia's existence. Would they be thrilled to hear about Luciano's illegitimate child? Or would they be shocked and dismayed?

She fiddled with the strap of her bag that now lay on the adjacent chair. The envelope holding Nonna's picture was safe inside. How would Luciano's fiancée react when she knew of it? She had looked so kind and gentle and so obviously excited to be marrying again. Had Luciano told her about his past? Or had he kept quiet about the young girl he had abandoned all those years ago?

Pia ate her way through the plate of *crostini*, one hand resting on her canvas bag. She had hoped that 'L' would treat the portrait as a long-lost gem. Now she feared she was holding a hand grenade that could shatter Jane and Luciano's lives.

Chapter Nineteen

The aroma of freshly baked bread rolls was hard to resist. It took every ounce of Lisa's willpower to bypass the laden wicker basket on the hotel buffet. She ladled a small scoop of fresh fruit salad into a bowl and carried it out to the terrace. She tore her eyes away from Cassie's laden plate and ordered a cappuccino from the waiter who was placing her sister's latte on the table.

'Not hungry?' Cassie tore the corner off a custard-filled *cornetto*. Tiny dots of icing sugar clung to her pink lip gloss.

'I'm meeting Matteo in twenty minutes. He told me not to have breakfast but . . .'

'Impossible not to have something.' Cassie's smile didn't quite reach her eyes. She pulled off another piece of pastry and dipped it into her coffee.

Lisa frowned. Something wasn't right. Cassie always used cutlery. Even as a small child she had insisted on knives and forks at her birthday parties, cutting her food up daintily whilst her friends crammed pizza into their mouths with their chubby fingers.

Lisa ate a spoonful of the chopped peach and strawberries; they were as delicious as the pastry would have been. Whatever Matteo had planned, Lisa wasn't going to risk going out on a completely empty stomach. Her insides had a horrible habit of gurgling alarmingly on the rare occasions she missed breakfast. She ate her meagre bowl of fruit slowly. The sun was warm on her bare arms; it was going to be a hot day.

She flicked a tiny speck of strawberry from the skirt of her favourite sundress. The faded blue and orange pattern always made her smile. An armful of silver bangles and friendship bracelets jangled as she lifted her coffee cup. The sounds of children chatting and laughing came from the pavement on the other side of the hedge. They sounded happy. Who wouldn't be happy on such a beautiful day? Lisa smiled to herself. She wondered what Matteo had planned.

Cassie continued to shovel down her breakfast, her eyes fixed on some spot in the distance.

Lisa studied Cassie's face carefully. Her eyes looked slightly puffy; perhaps she had slept badly. 'You're not upset, are you?' she asked.

'No, of course not.' Cassie took a huge bite of her sticky *crostata* as if to discourage further conversation.

'I didn't think you'd mind . . .'

'Mind what?' Cassie mumbled through a mouthful of tart.

'That I'm not coming with you and Jane to Montecatini today. It's just that Matteo has a few days free before he leaves for his concerts in Vienna. I could have put him off until tomorrow but that's when we're seeing the wedding venue.'

'I wonder what it's like.'

'I think it's quite a simple restaurant and function room but Jane says the views are really something,' Lisa said.

Cassie ripped the lid off the top of her yogurt and deposited the foil on the side of her plate. 'It will be good to spend some more time with Jane, especially since I ducked out of that shopping trip. Did you find any wedding shoes? I clean forgot to ask her last night.'

'Everything cream or white was too high or too flat. Jane doesn't want to totter around but she's quite small; she doesn't want to look silly standing next to Luciano in the photographs.'

'Anyone would look diddy standing next to him. He's like a great bear. A big, friendly bear.'

Lisa smiled. It seemed that Cassie was warming to Luciano at last. So, if neither Luciano nor Aunt Jane was the cause of Cassie's agitation, it must be something that Lisa had done, but she couldn't think of anything that could have upset her sister. 'So, you're really sure you don't mind that I'm not coming with you today?' Lisa said.

'Honestly, Lisa! Jane and I aren't six years old. I think we can just about manage to catch a train to Montecatini without you.' Cassie's eyes flashed.

Lisa put her hands up in mock surrender. 'Okay, okay.'

'You might as well make the most of the next couple of days with Matteo,' Cassie added. 'It's not like you'll see him again once we're back home.'

Lisa winced and bit back a sarcastic retort. She'd vowed last night to rebuild her relationship with her little sister but Cassie didn't always make it easy. She pushed away the remnants of her meagre breakfast. 'I'd better run. Matteo will be here any moment.'

Cassie swallowed her mouthful of *cornetto*. 'Have a good time.'

'I will. Have a great time in Montecatini.'

Lisa left Cassie sitting on the sunny terrace. She checked her appearance in the mirror on the wall of the small cloakroom just off the corridor that led to the hotel lobby. Her bangles and friendship bracelets glittered in a shaft of sunlight from the small window high up on the wall. She loved them but now they looked a bit teenage and unsophisticated. She never usually worried about what she wore but the excitement of spending the day with Matteo had her geed up with nerves. She wiped her hands on the front of her sundress and checked the time. Again. Matteo would be here any minute.

She stood in the empty lobby, twiddling her silver and turquoise ring.

'*Ciao, bella!*' Matteo strode into the Hotel Tosca, his hand on the shoulder of a short, wiry man with the deep tan of someone who spent all day outdoors. He dropped a soft kiss on her lips. Lisa's heart gave a little jump. 'This is my friend, Carlo,' he said.

'Hi . . . I mean *ciao!*' Lisa said.

'Matteo's told me all about you.' Carlo grinned. 'Now come and meet Gaia. She's waiting around the corner.'

'Great.' Lisa forced a smile. Matteo hadn't said anything about meeting other people. She had thought it would be just the two of them doing something romantic together.

'You're going to love her.' Matteo took her hand. They followed Carlo out through the revolving door. Carlo turned the corner where a horse and trap were waiting patiently by the side of the road. He stepped towards them.

'Here she is – my lovely Gaia.'

Lisa felt all the tension in her body evaporate. Gaia was beautiful. A big chestnut mare with four white legs and a wide white blaze as though someone had poured a pot of white paint down the centre of her long nose. A thick flaxen forelock almost reached her big brown eyes; her mane was secured in neat plaits each finished off with a crimson ribbon. Lisa ran her hand over the horse's gleaming coat. She turned to Matteo; his eyes were sparkling.

Gaia lifted her head and whinnied softly.

'Madam, your steed awaits,' Matteo joked. He took Lisa's arm and helped her step up and into the wooden open-topped carriage. It would have been easier if she had been wearing trousers, but she was glad she had chosen her favourite sundress for such a special outing.

'A drink?' Matteo asked.

Lisa gasped. She had been too busy admiring her new four-legged friend to notice the small wooden table groaning with an array of fruit, cakes and pastries. A bottle of Prosecco, and one of fruit juice were secured in purpose-built holders. Matteo carefully poured out two glasses.

'All set?' Carlo asked. He hopped up into the driver's seat and with a quick shake of the reins they were off. Gaia's large behind rolled from side to side as her hooves clip-clopped loudly along the road, through the archway into the Piazza Anfiteatro, past the coffee drinkers outside Café Europa across the piazza. Pigeons pecking crumbs from the paving swooped up and away. Viviana waved from the doorway of the Galleria Guinigi.

'*Ciao!*' Carlo called. They exited through another archway into the winding via Fillungo, where Lisa and Jane had wandered looking in vain for Jane's wedding shoes.

Carlo skilfully negotiated a path through the bicycles, window-shoppers and dog-walkers who meandered across the pavement-free road. 'Gaia wears blinkers so she is less distracted by what is going on around her. I have to keep a careful eye out so that no one steps straight in front of us,' he said.

'And that funny little crochet hat she wears over her ears, what's that?' Lisa asked. She didn't remember the donkeys wearing those on her childhood outings to Blackpool. Or perhaps their ears were too big to fit.

'They stop insects getting caught in her ears and make it a bit less noisy for her.'

Lisa nodded. She thought of Luciano marching along singing. He wasn't the only Italian who liked to live life at full volume.

'That's the clock tower ahead of us. It's the tallest in Lucca, taller than the Guinigi Tower,' Matteo said.

Carlo looked over his shoulder. 'Next we'll pass by San Michele, my favourite of all the churches.'

'We cycled this way with Aunt Jane,' Lisa said.

'Before Cassie had that argument with a tree,' Matteo joked.

'Yes!' Lisa could laugh about it now.

Carlo flicked the reins. Gaia walked on, passing a young family pulling their suitcases along behind them. Their smallest child, a girl in striped dungarees, jumped up and down pointing at Gaia.

'Horsey! Horsey!' the little girl cried, waving her pink teddy above her head in excitement. Her father laughed and waved too; her mother patted the girl's blonde curls. Lisa felt a small pang. She had never imagined having a family of her own but last night she had had the strangest dream: she and Matteo were cycling through Lucca on a tandem with a small child perched on the handlebars.

'We'll head for a ramp that will take us up onto the walls and we can make a circuit of the town,' Carlo said, breaking her reverie. 'It's better up there as we can keep Gaia away from the traffic. And of course you will have lovely views.'

'Gaia really is beautiful,' Lisa said.

'Like you,' Matteo said quietly.

Lisa flushed with pleasure. She took a sip of water. The fizzy Prosecco was making her feel quite light-headed. Or perhaps it was the way Matteo looked at her, the feel of his hand in hers.

The mare had no trouble pulling the carriage up the sloping road to the top of the wall.

'It's not too hot for her at this time of the day.' Gaia's ears pricked as though she knew Carlo was talking about her. He rubbed her neck affectionately. 'I don't let her work in the middle of the day when the sun is too strong. *Walk on, Gaia!* She would be happy to trot but it's nice to take it easy, don't you think.'

Looking out over the walls from her position up in the carriage was a totally different experience from the adrenaline-powered bike ride with Cassie and Jane. This time Lisa could really take in the beauty of her surroundings: the terracotta tiled roofs, the jumble of houses and churches on one side and the mountains in the distance. She fancied she could see a trace of snow in one or two of the crevices. From time to time she sneaked a sideways look at Matteo's face: his long eyelashes, his sharp cheekbones, the small bump on his nose. He seemed to become more attractive every time they met.

'The Palazzo Pfanner,' Carlo said, bringing Gaia to a halt. Lisa had a fantastic view of the gardens and the soft cream and grey façade of the Palazzo.

'Are you thinking what I'm thinking?' Matteo said.

'About meeting you in those gardens? It was so lucky to bump into you again.'

'It was fate, to meet you again in one of my favourite places in Lucca.' Matteo's melting brown eyes looked at her so tenderly her stomach flipped over.

'I was so stupid that morning outside San Frediano, assuming you were an actor.'

'You weren't stupid. When someone has hurt you, it is natural to fear being hurt again.'

'It was so long ago; I was a child when Dad left us.' Lisa fiddled with her turquoise and silver ring.

'Those experiences can stay with us for a long time. But that is all in the past. You are here with me now.'

He squeezed her hand but the happiness she felt was tinged with sadness. They were together today but Matteo was off to Vienna soon, playing in the first of many concerts all over Europe.

Gaia tossed her head, impatient to get moving again. Carlo flicked the reins and the mare walked on, her hips swinging. She broke into a trot to pass a small group of tourists with audio guides in their ears and matching orange baseball caps. A woman with sunburnt shoulders, who was wobbling along in her too-high wedge-heeled espadrilles, looked enviously at Lisa's mode of transportation. A few of the tourists snapped photographs and a young woman with a hooped nose-ring lifted her camera phone and followed their progress. It was funny to think that strangers might be watching her and Matteo on YouTube one day.

Carlo drove the carriage back through the town by a circuitous route, carefully guiding the horse and trap down the narrowest of the old streets. Eventually they halted opposite the wedding-cake façade of the cathedral.

Matteo carefully helped Lisa down from the carriage. 'Thank you so much, Carlo. *Grazie mille!*'

'Would you like to give Gaia a carrot? Here you go, hold your hand flat so you don't lose any fingers.'

Lisa put her palm just under Gaia's nose. The carrot disappeared in a trice.

'All in one go! That wasn't very ladylike.' Lisa rubbed the mare's silky neck, reluctant to turn away. Jane and Cassie would be gone for hours but she didn't know if Matteo intended to include her in his plans for the rest of the day.

'Thank you for arranging this – it was wonderful,' she said.

'I am so glad you enjoyed it.' Matteo's smile did something to her that she couldn't explain.

'I loved it,' she said. *And I love you.* The realisation shocked her. And scared her. She knew the wonderful time they were having together was just a prelude to heartbreak.

'So where to now?' he said.

Lisa hesitated. If she had any sense she would walk away before she got in any deeper. But she couldn't bring herself to cut short their day.

'Anywhere you like,' she said. 'Hold on, did you feel that?'

'Rain?' Matteo glanced skywards. 'It will only be a shower.'

A big spot of water splashed on Lisa's bare arm. 'Are you sure?'

'Quick, run!' Matteo grabbed her hand. Lisa ran besides him, laughing, as they tried to dodge the sudden downpour. The soles of her leather sandals flapped against the road; she was not sure they would last out much longer. They ducked and dived through a maze of streets until they were halfway along a narrow road in a residential part of the town.

Lisa didn't recognise where she was but behind her she could still glimpse the holm oaks on the top of the Guinigi Tower. 'Where are we?'

'My home. Shall we go in for a few minutes and wait for the rain to stop?'

He stooped down and unlocked the door. He chucked his keys into a brass pot on the narrow shelf below the oak-framed mirror that dominated the cramped hallway. Their eyes met in the dim light. Lisa felt a rush of heat. She suspected Matteo had more on his mind than sheltering from the weather.

'Come through to the kitchen.'

Lisa picked her way past a bicycle that was leaning against the wall. Matteo grimaced. 'Sorry about that. It drives Mamma mad when Viviana leaves her bike in the hall like this.'

'Is this is your family's house?'

'Yes, of course. Where else would I stay when I am back in Lucca? It would be more luxurious to stay in a hotel than sleep in my old childhood bedroom but Mamma would be mortified.' Matteo smiled.

Lisa followed him into a galley kitchen. The gap between the appliances and the units on the opposite wall was scarcely wider than the hallway that preceded it. The pale green fridge in the corner looked as though it had been there since the 1950s.

'A beer? Or would you prefer to warm up with a coffee?'

'A beer's great. I got a bit wet but I'm not cold at all.' Lisa was quite warm enough thanks to Matteo's close proximity.

Matteo took a bottle opener from a drawer and prised off the two lids. He opened the pedal bin with his foot and flicked the metal caps straight in.

'Good shot.'

'Sorry, I'm showing off.' He gave a rueful grin. 'The lounge is through here.' He ducked out of the kitchen and into a cosy living room.

A slightly battered green leather sofa and two mismatched armchairs were arranged around a woven cotton rug. Framed family photographs were arranged on an embroidered cloth on top of a carved chest in the corner. The soft apricot-coloured walls were home to a series of botanical prints and a collection of drawings and paintings in a bewildering variety of styles.

'This is what happens when your sister works in a gallery,' Matteo quipped.

'I like it,' Lisa said.

'So do I.' He sat down on the couch and handed her one of the beers, the bottle slippery with condensation.

She sat down next to him. He wiggled along the couch to bridge the small gap between them, draped one arm over her shoulder and pulled her closer. She breathed in the scent of his fresh, clean hair mixed with drops of rain. She could feel the heat from his body. Her heart was racing. He turned her face towards his and traced the outline of her lips with his index finger. Lisa's breath caught in her throat. They kissed for a long time. Matteo's hand traced the top of her spine, slowly inching downwards until his fingertips were beneath the thin fabric of her sundress. He looked at her questioningly.

'Yes,' she murmured.

'Not here,' he said.

Lisa tensed. She hadn't thought of the possibility that Viviana or her mother could walk in at any moment.

'Don't worry, Mamma's out visiting a friend; she'll be gone all day, and my sister always has lunch at the gallery when she's working. I thought we should move somewhere more comfortable, that's all.'

She stood up, adjusting the strap of her dress which had slipped off her shoulder.

Matteo grinned. 'I don't think that will be staying on much longer.'

They paused in the doorway of the bedroom, leaning against the doorframe. Lisa could just catch sight of a small desk in the corner, football posters on the wall, a shaggy rug on the floor.

Matteo fumbled with the catch on her dress.

'Oh, Lisa.' He undid the long zip.

She stepped out of her dress and left it in a heap on the floor.

Chapter Twenty

Cassie brushed her teeth and reapplied her pink lip gloss. She picked up her *Day Trips from Lucca* leaflet and descended the stairs. She wasn't meeting Jane for more than half an hour but there was no point in hanging around her hotel room when the maid was banging her trolley up and down the corridor waiting to replenish the toiletries and change the towels. There were a few comfortable seats in the little hotel bar where she could while away the time until their trip to Montecatini.

Montecatini looked beautiful with its gardens and old-world spas and she was looking forward to a day with her aunt. And a day without Lisa. Cassie was trying to be kinder to her sister since Lisa had unexpectedly revealed her childhood struggles but it was hard not to slip back into old patterns and make little digs at each other. Cassie wished she hadn't made that comment about Matteo over breakfast. After the stupid way she'd behaved towards Alonzo, she had no right to judge Lisa's relationship, even if it was just a holiday fling. Cassie's phone vibrated on the table. She didn't pick it up. It was probably Paul. She thought guiltily of his last unanswered text.

The bar was a little dim; no one had switched on the lights, perhaps assuming that none of the guests were likely to fancy a drink straight after breakfast. Cassie had expected to have the place to herself but someone was already sitting in the corner. A girl was curled up against a purple cushion, her striped canvas bag wedged between her body and the arm of her chair. A buff-coloured envelope lay on the coffee table in front of her. She caught Cassie's gaze and lay down the sheet of paper she had been studying. It was a drawing of a young girl's face in blue pastel. It looked like a portrait of her; the likeness was unmistakable.

'*Buongiorno.*' The girl picked up her envelope to slide the drawing inside.

'*Buongiorno.* Did you draw that? It's really good, I can tell it's you,' Cassie said. She knew she was being nosy but if the girl spoke enough English, it might be more interesting to while away a few minutes talking to her than reading through *Day Trips from Lucca* again.

The girl paused, the drawing half-in, half-out of the envelope. 'No. It is my nonna Concetta.'

'You're so alike,' Cassie said. 'Are you going to get it framed?'

'Not yet.' The girl handed her the drawing. 'Want to look?'

'Dated 1965,' Cassie said. 'But what does this inscription say?'

'*The most beautiful girl – Florence.* I think the artist might be my real nonno. I'm here looking for him.'

'How interesting.'

'Nonna did not tell us about Mamma's real father until she was on her death bed. She was only a teenage girl when she became pregnant. She wasn't able to tell Mamma much about the circumstances, but this drawing was made nine months before my mamma was born, so we think perhaps the artist was her father.' The girl bit her lip as though she had said too much.

'It says Florence, so why did you come here?' Cassie asked.

'Someone recognised the little doodle of the Guingi Tower on the back. It's the only clue I have. That and the letter "L".'

'L?' Cassie ran a finger around the inside of the collar of her dress. She was feeling a little warm.

The girl leant forward. 'I wish the artist had signed his full name. But there's a man who runs a gallery in the Piazza Anfiteatro. His name is Luciano Zingaretti. I think it might be him.'

Cassie fanned herself with the Day Trips leaflet. She swallowed hard. 'Have you spoken to him?'

'No.' The girl fixed her sincere, dark eyes on Cassie. 'Yesterday, three times I went to the gallery. Yet each time I could not walk through the door. I am scared. Scared that it is him and scared that it is not. Does that sound strange? I met his fiancée working in the gallery, the day before yesterday. Her name's Jane. What if she doesn't know about Luciano and my nonna? She seemed so nice; I wouldn't want to upset her. But if Luciano is the man who deserted my nonna when she was pregnant, shouldn't Jane know what kind of a man she is marrying? I shouldn't be bothering you with my troubles, but I just don't know what to do.'

Cassie spoke carefully. 'Don't worry about that at all, it's good to talk to someone. In my experience the answer to a big dilemma comes when you're busy doing something else. If I were you, I wouldn't go near the gallery today. Take a look around the town – there's so much to see – and by this time tomorrow I'm sure you'll know what to do.'

'Maybe you're right. You've been so kind . . .'

'Cassie,' Cassie said. 'I wish I could talk for longer but I'm meeting someone. I have to go.'

'Nice meeting you, Cassie. I'm Pia,' the girl replied.

Cassie walked out into the sunshine. She stood on the doorstep of the Hotel Tosca trying to compose herself. She hoped she had convinced Pia to spend the day exploring Lucca; she didn't want the young girl to go anywhere near the gallery. Not until Cassie had spoken to Luciano herself and found out the truth.

Jane stowed her tote bag between her feet so that Cassie could take the seat next to her. Cassie balanced her white handbag on her knees. It had accumulated a few scuff marks since she'd arrived, probably during Chiara's after-party, Jane guessed. According to Viviana it had been quite a lively do. It was strange that Cassie was reluctant to talk about that evening even though Lisa reported that her younger sister had enjoyed herself, dancing and drinking all night. Perhaps that was the problem: Cassie had never liked losing control.

'I'm so looking forward to seeing Montecatini,' Cassie said.

Jane glanced out of the train window. 'It's not far. I'm so glad we've got the chance to spend today together. I do hope you're not going to be bored.'

'Of course not!' Cassie's voice rose a little. 'What a silly thing to say. I picked up this brochure from the hotel lobby. Montecatini looks wonderful. I'm surprised you haven't been before.'

'I was waiting until I could go with Mary. You remember my old friend, don't you? She planned to come and stay for a couple of weeks but then she wasn't well.'

'How is Mary?'

'Her health's much better, thank goodness, though her walking still isn't good. She uses a stick these days. Us old ladies . . .' Jane let the sentence drift away. Jane had never thought of herself as old until some of her friends started suffering from this and that. It hardened her resolve to make the most of her new life.

'Seventy isn't old these days,' Cassie said.

'Mary is a good few years older than me of course,' Jane said. 'I don't suppose she'll make it out here before the wedding, but she's determined to get here for that even if she has to be pushed around in a chair.'

'The wedding . . . hmm.' Cassie looked as though something was on the tip of her tongue but instead she unzipped her bag and fished out a glossy brochure. She spread it across the top of the bag. 'Good. I thought I might have left this behind.'

'*Day Trips from Lucca*. Does it say much about where we're going?'

'*The healing waters of Montecatini Terme were known to the Romans but it was in the late 1800s that Grand Duke Leopold developed the spa resort we see today*,' Cassie read.

Jane leant over to look at the pictures. 'How pretty. I know we're going to love it.'

'I should hope so. If Lisa is off on some romantic surprise outing with Matteo, the least we deserve is a special day of our own.' Cassie pouted.

'Jealous of your sister? That will be a first,' Jane joked.

Cassie didn't laugh. She shrugged and turned to look out of the window.

'May I?' Jane reached for the leaflet. She peeked at Cassie from the corner of her eye. Cassie's jaw was stiff and her knuckles were white where she gripped the handle of her bag. Jane took her reading glasses from their tapestry case. That was better. *Four different types of water come from underground springs, each has its own medicinal powers*, said to *cure disorders of the liver, digestion* . . . she read to herself.

'What shall we do first?' Cassie asked.

'Oh, a stroll to find a nice piazza and a cup of coffee, don't you think? Then we'll do whatever you like. There's enough to see in the main town. I'll save Montecatini Alto for another day.'

'I'm sure we'll have time for everything. We're not in any rush, are we?' Cassie took back the brochure and flicked over a page. 'That's Montecatini Alto – just look at the views!'

'You have to get a little train up there – I know how much you hate heights,' Jane said.

'That red thing in the picture? Hmm . . .' Cassie studied the brochure. '*The funicular railway was opened in 1898.* Goodness, it's been there more than a hundred years.'

'It's carried a lot of people up and down.' Jane gently tried to encourage her niece, but she knew she was onto a loser. Cassie hated heights. There was no way that Jane was going to persuade her to ride on a steep, narrow-gauge railway that climbed four hundred feet.

'*Restaurants surround the main square, a narrow alley leads to the church of St Peter.* Let's go there, Jane. We'll take that little train.'

'If you're sure.' Jane looked at her niece.

'I'm quite sure. Let's go there first, straight after we've had our coffee before I have time to talk myself out of it.'

Cassie leant against the rail of the open viewing platform as the one-car train climbed the track. Her eyes were shining; a huge smile lit up her face as they passed the waving passengers on another train going back down the track. Jane couldn't help laughing at her niece's delighted expression.

'Glad you took the plunge?' Jane asked.

'Yes, it's such fun. I don't know why I never did things like this before. I'm not at all scared even though it's such a long way down.'

'Sometimes when you take a leap of faith you can surprise yourself,' Jane said. An image of Florence flashed before her eyes: Luciano singing as they walked across the Ponte Vecchio as people stared; his invitation to the Puccini concert in Lucca; the surge of adrenaline when she agreed to go. One leap of faith had transformed her life. 'Luciano says . . .' Jane began. But the strange expression that crossed Cassie's face discouraged her from continuing.

The train pulled into the platform. The passengers were disembarking in a colourful jumble: loud voices; camera phones being held aloft; children running ahead, ignoring their mother's cries.

'Let people go first,' Jane said. She moved out of the way to allow a large lady with a walking frame to edge her way past.

'I think this way leads to the Piazza Giuseppe Giusti – I believe that's the main square,' Cassie said.

'I can see why everyone was heading this way.' Jane looked around the piazza. It was a long, rectangular shape lined with restaurants shaded by light-coloured awnings. The Italian flag beside the war memorial fluttered in the gentle breeze.

'Wow! Look at the views!' Cassie exclaimed. She flung out her arms and spun around on one heel.

Jane laughed at Cassie's exuberance. She looked out over the rolling hills and valleys. The shades of green were broken up by terracotta roofs and clusters of white buildings. The town of Montecatini Terme lay below them.

'Isn't it strange how the hills in the distance look blue,' Cassie said.

'You're right – they do.'

'I love this piazza,' Cassie said.

'So do I. Look at that interesting building with the balcony.'

'I saw a photo of that in the brochure; it used to be a theatre,' Cassie said. 'Doesn't that restaurant over there with the check tablecloths and the pots of pink geraniums look perfect. Can we come back here for lunch?'

'Of course. Shall we take a walk? There's supposed to be an old church up here that's worth seeing.'

Cassie slipped her arm through Jane's. The white bag dangling from the crook of Cassie's elbow knocked against Jane as they walked, but Jane didn't mind.

It was a shame she hadn't been able to come to Montecatini with Mary, but the church was as pretty as Jane had hoped it would be, the views from the top of the town were stunning and the weather was perfect. She and Cassie even came across one of the surviving old stone towers that used to protect the town. So far, it was proving to be a satisfactory outing in every way, but one worry was seeping into the edges of Jane's happy picture: there was something odd about Cassie. Not only had she thrown caution to the wind and jumped on the funicular railway, she'd pounced on a bright red slogan T-shirt hanging on a souvenir stall that was nothing like her normal wardrobe of girlish, pastel-colour clothing. Cassie had always been so predictable. Something wasn't right.

'Lunch?' Cassie said.

Jane looked at her watch. 'Yes, why not? Shall we go back to Piazza Giuseppe Giusti?'

'Oh yes, let's.' Cassie picked up pace in the direction of the restaurant with the pink geraniums. 'Oh, look, Jane, they've got a free table.'

Jane was relieved. She could do with a sit-down. Mary wouldn't have been able to manage half the walking she and Cassie had done.

'Shall we have some wine?' Cassie said.

Jane tried to hide her surprise. 'Why not? White?'

'Yes please.'

The smiling waiter deposited a half-litre carafe on their table and two large glasses. Jane poured the wine.

'*Saluti!*' Cassie said. She took a large swig.

Jane took a dainty sip; it was deliciously cold. 'Just pasta, I think, don't you? Can you read what's on the board?'

Cassie peered over Jane's shoulder. 'Yes, just about. I'll have that special, the second one down. How about you?'

Jane swivelled around. 'Same here.' The aroma of garlic from the next table was making her terribly hungry. She tore the end off a packet of *grissini* and offered one to Cassie.

Jane was glad that whatever was going through Cassie's mind was not affecting her appetite. Her niece munched through several *grissini* and ate her pasta with gusto. Jane didn't take long to clear her plate either. She was now quite accustomed to spinning pasta around her fork.

'That *pici alle briciole* was an inspired choice,' Jane said.

'I can't believe just mixing a few breadcrumbs with garlic can make pasta so delicious.'

'Dessert?' Jane said.

'Let's grab an ice-cream from that *gelateria* near the entrance to the funicular before we go back down to Montecatini Terme,' Cassie said.

'My mouth is watering already.' Jane paid the bill. She didn't bother to wait for the change. She pushed back her chair. 'Ready?'

The *gelateria* was cool and the light was dim compared to the bright sunshine bathing the square. Jane studied the contents of the metal trays.

'Melon and raspberry for me. *Melone e lampone per favore.*' Jane smiled at the man behind the counter; she was getting more confident at speaking the language.

The man nodded and started filling Jane's cone. Jane opened her mouth to request Cassie's usual strawberry and vanilla; she had eaten the same flavours since she was a little girl.

'That one with the chocolate shards in. *Stracciatella*? Is that how you pronounce it, Jane? And I'll have the raspberry, umm, *lampone*, as well.'

'Very good.' The man behind the counter took a scoop of the ruby-red ice-cream.

'Shall we sit on a bench before they melt?' Cassie said. The sun was the hottest it had been all day.

Jane nodded. Her *melone* was beginning to drip down the cone.

Cassie dived into the ice-cream as if she had not had any lunch at all, let alone a steaming great plate of *pici* pasta. 'Mmm. Delicious.'

'Where shall we go next once we're back down in the main town?' Jane asked.

'That's an easy decision. Let's go to the park with the thermal spas. I'd love to visit Terme Tettuccio, that's the best-known one.'

Jane gulped on a cold mouthful of ice-cream. A spa visit. She hadn't been expecting that. Lying on adjacent couches smothered in oil and wearing paper knickers or – heaven forbid! – nothing at all was taking aunt-niece bonding a little too far.

'Oh, don't you fancy it?' Cassie frowned.

Jane hesitated. Maybe Cassie shouldn't be the only one to step outside her comfort zone today. And the tale would certainly make Luciano chuckle. 'Well, we are in a spa town . . .'

'Exactly,' Cassie said. 'But you don't sound that convinced.'

'I was just wondering about the level of . . . um . . . nudity.' Jane was sure her cheeks matched the colour of her raspberry ice-cream.

'Nudity?' Cassie spluttered on the last bit of her cone. 'I don't think we have to worry about that. I wasn't going to sign us up for a naked massage. Apparently, they drink the water cures at Terme Tettuccio but I'm not sure I fancy that either – downing a glass of hot sulphurous water doesn't really appeal, especially in this weather. I thought we'd go and have a look around, that's all. Apparently, you can get a ticket for the gardens in the afternoon; they're supposed to be beautiful.'

'Phew!' Jane jokingly mopped her brow.

'Nudity!' Cassie laughed. 'Honestly, Jane – can you imagine me doing that?'

'I suppose not,' Jane said. Normally she couldn't imagine any such thing. But the way Cassie had been acting the last few days, nothing would surprise her.

Chapter Twenty-One

'Where are we going?' Lisa dodged around a couple of parked mopeds as she followed Matteo down the narrow street.

'It's a bit early for lunch but I have worked up a bit of an appetite.' Matteo grinned.

Lisa blushed. She blinked away a memory of Matteo's naked body. She didn't regret her impulsiveness but now it was going to be ten times harder to go back to England and forget him.

'We saw the Palazzo Pfanner and the Guinigi Tower this morning but I wanted to take you back somewhere we've been before,' he said.

'Ilaria's Tomb?' They'd stopped outside the cathedral that morning, but they hadn't been inside.

Matteo laughed. 'How could you forget my other favourite place, Gelateria Gabriele? If you don't mind walking for a bit first, we'll make a bit of a detour. I love browsing the old books and prints on the stalls in the Corte del Biancone when I've got the time.'

'Sure,' Lisa said. She was happy to go anywhere.

She followed Matteo through the shady streets in the direction of the Piazza Napoleone. His hand was warm in hers as they strolled along. The showers had cleared and the sky was a picture-book blue. Lisa hoped Cassie and Jane's outing to Montecatini had brightened her sister's mood.

She didn't like to think of her being worried or unhappy on such a beautiful day.

They turned into the Corte del Biancone. A group of stalls was set up at the back of an old church.

'*Ciao*, Matteo!' An old man looked up from behind a pile of books he was busy pricing.

'*Ciao*, Pietro!' Matteo walked over. The man put the pencil he was using behind his ear. His face was so deeply lined he could have stored the pencil in any one of its innumerable folds. '*Questa è Lisa.*'

The man responded in rapid Italian. Lisa smiled politely. He carried on speaking, apparently not discouraged by her lack of response.

Matteo finally got a word in.

'*Allora*, English.' The man gave Lisa a toothy grin.

'Will you excuse me for a moment,' Matteo said. 'Pietro has something special to show me.' The old man picked up a vicious-looking knife and sliced through the parcel tape securing a rather battered cardboard box. He placed a pile of prints on the table and fanned them out. Each depicted a musical instrument in extraordinary detail, but the papers were slightly yellowed and many were spotted with age like the man's own hands.

Matteo nodded along as Pietro talked. Pietro laid three drawings of violins side by side.

'One of my contacts found these in a house clearance in Cremona.' He handed one of the prints to Matteo for his closer inspection. It was only a little discoloured at the very edge.

Matteo's face softened. He turned to Lisa. 'An instrument by Guarnerius del Gesu. Some say he was Italy's greatest violin maker, even greater than Stradivari. A master of his art. It is my dream to play one of his instruments one day, but for now this etching will have to serve as an inspiration for me.'

The two men continued to converse in their own language. Lisa smiled. Ordinarily she would have been bored but it was a pleasure to see Matteo so absorbed.

Matteo shook Pietro's hand. '*Ciao*, Pietro!' He put his arm around Lisa and walked away.

'He didn't persuade you to buy anything?' Lisa was surprised. Matteo's face had lit up at the sight of the drawing, like a small boy presented with a new toy.

'I'm afraid he has. That wonderful Guarnerius del Gesu and the two other prints. One is a violin by Niccolo Amati, another great artisan from Cremona. Pietro will get them framed by Old Alberto; he has a workshop up in the hills. Let's get our ice-creams, but before that there is something I want to buy from Maria's stall over there.'

Maria's stall stood out from the others. Amongst the vintage maps and books were bright piles of guidebooks and posters that had attracted quite a crowd. They had to wait for a group of tourists to depart, all clutching their souvenirs.

Matteo spoke to the woman and she reached into her apron to give him a couple of coins in exchange for his ten-euro note. She handed over a large white envelope.

'For you.'

Lisa was chuffed; she didn't know what Matteo had bought but she hadn't expected to receive any sort of present. 'Shall I?'

'Yes, please open it.'

'A calendar?' It was only July.

'They print them early here so that they can sell them to the tourists. All the months show views of Lucca.'

Lisa flipped through the thick, cream pages. 'These are beautiful. Look at that view from the walls, just like the one we saw this morning.'

'For when you are back in England. You will think of this wonderful city. And you will not forget me.'

'There's no chance of that.'

Matteo put his arms around her waist. Lisa ran a hand through the back of his hair. She leant into his embrace. They kissed as though no one was watching. Finally, they pulled apart.

'*Bravi!*' Maria clapped her hands. Old Pietro made a thumbs-up sign from behind his stall.

Lisa clapped her hands over her burning face, half thrilled, half horribly embarrassed. Even Matteo reddened. He pretended to fan himself. 'Time to get that ice-cream. I need to cool down.'

He took her hand and led her down the road to the gelateria.

'There you go,' Matteo handed her a laden cone. 'These will melt in no time if we stand in the sun.'

'There's no one on that bench over there,' Lisa said.

'Quick! Before those teenagers get it.' They dashed across the piazza and flopped down laughing.

'What a perfect day,' Matteo said. His eyes met hers. Her heart lurched. She would have kissed him again if she hadn't got a fast-dissolving double ice-cream to consume. 'Try some of this.' He held out his cone. She leant in to take a bite.

'Delicious . . . I wonder what Cassie and Aunt Jane are doing now.'

'Not having as much fun as we are.' He kissed the tip of her nose. 'Where did you say they were going today?'

'They were taking the train to Montecatini.'

'That's not far. I think they'll like it there. It's nice to take the funicular railway up to Montecatini Alto and have lunch in the main square. I'm sure Luciano will have recommended somewhere. There's a place that does the most amazing *pici alle bricciole*. It was Luciano and Frankie's favourite pasta dish when they were children. He still loves to eat it but it brings back such bittersweet memories.'

'Poor Luciano. A tragedy like that must overshadow your life.'

'That's why it's so important to enjoy life today – there's no guarantee what will happen tomorrow.'

'So, you'll keep travelling, never looking more than a few weeks ahead?' Lisa said quietly.

'Vienna, Munich, Warsaw . . . so much to see.' He smiled. 'I'm playing in so many different places this summer. I would love to explore some of them with you if you can get away and join me.'

So, that was how he saw their future. A few days of fun here and there before he packed his bags and left. Again. Why had she dreamt of anything different?

'How about meeting me in Prague?' Matteo said. 'I've never been there before. I've heard it's beautiful.'

Lisa had seen pictures: the baroque buildings, the quaint cobbled streets, the statues on Charles Bridge. It looked so romantic. But a few days there would only prolong her heartache. She couldn't allow Matteo to flit in and out of her life. It was better to cut and run.

'I'm sorry.' She avoided his eyes. 'Cassie and I are leaving the day after tomorrow. I expect we'll see you again at Jane and Luciano's wedding but I don't think it's a good idea to meet before.'

'What do you mean? I can't believe this! Look at me, Lisa!'

His face was pale. She didn't dare speak. She drove her nails into the palms of her hands.

Matteo stood up. 'I thought you were different,' he muttered.

He turned and walked away.

Tears filled Lisa's eyes. She wanted to run after him. She wanted to tell him she was falling in love with him. But she had to be strong. She had to let him go. Matteo was a free spirit, like she was. She could fly off any time, as unencumbered as a bird. That was how she had chosen to live her life. But it was no longer enough. She no longer wanted to be someone's passing fancy. She wanted something more. She wanted to love and be loved for a lifetime.

Chapter Twenty-Two

'Weren't the spa gardens gorgeous?' Jane said. 'I'm so glad you suggested we went.'

'That building with the elegant columns and the colours in those tiles were just beautiful,' Cassie said.

'I believe they call it "liberty style".'

'I wasn't expecting those musicians to be playing under the cupola though, were you?'

'That really was a treat. I was quite transported to a more elegant age.'

'It's been a wonderful day. I can't imagine Lisa's day can have been half as good.' Cassie looked so pretty when she smiled, and a smattering of freckles had appeared on the bridge of her nose, softening her face.

'There are so many interesting places in Tuscany. Perhaps you and Paul can tour around a little when you come back to Lucca for the wedding. I'm told Pistoia is definitely worth visiting.'

'Paul?' A shadow crossed Cassie's face.

'He is coming to the wedding, isn't he?' It dawned on Jane that Cassie had not yet sent a formal reply; she'd just assumed that her niece and husband would both be attending.

'Umm, yes . . . er, of course,' Cassie mumbled. She looked straight ahead as she and Jane walked along.

'He's a good man,' Jane said. 'Marriage isn't always easy.

You have to take the rough with the smooth. Even Eddie and I had the odd disagreement.'

'I can't imagine Uncle Eddie ever arguing about anything.'

'Hmm,' Jane said. Cassie was right. She and Eddie had never actually argued but occasionally he had looked a little hurt when she suggested going somewhere or doing something a bit out of the ordinary and so she had brushed her feelings aside. She had been happy to bend a little. It was a small price to pay for their long and happy marriage. And now she was experiencing such an extraordinary new life, she could look back at her former solid, ordinary life with a pleasant nostalgia. But she didn't know how to explain that to Cassie without sounding disloyal. Eddie had been one happy chapter. Luciano, with all his differences, was another. One she was determined to see through to the end, even if sometimes she felt she was walking along the very edge of a cliff: thrilled by her own daring and fearful of falling, but oh, so alive!

'Look, up there, Cassie – you can see Montecatini Alto,' Jane said instead.

'So you can.' Cassie visibly brightened at the change of subject. 'You can see all the little white buildings. I can't believe how high up it is!'

'You went all the way up there on that funicular railway.'

'I don't know why I was so nervous before. I want to do more things like that.'

'That's good to hear.' Jane patted her niece's arm.

Cassie turned towards her. She grasped Jane's hands in hers. 'Oh, Jane, there's so much that I want to do. So much more. I want to live, really live!'

'Goodness! That's um, great.' Jane's heart sank. Cassie's words had brought back an echo from Jane's past. She had almost forgotten Simone, her old next-door neighbour.

Three weeks after a holiday to Turkey, Simone had upped and left her bewildered husband and daughter for a new life with a boat builder from Bodrum. Jane had bumped into her as she loaded her possessions into the back of her old Mini. 'I want to live, really live,' Simone had said. Then she had put her foot down and accelerated away from Honeypot Lane leaving Jane to try to pick up the pieces with homemade casseroles left on the doorstep and lifts to school with a sobbing teenager on the back seat.

'I haven't been living. I've just been drifting through life merely existing,' Cassie continued.

'I wouldn't say that,' Jane said carefully. 'You've always had goals and plans. Both you and Paul.'

'Work promotions, home improvements.' Cassie kicked at a twig lying on the pavement.

'Planning for a family, building a home. Those things are important.'

'I know,' Cassie said. Her bottom lip stuck out the way it used to do when she was small.

'Maybe your life has been a little "all work and no play",' Jane admitted. 'Maybe it's time that you and Paul sat down together and talked about what you both want from life. You've built a solid foundation, perhaps it's time to add one or two frivolous touches.'

'I'm not sure Paul could ever be frivolous,' Cassie sighed. 'I've had such fun here, Jane. I can't go back to being my old self.'

'Yes, you have, haven't you,' Jane said more gently. 'I never thought I'd see you get on the back of that tandem with Alonzo.'

'This has nothing to do with Alonzo,' Cassie snapped.

'I didn't say it had.'

Cassie strode on ahead. Jane hurried along beside her wishing she would slow down; her feet were sore after all the walking. 'Cassie, please wait!'

Cassie stopped abruptly.

'What's wrong?' Was it the mention of Alonzo that had put Cassie into such a spin? Jane couldn't imagine what could have occurred between the handsome young man from the gallery and her usually oh-so-sensible niece.

'Nothing.'

The way Cassie's face flushed bright pink told Jane all she needed to know. Suddenly everything began to make sense. Alonzo was the cause of Cassie's restlessness. Cassie had fallen for Alonzo. Fallen for him hard.

Jane pursed her lips. Nothing good could come of this. There was nothing she could say, but there was something she could do – but that would have to wait until they got back to Lucca. For now, she would act as if she suspected nothing. She cast her mind around for a neutral topic of conversation.

'Just look at that mass of purple flowers over there,' she said.

'I should get something like that for the garden.' Cassie made a show of leaning down to examine the blooms. Jane strongly suspected Cassie wasn't thinking about gardening. She was sure Cassie's head was full of a dark-haired green-eyed jeweller.

Lisa wandered blindly through the streets, barely conscious of the other pedestrians and cyclists. Before long she had reached the church of Santa Maria Bianca. She crossed over the narrow canal that ran down via del Fosso. She avoided the turning that led to Luciano and Jane's flat and took the road to the botanical gardens. Lisa had no particular interest in flowers or plants, but she needed to do something to pass the time; she was in no mood to make her way back to the Hotel Tosca and sit alone in her room.

She rummaged in her purse and found some small change. The smiling woman at the counter handed her a printed ticket. She wandered amongst the cacti, soaring pine trees and the innumerable potted shrubs and palms trying to sum up some enthusiasm. Even in her current frame of mind she couldn't help but be impressed by the huge cedar tree that was being photographed by a woman in a large-brimmed yellow hat. She stretched her arms wide to try to get an idea of the tree's circumference. A man pushing a wheelbarrow caught her eye and smiled.

'How big?' She took the chance that he would speak English.

'About six metres wide.'

'Twenty metres high, I'm told. They say the pine trees here reach thirty,' the woman in the yellow hat added in an American accent.

'*Grazie.*' Lisa smiled, nodded and moved on.

She took the crazy-paving path down to the pond at the far end of the gardens and stopped on the narrow ledge that ran around it. Something moved amongst the lily pads – a sleepy-looking turtle.

Lisa glanced at her phone. There was no message from Cassie to say that her aunt and sister were on their way but she'd exhausted the gardens. She was surprised to find the *Lucca Attractions* leaflet in the bottom of her handbag; she hadn't remembered putting it there. She was pretty sure they'd seen all the attractions, but it seemed there was one site nearby that the three of them hadn't visited. She made her way listlessly up the road to Villa Bottini. At least it would give her something to talk about over dinner. She certainly didn't want to discuss her outing with Matteo.

Arguably the most attractive and significant villa in the region, Lisa read. *The frescoes in the vaults above the porch and the main hall are the only surviving sixteenth-century frescoes in a Lucchese villa.*

She stood in the loggia staring up at the painted ceiling for a long time, picking out all the details: the soft-buttocked nudes, reclining cherubs, a winged horse. She spotted a woman holding a golden violin and quickly looked away.

She shook her head to get rid of the crick in her neck.

'Fabulous isn't it? I adore this place. I've come all the way from Chicago.' It was the woman from the botanical gardens.

'Yes, it's beautiful,' Lisa said.

'I just love this whole town, don't you?' the woman chattered on. Lisa nodded distractedly, wishing she would go away.

Eventually the woman wandered off. Lisa walked through the archway into the grounds. She made a cursory tour, but it was impossible to focus. A message pinged on her phone. Jane and Cassie would be back in an hour. Soon Lisa would be sitting outside Café Europa with a large glass of wine in her hand. She would try to blot out the memory of her break-up with Matteo. And the hurt look on his face before he walked away.

She made her way back alongside the narrow canal cut into the via del Fosso. She didn't need to consult her map to find her way back to the hotel; she could see the trees on top of the Guinigi Tower to guide her way. As she neared the turning towards the Piazza Anfiteatro, a familiar figure came cycling towards her.

Viviana slammed on her brakes so suddenly she almost pitched over the handlebars. She yanked the front wheel to one side, blocking the narrow road. She swung her black-clad leg over the saddle and stood with the bicycle in front of her like a barricade. Her perfectly painted scarlet lips were pressed together.

'Er . . . *ciao*,' Lisa said.

'Don't "*ciao*" me like I'm your friend.' Viviana's eyes were cold.

'I . . .' Lisa swallowed. She wiped her hands on the front of her sundress.

'How could you? How could you treat my brother like this? He really liked you, Lisa. I thought you liked him.'

'I did . . . I do.'

'Yes, you liked him. You liked him for a nice holiday fling.' Viviana jerked her head as though Lisa was an insect she wanted to shake off. 'Yes, a bit of fun for a few days . . . Women like you . . .' Viviana gave a dismissive half-snort. She swung her leg back over her bicycle.

Lisa grabbed hold of the wicker basket, anger bubbling up inside her. How dare Viviana talk to her like this? How dare she judge her? 'Yes, we've had a holiday romance; there's nothing wrong with that. But how could it be anything else? Matteo's a travelling violinist, he's off to Austria and Germany next week. He goes wherever the music takes him. You know that.'

'Yes, he travels a lot. He enjoys seeing the world. He told me you did too. He thought you understood.'

'I do. I understand completely – Matteo doesn't want any ties. He's like a sailor with a girl in every port.'

'Matteo's nothing like that. Why do you say these things? Of course he has had girlfriends in the past but only one at a time. My brother has never been unfaithful. You're so suspicious, just like her.'

'Her?'

Viviana got back off her bicycle and leant it up against the wall out of the way.

'Matteo's fiancée. She never trusted him although he gave her no reason to doubt his love. She was controlling, possessive. Gradually she placed more and more demands on him. He travelled to concert venues at the last minute, missed as many rehearsals as he dared. He rushed back from every assignment exhausted. He never got to see the beautiful places he played in; he saw only the hotel room and the concert venue. Still, it wasn't enough for her. She wanted him to give up his violin and his music. He loved her so much, but he realised deep down that giving up the thing that brought him such joy still would not be enough to satisfy a woman like that. Something else would fuel her suspicious mind. He had to let her go, although it broke his heart.'

'What happened to her?'

'She's married now. Two children and a haunted-looking husband who can barely walk to the local bar without her permission. Whether or not she's happy, who knows?' Viviana shrugged. 'You don't know how hard it has been for him to open his heart again after that.'

'I've dated free spirits before, Viviana. I know the score.'

'Do you know what it takes to become a classical violinist?' Viviana said. 'The hours of practice, the sacrifices one makes? That's loyalty. That's commitment.'

'I suppose . . .' Lisa muttered.

'My brother has travelled the world but he always comes back here, to Lucca, even if sometimes it would be easier to stay elsewhere. And since our father died, he has phoned our mother every day, no matter where he is. That's constancy. That's devotion. That's the sort of man you've thrown away.'

'My father was an actor, a charismatic handsome man. He led our mother a merry dance.'

'And you judge Matteo by his standards. Everyone's an individual, Lisa.' Viviana sighed. The anger in her eyes replaced by sadness. She took hold of her bicycle.

'Please tell him . . .' Lisa began. But Viviana was already pedalling away.

It didn't matter. Lisa didn't know what she could say. It was all too late.

'Luciano!' Jane didn't know why she bothered to call his name; she already knew that he was not at home, the apartment was far too quiet.

There was always some sort of noise when Luciano was about: loud singing in the shower; Puccini blasting from his old record player; the sound of his easel scraping across the floorboards as he dragged it nearer to the upstairs window to try and capture the light. He couldn't make a pot of coffee without banging the cupboard doors or go to sleep without an accompaniment of snuffles and snores. Jane was used to it now but it had been quite a culture shock after years by herself with only the gentle hum of Radio 4 breaking the silence.

Luciano hadn't been gone long. The aroma of fresh coffee still hung in the kitchen. Jane moved a plate and a knife into the sink; she brushed a few crumbs of cake – *buccellato*, she guessed – from the wooden worksurface into her hand then tipped them into the bin. There was a note leaning against the rose-patterned caddy that held her favourite Earl Grey loose-leaf tea. *Gone back to the cathedral to paint. The light today is perfect!* Six extravagant kisses had been added to Luciano's distinctive scrawl. Jane smiled. She lifted the lid on the caddy and hesitated. She grabbed a teabag instead; she was too impatient to wait for a pot to brew. She wanted to make her phone call straight away before Luciano returned. She loved Luciano; she could talk to him about anything. But when it came to this matter of the heart, she wasn't sure he'd understand.

Jane punched in Mary's number and held her breath. There was every chance her friend was out of earshot of the phone, at the bottom of her garden tending to the plants in her beloved raised beds but Jane was in luck — Mary answered almost immediately.

'Jane! How wonderful! I didn't think I would hear from you this week. I know how busy you must be with the girls visiting.'

Jane leant back on Luciano's ancient couch and kicked off her slip-on shoes. How glad she was that Mary had picked up the phone. Her old friend's voice was as comforting as a slice of her legendary Victoria sponge.

'It's not something to do with the girls, is it?' Mary said.

Jane heard the clink of a china cup, the rustle of the wrapper of one of Mary's favourite barley sugars. She imagined her friend adjusting the bolster cushion in her high-backed winged armchair, getting herself nice and comfortable before settling down to hear Jane's story.

'You know me so well.' Jane had planned to have a general chit-chat before she regaled Mary with her concerns but her friend was shrewd enough to guess the reason for Jane's call.

'Lisa, is it? I can well imagine her getting herself involved with some raffish Italian stallion.'

Jane coughed and spluttered.

'Are you okay, dear?' Mary said.

Jane patted her mouth with the cotton handkerchief she kept up her sleeve. Her tea had gone down the wrong way. 'Italian stallion! Where on earth did you get a phrase like that from?'

Mary chuckled. 'I asked the new librarian to recommend me another book from the Romance section. Rather an eye-opening read, I must say, but never mind about that, now. Who is Lisa embroiled with? I do hope he's not married.'

'Lisa *has* met someone . . .'

'I knew it!'

'Matteo. He's a lovely young man, but you know Lisa – she's in no rush to settle down.'

'As long as she's happy,' Mary said. 'But something's wrong. I could tell as soon as I picked up the phone.'

'Oh, Mary, I do need your advice. But it's nothing to do with Lisa. It's Cassie.'

'Cassie? Surely she's not in trouble. That would be a turn-up for the books.'

Jane sighed. She didn't know where to begin.

Mary nodded and made encouraging noises as Jane talked. At least, Jane assumed Mary was nodding. She could almost see her dear friend as if they were sitting opposite each other in Mary's cosy sitting room at Dapple Cottage rather than at opposite ends of a phone line hundreds of miles apart.

'So, you're sure I'm doing the right thing?' Jane asked. Again.

'Absolutely.' Mary's tone was brisk but still warm. 'Marriage isn't something to be thrown away lightly, no matter what the divorce statistics say. I'm quite surprised Cassie has got herself into this pickle. It's time to stop wondering if you're doing the right thing and just pick up the phone and do it. She'll thank you one day.'

'Luciano would say . . .'

'No disrespect, but I doubt Luciano would be the best person to ask. This needs a woman's intuition. Isn't that why you called me?'

'Yes, it is,' Jane said.

'Well then?'

'I'll do it. Thank you.'

'No need to thank me, that's what friends are for. Now, I'd love to keep you on the phone and find out what progress you've made on your wedding plans and hear about all those wonderful birds you've been spotting, but now you have another call to make so I'll say goodbye.'

'Goodbye, Mary.' Jane put down the telephone feeling more resolute. She lifted her mug to her lips. Her tea had gone cold but she resisted the temptation to make another one. If she didn't act now she'd lose her nerve.

She rang Paul's number. He answered almost at once.

There was a chink of light visible under the hotel room door. Cassie rapped on the door for a second time.

'All right, I'm coming!' Lisa shouted.

The door opened. Lisa looked strangely small, bundled up in the hotel's white towelling dressing gown. 'Hi! Did you have a nice time? How's Jane?'

'Montecatini was amazing . . .' Cassie began. 'Lisa, what's wrong? Why aren't you dressed?'

'I had a shower. I thought it would make me feel better but it didn't.'

Cassie looked into her sister's red-rimmed eyes. 'What's happened? Is it Matteo?'

Lisa sank down onto the bed. She grabbed at a hank of her hair. 'Oh, Cassie! It's all over.'

Cassie sat down next to her. 'Come here!'

Lisa flopped limply into Cassie's arms. All Cassie's worries about Paul, Jane's impulsive wedding and Luciano's secret love child seemed trivial compared to her sister's anguish.

Cassie stroked Lisa's hair. 'It's all going to be okay. I'm sure Matteo really likes you.'

'Not enough,' Lisa sniffed. 'I envy you, Cassie. Having Paul, knowing how much he loves you.'

'You'll meet someone else.'

'Who? I don't want anyone else.'

'Maybe Paul's got a friend. There's someone for everyone,' Cassie said, aware that she probably wasn't being very helpful.

'Even Aunt Jane,' Lisa sighed. 'You'll be suggesting she fixes me up with a friend of Luciano's next.'

'An Italian pensioner with loud shirts and paint in his hair. I can see it now.'

'Oh, do shut up!' Lisa laughed. She gave her sister a poke in the ribs.

'Just trying to help,' Cassie said.

'Well don't.' Lisa grabbed a quilted cushion from the bed and lobbed it at her sister's head.

Cassie ducked. The cushion sailed over the bed. 'Hey! What are you doing?' She grabbed a pillow and hurled it back.

'Right, that's it!' Lisa grabbed two pillows at once.

'That's cheating!' Cassie snatched one back. They fell into the bedclothes wrestling until they collapsed in a tangle of limbs.

'You're too good at this!' Cassie lay back, red-faced and panting. She couldn't believe they'd actually had a pillow fight. They hadn't done that since they were kids.

'Did you forget I had a hidden talent?' Lisa said.

Cassie sat up and turned towards the mirror. Her hair was a hot, sticky tangle. 'Ugh! I'm definitely going to have to have a shower before we meet Jane and Luciano for dinner.'

'Serves you right for being an interfering little sister,' Lisa said, smiling.

'I was only trying to help.' Cassie put on a mock-hurt voice.

Lisa rested her hand on her sister's arm. 'You can't help me. But at least you made me laugh. And, Cassie . . .'

'What?'

'I'll never regret this trip. It's been good to spend some time together; I feel like we've got to know each other all over again. I think Mum would be proud of us. I really am glad you're here.'

'Glad enough to lend me your denim jacket tonight?'

'Don't push it,' Lisa picked up a pillow and held it above her head.

'No more!' Cassie shrieked. She escaped into the bathroom, switched on the shower and let the hot water gush over her. She lathered on some shower gel; the room filled with grapefruit-scented steam. Cassie cast her mind over Paul's old university friends. It was hard to envisage Lisa dating any of them.

Chapter Twenty-Three

Lisa took a peach yogurt from the breakfast buffet. She couldn't face eating anything else. She had struggled to pick her way through the three-course meal with Jane and Luciano last night. The rich *tordelli Lucchese* pasta had smelt delicious but she had completely lost her appetite. It had been hard enough to keep a smile on her face whilst she described her carriage ride with Matteo in a few bland phrases. She didn't want to tell Jane and Luciano what had happened after that. She hadn't wanted to put a dampener on the evening, not when the others were so excited about visiting the wedding venue today.

Lisa stepped out onto the terrace and did a double-take. Cassie was already sitting at their usual table in the corner by the potted lemon tree. Cassie had got ready so quickly that morning she was out of their hotel room and downstairs before Lisa had finished in the bathroom. Cassie's skin was free of make-up and her hair wasn't pulled back in its usual tightly controlled French pleat. It hung over her shoulders, a loose, golden curtain. She was wearing a bright red T-shirt with a white slogan across her chest that read: *Ciao Bella!* Lisa would have been less surprised if Cassie had been sitting there naked.

Cassie twisted a piece of hair behind her ear as Lisa approached. 'Hi!'

'Hi!' Lisa put her yogurt pot down on the yellow tablecloth.

'Is that all you're having?'

'I'm not hungry,' Lisa said. 'Where on earth did you get that?' She nodded her head towards the T-shirt.

'In Montecatini, yesterday. It's a bit touristy but don't you think it's kind of cool?'

'I like it but . . .'

'I know it doesn't really go with this skirt but it would look good with a denim mini don't you think? I thought I might look out for one.' Cassie popped the last mouthful of cherry *crostata* into her mouth. She nodded at the hovering waiter. 'Cappuccino, Lisa?'

'Umm, yes, please.'

'*Due cappuccini per favore*,' Cassie said. It was the first time Lisa had heard her try out any Italian.

'You don't want a latte?' Lisa peeled the foil from her yogurt.

'Fancied something different. Are you sure you don't want anything else? Try a bit of this . . .' Cassie cut the corner off a slice of cake spiked with raisins. '*Buccellato* – apparently it's a local recipe. It's got this kind of aniseed flavour.'

'No, I'm fine.' Lisa looked at Cassie's plate. 'Are you really eating all those cakes for breakfast?'

'Why not?' Cassie shrugged. 'Mmm, I can smell our cappuccinos coming from here.'

Lisa sipped her coffee and toyed with her yogurt. She forced a smile. 'Looking forward to seeing the wedding venue today?'

'Yes, it will be nice to head out to the country. But I'd like to squeeze in a bit of window-shopping in via Fillungo before we meet Jane and Luciano.' Cassie glanced at her watch. 'We've still got over an hour. That's if you don't mind, of course.'

'Not at all.' Lisa felt some of the tension in her shoulders ebb away. A whole hour of not having to pretend she was okay. A whole hour to herself. She knew exactly what she was going to do.

Lisa took the steps of the Guinigi Tower two at a time. Climbing up high was the only way she knew to calm her whirring mind. If she stood at the very top and looked out over the town, she might be able to get some perspective on the events of the last twenty-four hours. It had worked for her in the past, whenever she wanted to clear her mind of the unwelcome memories of Dad's betrayal that surfaced from time to time. And the distressing thought that Dad loved his youngest daughter – the half-sister they never spoke of – more than he had ever loved them.

The viewing platform was almost deserted. Most of the town's tourists were probably still enjoying their breakfasts and the day-trippers and coach parties had not yet arrived. A delicious breeze was blowing. Lisa inhaled through her nose, counted slowly and exhaled. There was something calming about looking down from a great height with a commanding view of the yellow and white buildings and maze of streets. She could see the cathedral and the soaring clock tower, the mountains on the horizon. Beyond them lay other towns, other provinces of Italy, other countries. Lucca was just a dot on a map of Europe. She was a speck of dust.

Usually Lisa was comforted by how large the universe was; it made her problems seem tiny and insignificant. But not today. There were nearly two hundred countries in the world, more than seven billion people. So why did it feel as though Matteo was the only one for her? No matter how far she roamed, she couldn't imagine that she would ever find someone who made her feel that way again. She stared at the horizon, willing herself to recapture that wonderful feeling of freedom she had discovered as a child, standing on the climbing frame and believing she could see the skyscrapers and yellow taxis of New York.

It was no use. Her eyes kept returning to the old ramparts where Carlo and his horse Gaia had taken them on that magical carriage ride. What use was a whole world of adventure if her heart was stuck here?

She walked slowly around the perimeter of the viewing platform looking at the city from every direction. It was going to be so hard to leave. Lisa rested both elbows on the railing and put her head in her hands. She felt someone come up behind her. A hand on her arm. A familiar scent made her heart leap.

'I'm sorry,' Matteo said.

She spun around. 'I'm the one . . . I mean . . . I didn't mean,' she began.

'No.' He held up his hand. 'My pride was hurt but I should have behaved better. It was rude and childish of me to walk off. I am glad to see you here and get a chance to apologise. I would not miss Luciano and Jane's wedding for anything, and I could not bear for any awkwardness between us to overshadow their day. I wish you well. Goodbye, Lisa, have a safe flight home.'

'Matteo, please.' Lisa touched his arm.

Matteo flinched but he didn't move away. He turned his head and stared out across the rooftops. 'You know, it is funny, a day or two ago I would have thought it was a good omen that whenever I bump into you it is always in one of my most favourite places.' A flicker of sadness crossed his eyes.

'I love it here, amongst these trees, above the town,' Lisa said. It wasn't the conversation she wanted to have but talking about the tower might keep Matteo with her for a few minutes longer. And every moment she shared with him was precious.

'My papa used to bring me here when I was a child. It was a wonderful treat to spend time with him, wherever he took me; he was away travelling so much. But every time we came here it was extra special. Even more special than our trips to the gelateria.' Matteo smiled. 'He would lift me up on his shoulders and point out all the places we could see. I used to imagine that I could see the whole world from here. I would look into the distance and believe I could see . . .'

'America,' Lisa murmured.

'America?' Matteo laughed. 'No, not there – Japan. When I was a little boy, it was the most exotic place I could imagine. My nonna had a silk kimono that my great-grandfather had brought back from there. I used to stand up here and imagine I would go there and all the places I would visit when I was old enough.'

'And did you ever go to Japan?'

'No. Perhaps one day. And you, did you ever see New York?'

'Not yet.'

'Nor me. There are so many places I still want to see, but to travel you need somewhere to come back to, somewhere to call home, the place where your heart is. But some people cannot bear to have any ties. It was foolish of me to hope that you wanted more from me than just a holiday fling. You have had a fun time in Lucca – why would I blame you for that? I understand that you don't want anything to tie you down.'

'You're so wrong.' Lisa's voice was barely above a whisper.

'Please don't make this any harder.'

'It's true.' It was difficult to speak with the lump that had formed in her throat. 'Please, Matteo, give me a chance to explain. I ran from you because I was scared. I've never let myself get close to anyone, but before you it's never mattered, no one meant that much to me. And I've been let down so many times in the past. I didn't dare believe that you weren't like the others.'

'Like your father.'

'My father?' Lisa stiffened.

'Remember, Cassie told me about him. He let you down so badly. I should have realised that had something to do with it.'

'Why would you? You're nothing like him, nothing like him at all.'

'Perhaps not.' Matteo took her hand in his. 'But the experiences we have, they cloud our judgement. Sometimes they make things seem different from what they really are. Then we throw away something valuable.'

Lisa bit her lip. She felt tears pricking her eyes. 'I didn't want things to end. I wanted to meet you in Prague but I don't want us to savour a few days together then not see each other again for weeks or months.'

Matteo moved closer. She held her breath, her heart racing. His finger traced the outline of her top lip. 'I'm going away tomorrow to Austria. Then to Germany. I won't be back in Lucca for a while. I'll miss this place. But this time part of my heart will be in England. But if you felt the same way . . .'

'I do.'

He pulled her close and kissed her softly.

'This summer I am on tour, but it doesn't always have to be like that.' He kept his arms around her waist.

'But how? I couldn't ask you to give up your music.'

'Not being able to make a living from my passion would make me miserable but there is another way. There's a wonderful orchestra based in Florence. The director of music has been trying to persuade me to join for a while; their first violinist is ready to retire. They rarely tour but they do have a three-month residency at the end of the year. In London. And after that, who knows, but we could find a way to be together. We'll work something out.'

'But what about seeing the world? What about your dreams of Japan?' Lisa waved an arm towards the rooftops.

'Even musicians get holidays,' Matteo said.

'I wish we could spend today together . . .'

'But you're going to see Jane and Luciano's wedding venue. You can't miss that.'

'No, you're right. Jane is so excited to show us.'

'Luciano's car takes five.' Matteo grinned.

Lisa was sure her smile was almost as wide. 'I'm sure Aunt Jane wouldn't mind.'

'I know she wouldn't; she invited me yesterday evening. I told her I couldn't make it.'

'She'll be happy that you've changed your mind.'

'Not as happy as I am.' He kissed her again. She held him tightly. She never wanted to let him go.

Cassie breathed a sigh of relief. Lisa had fallen for her story about going window-shopping on via Fillungo. At last, she had managed to get away. She had to track down Luciano and find out the truth of Pia's allegations. And she had to do it alone; Lisa would only tell her not to interfere.

Yesterday in Montecatini it had been hard to keep Pia's revelations to herself but Cassie couldn't risk causing Jane any anguish until she was sure that Pia was really Luciano's secret grandchild. The letter 'L' and a few doodles on the back of an old portrait didn't amount to sufficient proof. The girl could easily be mistaken. Cassie needed to hear the truth from Luciano himself. If he was concealing an abandoned love child from his new fiancée, what other secrets were lurking behind his amiable bear-like façade?

Cassie didn't have much time before the four of them left to view the wedding venue but she knew where Luciano would be found. He would be up on the walls sketching, capturing the morning light falling on the terracotta rooftops.

Cassie hurried along to the steps that led up to the wall. She loved this wide avenue with its views across the town and its sturdy, leafy trees that dappled the paths. It was so tempting to flop onto a bench and watch the dog-walkers, joggers and cyclists passing by. This morning she had no time to dawdle. In the distance, a large man with orange plaid shorts was leaning against the wall. It had to be Luciano. She picked up her pace, repeating to herself the conversation she had rehearsed in her head.

She was right – it was Luciano. His head was bent, his pencil flying over the page of his small sketchbook. Cassie slowed down and took a couple of deep breaths. She needed to look as though she was in control although she felt anything but.

Luciano swung around. Someone had called his name. It was Alonzo, approaching from the other direction. The heat rose to Cassie's face; she couldn't bear the embarrassment of running into him again. She ducked behind the protective girth of a large plane tree and prayed that neither man would look around and see her skulking there.

The minutes ticked by. Finally, Alonzo turned to go. Cassie exhaled. Too soon. Luciano followed the younger man to a nearby bench. Alonzo pulled something from his jacket pocket. A packet of playing cards. Cassie let out a sharp breath of irritation. She had no chance of speaking to Luciano alone. She would have to go window-shopping on via Fillungo after all. Quietly, she crept away.

Chapter Twenty-Four

Matteo wound down the window.

'Thanks,' Lisa said. It was rather hot being squashed in the middle of the back seat of Luciano's car. Feeling Matteo's thigh pressed against hers, she felt even hotter. She sneaked a peek out of the corner of her eye; Matteo's dark hair was ruffling in the breeze from the open window. She looked at his aquiline nose, his olive skin and sharp cheekbones. How had she ever thought he was just ordinary?

He caught her looking at him. Their eyes met. He smiled that wonderful smile of his. She couldn't resist the urge to place her hand on his knee and give it a quick squeeze. Beside her, Cassie stared straight ahead.

'Look, vineyards.' Aunt Jane swivelled around in her front seat.

Rows and rows of vines stretched for what seemed like miles. Lisa could see a yellow farmhouse on the horizon. Poppies bobbed their red heads by the side of the road.

Luciano seemed to read her thoughts. 'The Tuscany of a thousand postcards.'

'That view reminds me of one of Chiara Marinetti's paintings,' Jane said.

'A wonderful exhibition. A sell-out I hear,' Luciano said.

'Is it far?' Cassie asked. She fanned herself with her now rather dog-eared copy of *Lucca Attractions*.

'Only a few miles,' Jane said. 'I can't wait for you girls to see it.'

'The views are very romantic,' Matteo added. He let his hand brush against Lisa's. Her stomach flipped. She turned towards him and smiled. She still couldn't believe how close she had come to losing him.

Luciano turned the car into a narrow lane.

'Wait a minute. This isn't the right way,' Jane said.

'There's been a change of plan – I hope you're not going to be too upset.'

'What do you mean? There isn't a problem with the venue is there?' Jane's voice wobbled slightly.

'I found out yesterday that our venue is double-booked but please don't be distressed. I have arranged for us to view another place. Somewhere I am sure you will love even more.'

'Oh,' Jane said. Her voice was quiet. Lisa's heart went out to her aunt. Jane had put so much effort into her wedding plans.

They drove past more vineyards until their way was barred by a set of tall, wrought-iron gates. 'This is it,' Luciano said. He clambered out and unhooked a latch. The gates swung open. Lisa was surprised they weren't locked.

Luciano squeezed back into the driver's seat and drove up a long avenue lined with cypress trees. 'The housekeeper is expecting us,' he said.

'Luciano has known the owner of this villa for many years,' Matteo said. 'I'm sure you will all love it.'

'Are we meeting the owner?' Jane said.

'No . . . no, he is . . . um, away. But he trusts us to look around,' Matteo said.

Luciano fumbled in the pocket of his orange shorts, drew out a red spotted handkerchief and mopped his brow with one hand. The other rested on the steering wheel.

Cassie sat up straighter as the car slowly approached the house. 'This looks very grand.'

Lisa winced at her sister's tone of voice. The words *how can a poor artist afford this?* hung in the air.

Luciano parked the car on the white gravel drive. Its slightly chipped paintwork and dented rear door looked rather incongruous against the palatial surroundings. Matteo helped Aunt Jane out of the passenger seat. She smoothed down her pleated skirt and patted her auburn hair.

Lisa didn't know what she'd been expecting, but she hadn't been expecting *this*. The white gravel drive that led to the villa was flanked by manicured lawns. Weathered statues of naked nymphs peeked coyly from between the gaps of immaculately neat box hedges. Blowsy, pink roses spilled out over huge stone urns. A double stone staircase led up to the entrance of the four-storey villa. Lisa started counting: eighteen windows all shaded by smart grey shutters were set into the splendid soft apricot façade.

'Welcome to Villa Melograno!' Luciano flung his arms apart.

Luciano turned to Lisa and Cassie, who was gazing open-mouthed. 'When I discovered we had a problem with our venue I thought it worth making some enquiries to see if it was feasible to hold the wedding here. Forgive me, dear Jane, for springing this on you but I did not want to say anything about our thwarted plans until I was sure that we had a better alternative.'

'Oh, Luciano! What an amazing place! This is more than I could ever dream of!' Aunt Jane beamed.

'Look!' Matteo pointed to a peacock strutting across the lawn. It stopped a few feet away from them, fixing its beady eye on Lisa. She stepped backwards away from it, her sandals crunching on the gravel. Matteo slipped his arm around her waist. She leant against him, savouring the scent of his sun-warmed skin.

The peacock's tail slowly unfurled. His iridescent blue and green feathers shimmered in the sunshine.

'Wow! He's beautiful,' Lisa said.

'They don't often display their tails to visitors like that,' Luciano said. 'He must like you.'

'He's not the only one,' Matteo whispered.

Cassie looked down and fiddled with the clasp of her handbag.

The peacock paused for a moment or so, then, as if he deemed they had seen enough, he turned his back on them and stalked off.

'Shall we go inside?' Luciano said. The others followed him up the sweeping stone staircase.

'The frieze shows the scenes from Dante's *Divine Comedy*.' Matteo pointed to the carved reliefs on the architrave over the entrance. 'The shield in the centre is the coat of arms of the Contini family; they were the original owners.'

'They must have been terribly important,' Cassie said.

'Not important, just successful in business – they were silk merchants. That has been a significant trade here since the eleventh century,' Luciano said.

'It really is something.' Cassie tipped her head back and stared up in awe.

Lisa suppressed a smile. Her sister might not be convinced by Aunt Jane's hasty engagement but she was clearly impressed by the new wedding venue.

'*Buongiorno*. Welcome, welcome.' A short, slightly plump lady in a pink floral smock topped with a white pinny stood at the top of the stairs with her hands clasped together.

'*Buongiorno*. Welcome, Luciano, Jane. Jane, I am Velia.'

'Very pleased to meet you,' Jane said.

'These are Jane's nieces, Lisa and Cassie,' Luciano added.

'*Piacere*. Pleased to meet you. Do come in.' Velia waved her hand towards the open doorway and stepped aside.

Cassie gasped audibly.

Lisa felt her mouth literally fall open. Her own flat would fit into this space twice over. Yet, despite its size, there was something homely about it.

'You like it?' Matteo slipped his arm around Lisa's waist.

Lisa nodded. She wasn't often lost for words. She looked around the vast hallway, taking in the high ceiling, the round polished centre table with its curved legs tipped with lions' heads, the exquisite silk Persian rug lying on the stone flagstones worn by centuries of use, oil paintings in heavy, carved gold frames hung on the walls.

'These pictures,' she said finally. 'Family portraits, I suppose.'

'Not all of them,' Cassie said.

Lisa turned to her in surprise.

'Your sister is right,' Luciano said. 'You recognised this one, perhaps?'

'Puccini?' Cassie suggested.

'*Brava!* Very good.'

'And there he is again.' Matteo pointed out another picture, a double portrait this time.

'And is that his wife?' Lisa looked at the woman's strong features. Her so-real-you-could-reach-out-and-stroke-it fur-edged robe.

'Elvira,' Cassie mumbled. Lisa looked at her curiously, but Cassie was already moving away, her attention apparently sparked by a painting on the other side of the room.

'Yes, Elvira Gemignani,' Matteo said. 'She was the love of his life.'

'It's beautiful,' Lisa murmured. She knew it was soppy but when Matteo said the word *love* it made her insides turn to jelly.

'This way.' Matteo took her hand. He held open the door at the far end of the hall through which Luciano, Cassie, Aunt Jane and Velia had already vanished.

They entered a panelled dining room. Sun sparkled on the heavy chandeliers suspended above a long, polished wooden table dressed with a fine, embroidered linen runner. Statues were set in alcoves on each side of the room.

Cassie's eyes widened. 'Will you hold the wedding breakfast here, Jane?'

'It's beautiful but surely it's far too large; that table looks as though it seats nearly a hundred.'

'I believe we will be able to use the Garden Room,' Luciano said.

'It's at the end of the corridor,' Matteo added.

'You know the place well. Do you know the owner too?' Lisa asked.

'I've been here once or twice. This way . . .' Matteo strode ahead.

Lisa followed him into another large room where Velia was plumping up the cushions on a chaise lounge.

'This is perfect.' Jane's face lit up. The room was so light and pretty. The floor was inlaid marble and the walls were covered with delicate, pastel-coloured frescoes. A huge, foxed mirror hung above the flower-laden marble mantelpiece. A glossy, black grand piano stood by the doors at the far end, which opened onto a substantial terrace leading down to a sloping lawn. A gold-edged dish on top of the piano was piled with porcelain fruit.

Luciano's unruly hair, striped collarless shirt and orange plaid Bermuda shorts looked rather out of place amongst the elegant surroundings. Lisa couldn't help wondering what he would be wearing on the big day.

'It's a shame it will be too cold to keep the doors open in December, but this room should be just as beautiful in winter with the shutters closed and the curtains drawn,' Luciano said.

'Beautiful . . . and cosy,' Velia agreed. She ran her hand down the edge of one of the heavy silk-velvet drapes. They were an unusual colour – something between green and grey.

'Maybe we might hire some outdoor heaters so that we will be able to go out onto that terrace and take a few photographs,' Jane said.

'Whatever you wish, my love,' Luciano said. Aunt Jane beamed with happiness.

'Shall we go outside?' Matteo led them through the glass doors out onto the wide terrace and down the steps onto the great expanse of lawn dotted with substantial terracotta pots holding citrus trees.

Lisa looked around in wonder.

'There are more than a hundred lemon trees. When it gets too cold, they are moved into the lemon house, over there, until the weather warms a little,' Velia said.

'All this belongs to the villa?' Lisa asked. The grounds seemed to stretch for miles.

'Yes. All this, and beyond here is the lake – and of course the woods too – they are all part of Villa Melograno.'

'Gosh,' Cassie said. 'It must take a lot of looking after.'

'Talking of which, you must excuse me whilst you look around,' Velia said.

'Of course, thank you, Velia,' Luciano said. He ambled towards a series of geometric brick-edged flower beds. The others followed.

'*Teatro flora*,' Jane said. 'It means flower theatre – that's what they call this type of planting.'

'So pretty,' Lisa said. Geranium heads waved in the soft breeze, bees buzzed, the scent of freesias filled the air. Matteo's arm was around her shoulders. Had she ever felt happier?

'You should see the lake – it is the most beautiful part,' Luciano said. They passed under a rose arch and followed a path that curved away to the left.

Sun shimmered on the surface of the water, which was speckled with lily pads. A pair of pure white swans glided by.

'How wonderful to hold their wedding here,' Lisa said.

'Perhaps . . . one day we will do the same.' Matteo pushed his sunglasses up into his hair. He kissed her gently.

Lisa opened her eyes. The others had discreetly wandered away.

'Let's take a walk into the woods,' he said.

He took her hand as he led her through the canopy of trees that provided a deliciously cool shade. A bird chirped. Leaves rustled, a twig snapped. Lisa turned and saw a flash of something purple moving in the trees.

'What was that?'

'What was what?'

'There was someone over there amongst the trees.'

Matteo kissed her forehead. 'No, it was just a roe deer or perhaps a porcupine.'

'No, look over there.' Lisa pointed. It was definitely a human figure. A woman's figure – tall and upright – walking between the trees deep in the woods. A glimpse of a bright green handbag, the gleam of a metal hairclip in her black chignon as she turned away.

'I can't see anything,' Matteo said.

'I'm sure it was a woman.'

'It's easy to imagine things in these woods.' He smiled. 'Come on, the others will wonder where we are.'

Lisa wished she could look into his eyes but they were hidden behind his dark sunglasses. She was sure Matteo had seen the woman too. So why was he lying to her?

'Oh, there you are!' Luciano said. 'You don't mind if I borrow Matteo for a few minutes?' The two men walked off across the lawn, talking in Italian.

Aunt Jane and Cassie were standing by a weathered statue of Persephone, watching a gardener tending to the rose bushes. Jane smiled as Lisa approached. 'I thought you two had got lost,' she joked.

'We went for a walk in the woods.'

'Very romantic,' Jane said. 'Isn't it perfect! I think I must be dreaming!'

Cassie looked away. Lisa wondered, again, what was bothering her sister.

'Those woods are like something out of a picture book aren't they,' Jane said. 'I can almost imagine I can see fairies living there.'

'I thought I saw a woman amongst the trees, but Matteo insisted it was my imagination,' Lisa said.

'What did she look like?' Cassie asked.

'Tall, rather dramatic-looking, but I only caught a glimpse of her.'

The gardener paused in his work. 'That will have been Chiara Marinetti.'

'The artist?' Lisa said. 'Yes, you're right, I thought there was something familiar about her.'

'We saw Chiara's exhibition the other evening. What a strange coincidence.' Cassie frowned.

'A coincidence, but not a strange one. Chiara lives at Villa Melograno.'

'Chiara lives here?' Cassie repeated.

'That's right.' The gardener picked up his secateurs.

Lisa tried to hide her surprise. She looked at Aunt Jane. Judging by the expression on Jane's face, it was news to her too.

Chapter Twenty-Five

Jane looked from one niece to the other.

'I . . . I . . . just don't understand. Why didn't Luciano tell us?' Her voice quavered.

'Well . . .' Cassie began.

'I'm sure there's a perfectly reasonable explanation,' Lisa interrupted. She shot her sister a look. Cassie pursed her lips.

'Luciano says he's known Chiara for years. Why didn't he mention she lived here?' Aunt Jane wrung her hands together.

'Hmm,' Cassie said. She looked as though she wanted to say a lot more.

Lisa shifted from foot to foot. The awkward silence grew. Jane avoided eye contact; she couldn't face their pitying looks. The gardener continued his work blissfully unaware of the impact of his casual remark.

At last, Lisa spoke. 'This hot weather's making me ever so thirsty. Why don't we go inside? I'm sure Velia wouldn't mind fetching us some water.'

'Let's do that,' Jane said. She watched the peacock picking his way along the edge of the lawn. The sky was a cloudless blue and each bloom in the *teatro flora* was a little piece of perfection, but the garden had lost its appeal. Jane didn't care if the rain fell or the wind blew or every delicate pink petal turned crispy and brown. Everything was already spoilt.

Jane followed Lisa and Cassie into the house. She was glad of Velia's inconsequential chit-chat as they sipped iced water from heavy glass tumblers. Jane wished hers was a stiff gin and tonic.

How did Luciano think he would get away with not mentioning Chiara lived here? Chiara had to be more than just an old friend; why else would he be so secretive? She thought back to the strange way the artist had, seemingly deliberately, given her the wrong change when they had attended her exhibition. Her gut had told her that something was wrong but she had ignored the warning signs. Even when she discovered the photograph of Luciano with his arm around Chiara tucked away in the kitchen drawer, she had made excuses instead of confronting him. Jane felt sick. Luciano and Chiara were up to something. Were they having an affair all along? What was Luciano keeping from her?

She had been so convinced that she'd found lasting happiness. How blind she had been. Cassie and Lisa had been right to come out to Lucca to try to rescue her from her foolish, hasty marriage plans. Jane wasn't naive enough to think there was any other reason for the timing of their visit so soon after the wedding invitations had been received.

Jane stole a glance through the open glass doors. Luciano was still talking to Matteo by the path that led down to the lake. Jane turned away – it hurt too much to look at him. She loved him so much – that wouldn't change no matter what he'd done. Perhaps she was just an old fool but she would never regret their brief relationship. He had changed her life. Italy had changed her life. It had magicked her away from her predictable, quiet existence and opened up a world of opportunities.

Jane pushed her shoulders back. She sat up a little straighter. She had survived Eddie's death – that was the worst thing that had ever happened to her. Or could happen to her. If Luciano and Chiara were having an affair, she wouldn't crumble. She would terminate her engagement to Luciano and emerge a stronger person. She hoped.

'Some more?' Velia held out the water jug.

Jane snapped out of her thoughts. 'No, thank you. But that was most welcome.'

'Not for me either,' said Lisa.

Cassie shook her head. Velia gathered up the empty glasses and placed them on a lacquered tray. Jane immediately regretted not requesting a top-up. It would have given her something to do with her hands.

Lisa was chewing the skin around her thumbnail. Cassie unfolded the *Lucca Attractions* leaflet. She must know that off by heart, Jane thought.

Jane stood up. If she sat there any longer she might scream. She made a show of studying the frescoes on the Garden Room's walls.

'Have you considered engaging a harp player?' Velia asked.

Jane stiffened then forced a smile. She wasn't going to share her troubles with the kind housekeeper.

'I thought we might just be able to use that grand piano.'

'Do you remember those Sunday afternoons when we used to play yours?' Cassie said. She had visibly brightened up at the prospect of a nice, neutral Luciano-free topic of conversation.

'My poor neighbours.' Jane laughed despite herself.

'We did make a terrible racket,' Lisa said.

'*You* did. *I* practised,' Cassie said.

'And you got a merit in Grade Five whilst I never made it past Grade Two as you never tired of reminding me.'

'I was a terrible prig, wasn't I.'

'Not *all* the time . . .'

'You both play the piano?' Velia asked. 'Please . . .' she gestured towards the grand piano.

'Won't the owner mind?' Jane said.

Velia regarded her curiously. 'Not at all. The piano is regularly tuned but no one plays it anymore. It's such a shame.'

'That's a shame,' Jane said. 'Such a beautiful instrument. I had a small upright piano back in England but it's nothing like this.'

'Why don't you play something, Aunt Jane? You're so much better than us,' Cassie said.

'Oh, I couldn't . . .'

'Why not?' Velia said.

'Go on, Jane,' Lisa said. 'You always said it was the perfect way to unwind.'

Jane hesitated but not for long. Lisa was right: playing the piano always relaxed her. It had helped her through the many dark days after Eddie's death. She had spent hours lost in the music. And it would help her while away the time until she had to face Luciano. It might calm her frayed nerves in the absence of that large gin and tonic.

'Okay,' Jane said.

'There's some music in the piano stool.' Velia lifted the creaky lid.

Jane sat down on the padded yellow velvet seat and leafed through the sheet music. '*Puccini for Piano Solo*. I wish I'd brought my reading glasses . . . silly of me. I think it will be too difficult to sight-read without them. I don't know many pieces by heart.'

'You must remember one of those old ragtime tunes you used to play. I'd love to hear one of those after all these years,' Lisa said.

Jane wasn't in the mood for something so jolly but at least it would cheer up her nieces. She still couldn't work out what was the matter with Cassie but Lisa still looked shaken up by the realisation that Matteo had been less than truthful about seeing Chiara in the woods.

'Let's have "The Entertainer",' Cassie suggested.

Jane found middle C. She fumbled the first couple of notes but then started hitting the keys with gusto. *Tum-tee, tum-tee, tum, tum-tee, tum, tum* Jane mouthed silently. Cassie and Lisa started humming along.

'Stop!' Matteo shouted.

Jane's fingers froze on the keyboard. She swung around in alarm.

Matteo was standing in the doorway. He was red in the face and his hair was all dishevelled as though he had been running.

'I thought . . . Velia said we could . . .' Jane fumbled over her words. She caught sight of Luciano standing behind Matteo. All the colour had drained from his face. He looked as though he had seen a ghost.

Luciano's hands were trembling. Seemingly on the verge of tears, he struggled to compose himself. All Jane's anger at his deception evaporated. She had no idea what dreadful occurrence had caused Luciano to become so distressed; she couldn't bear to see the strong man she loved so deeply affected.

'The piano . . .' Luciano murmured.

'I am so sorry,' Jane said, though she could not imagine how the sound of the instrument had caused him such anguish.

'*I* am so sorry, I said she could play,' Velia said.

'Of course, of course . . . Jane, my darling, don't look so fearful. You have done nothing wrong. It is a joy to me that you should enjoy playing this neglected instrument.' Luciano put his large hand on the piano's smooth, black lid.

'Then, why . . .' Lisa began. Matteo gave an almost imperceptible shake of his head.

'It was that tune . . . it brings back such memories. Frankie loved those old tunes.'

'Oh.' Jane looked down. She knew from her own experience how easily a song or even a familiar scent could uncover a person's well-hidden grief.

Cassie glanced at Lisa.

'Frankie was Luciano's younger brother,' Lisa said quietly.

'He passed away many years ago. He was just a teenager. One moment he was playing football in the street; the next he was gone,' Luciano said.

'I'm so sorry,' Cassie murmured.

'He had so many talents: football, drawing – I'll never be half as good as he was – and music . . . It was such a shock to hear that tune. I know it sounds crazy but for a moment I thought he'd come home. Even though, of course it's impossible. Foolish . . .' He sank down onto the couch and put his head in his hands.

'Come home?' Jane took his big hand in hers. She didn't want to stir his grief but his choice of words threw her. 'Why would Frankie come home to Chiara's house?'

Luciano straightened up. 'Chiara's house? What do you mean?'

Jane paused. She hadn't meant to confront him like this. She wanted to pick her moment. 'Nothing . . . I . . .'

'Chiara owns this villa,' Cassie said.

'No, that's not true.'

Jane's heart sank. If he wasn't going to be honest with her, there couldn't be any future for them. She twisted her engagement ring around her finger. The symbol of the promises they had made. Had it all been based on lies?

Cassie gave a sniff of distaste. 'We know she lives here.' She jutted her chin out, daring him to deny it.

'Perhaps you could give us some privacy. I think your aunt and I need to talk,' Luciano said.

Matteo reached for Lisa's hand. 'It's okay,' he whispered. Lisa stood up.

'No!' Jane said.

Her nieces turned and stared.

'Whatever you have to say, Lisa and Cassie can hear it too.' Jane sounded much stronger than she felt. She bit her lip and started counting backwards slowly from one hundred, trying vainly to calm herself as her heart raced.

'I have some explaining to do.' Luciano folded his hands in his lap. His voice was quiet, all his usual flamboyance had deserted him. 'Jane, there is something I have been meaning to tell you. I just haven't found the right time . . . or the right words.'

Jane swallowed a big lump in her throat.

'You see,' Luciano continued. 'Chiara doesn't own Villa Melograno. I do.'

Chapter Twenty-Six

Jane could hardly believe what she was hearing. Luciano owned Villa Melograno. And Chiara lived there. He hadn't denied it. How he had come to own this property – which must be worth millions – she did not care. She only cared that he had concealed its existence from her. No wonder – his mistress was installed there! And he planned to marry Jane right under her very nose.

Jane could tell from Matteo's face that Matteo knew all this already. How many more people knew about Chiara and the villa? Viviana and her mother, Livia; all her other new friends and acquaintances. All of them in the know. All laughing at her.

Jane felt faint and weak, as if she might slide off her seat onto the marble floor. She gripped the arm of the couch. She stared at her engagement ring, sparkling mockingly in a shaft of sunlight.

'Let me explain,' Luciano said.

Jane nodded. She would hear all his justifications and excuses. It wouldn't be pleasant but at least she'd know everything. But if he believed his wealth would convince her to stay with him, he was wrong. She would rather be with an honest poor man than a duplicitous rich one.

'I was born in Bagni di Lucca, a small spa town not far from here. We had no money to speak of but when I think of my childhood, I have only happy memories. There were just the four of us: Mamma, Papa, me and my little brother Frankie. My mother worked in the local bakery. She was dressed and out of the house before we woke up, but she was always there to greet us after school. Not that we appreciated it at the time, we were off outside to play before she had the chance to hang up her coat.

'My father loved art and music; in fact, it was he who gave me my lifelong love of Puccini. But Frankie was the musical one. Papa scrimped and saved to buy him a second-hand piano. Papa was no musician, but he was artistic, though he didn't have much chance to show it. I sometimes saw him pick up a pencil and doodle on the corner of the newspaper and he drew funny caricatures of our neighbours to make us laugh, then he would screw up the paper and throw it on the fire. He would no sooner have tried to make a living from his talent as build a rocket to the moon. He had a wife and two children to support. He was a practical man; he used his hands to make a living as an electrician.'

Jane shifted on the couch. Were they going to have to listen to Luciano's life story before he got to the point?

'Papa needed a steady income. He and his four brothers and sisters had been very poor. His father, my Nonno Antonio, had trained as a carpenter but he gave that up to follow his dreams and try to make a living from his art. Papa grew up seeing the way his mother went without to put food on her children's plates. He didn't resent his father but he knew that the whole family suffered financially from Nonno's devotion to his art. Papa swore he would never put his own wife and children through such hardship.

'After Nonno Antonio died, Papa insisted that my nonna came to live with us. Mamma and Papa helped Nonna to go through my grandfather's things. They sifted through hundreds of sketches and framed the half-dozen that Nonna loved best.'

'The pictures in our hallway,' Jane said.

'Yes, the ones I showed you on your first visit. I have always kept those drawings close to me.'

'And then?' Cassie sounded rather impatient.

'And then all our lives changed.'

'It really is an amazing story,' Matteo interjected.

'One you will have to listen to again, my friend. Where was I? Oh yes, my parents were helping Nonna sort through Nonno Antonio's things. I was fifteen years old but I will never forget that day. Frankie and I were hanging around, bored. Nonna wanted to look at everything. Every last shirt and tie, every book, every drawing.

'At last my father came to the final drawer. There was another bundle of sketches, rolled up and tied with string. We had no idea what they were at first. The whole family admired Nonno's work; perhaps we were biased because of who he was, but even at fifteen years old I could tell that these drawings were made by more talented hands.

'When I saw the signatures I swear I began to shake: Picasso and Chagall . . . so famous – I had studied them at school.'

'But how . . .?' Lisa said.

'We were astonished. My parents stared at Nonna but she was equally baffled. At last she remembered a story from Nonno's past. When he was a young man he had travelled to France sometime before the outbreak of the First World War. He had heard about the artists working there and fancied that was the place where he could make a name for himself. He managed to stay there for a few months finding some carpentry work and acting as a handyman whilst he honed his craft. He hung around the cafés and bars where the painters liked to go and gradually got to know some of them. In those days they would sometimes pay their rent or bills with sketches and small paintings. He must have done some work for a few of them.

'I don't know if Nonno had forgotten about the sketches or just didn't realise their worth. At first, even Papa did not appreciate the magnitude of what he had found. He took the pictures to an art dealer in Florence. The man was on the phone to the auction house straight away. On the day of the auction Nonna was in tears. After a lifetime of struggle she was a rich woman. She knew immediately what she wanted to do. When she was a little girl she had once visited this villa. So we moved from a cramped flat to Villa Melograno. Nonna spent the rest of her days here.

'Papa still worked; it was in his nature, but Mamma left the bakery. She devoted herself to improving these wonderful gardens. I wasn't so sure about the move. I was a self-conscious teenager who just wanted to fit in with his friends. But when Frankie walked into this room and saw that piano – the previous owners had left it behind, you see – he was in heaven. He would play for hours with those doors open whilst Mamma worked on her flower beds and Nonna dozed in a chair. How happy we were . . .'

Luciano's voice faltered. 'Of course it did not last. A lifetime of hard work and stress had taken its toll on my mother and Papa wasn't far behind. I was just nineteen when Frankie and I inherited Villa Melograno. It was a ridiculous place for two teenage boys to live but Frankie loved it here so much. I knew it would break his heart to leave. Then one day . . .'

Luciano stopped abruptly. He gazed across the terrace to the sloping lawn beyond. Jane waited. Luciano had provided no excuse or explanation about Chiara, but Jane felt she must listen to his story. For better or worse, it would enable her to understand a little better the man who had turned her world upside down.

'Frankie was just seventeen when he died. And I was twenty. I could not bear to live here any longer. Luckily, when I met my late wife, Adelina, she was content to live in town where we had a small house. Adelina ran a little dress boutique in via Fillungo and had no desire to live out in the countryside. I wanted nothing to do with this place, there were too many memories. But still, I could not bring myself to sell it. Frankie had loved it so much. For his sake I could not allow it to become a ruin so I employed Velia so that it did not fall into disrepair. I could not bear to come here. I could not bear to speak of the place, not even to you, my love.'

Jane's heart went out to him. What did a big house and money matter when you had lost someone you loved? But none of this explained why Chiara was living here. There was only one reason for that.

'I was lucky, not all of our inheritance was tied up in Villa Melograno, and though Papa made sure Mamma had everything her heart desired, she wasn't interested in jewels and furs and he was never extravagant, it wasn't his way. Papa put a little money aside in shares and bonds to allow me to pursue the career I had always dreamt of. I'll never be a great artist but I create pictures that people enjoy. Perhaps that is enough. Sometimes I feel guilty that there are so many more talented people than me who do not have the luxury of devoting themselves to their art. Then I met Chiara . . .'

Jane held her breath.

'Chiara and I got chatting when she came into the gallery one day. She was painting some little framed views of Lucca back then. She thought we might be interested in selling some so I took her card and promised to go and take a look, the way I always did. A few days later I visited her at home. She was living in a tiny apartment in a village not far from here. Her pictures were skilfully done; I agreed to take some on the spot. But before I got back into my car I took a stroll around, it was a beautiful day and I was in no hurry. I was walking through an olive grove when I spotted something quite extraordinary.

'There were two easels propped side by side holding up a half-finished painting. The view the artist had captured astonished me. It was so real and yet so unreal at the same time; the colours were incredible. I stopped dead in my tracks. This was real talent, I had no doubt. I rushed back to Chiara's apartment to ask her if she knew where I could find the person who was capable of creating such a masterpiece. To my surprise, she was the artist, yet she had not mentioned a thing. She laughed and explained that these huge paintings were her hobby, she showed me some more, which she stashed in a neighbour's shed. She said: "I create the little watercolours for a living but this is the art that satisfies me. I never tire of painting the landscape. But I cannot make money from these. Who has space for such works? They are a little impractical, don't you think? Sometimes I destroy the canvases once I have finished. I have so little space to store them. But it is no real hardship; to me the joy is in the creation of my work, not viewing it after it is completed."

'I made up my mind immediately. I suggested she come and live at Villa Melograno. It was the perfect solution. There were so many rooms lying empty and she could paint in the grounds and outside in all the marvellous countryside around here. In poor weather she could use the lemon house. I could support a brilliant artist – someone far more talented than myself – and Villa Melograno would not be lying empty. Of course, she was suspicious at first. Who wouldn't be? But then she and her husband met with me and Adelina. We had a long dinner and by the time we had finished we were all agreed.'

Husband. Had Jane heard right? Was Chiara married? Was there nothing between her and Luciano after all? She was too nervous to ask.

'So does Chiara's husband live here too?' Lisa asked.

Jane shot her a grateful look.

'No, Stefano Marinetti is a playwright. He says he needs only a desk and a chair. Besides, he loves the village where he lives. He has been there all his life. Chiara lives at Villa Melograno during the week whilst Stefano locks himself away writing. She returns home at the weekends. I am pleased to say the arrangement seems to work perfectly.'

'But why didn't you tell me before?' Jane said.

'I wish so much that I had done so but I had shut that part of my life away. I did not want to share my pain; I did not want the past to overshadow our future together. And besides, when I met you in Florence you assumed I was a penniless artist wanting to draw your portrait.'

'And I didn't want it drawn,' Jane chuckled.

'I knew that my money would make no difference to you, Jane. You loved me for who I am, not for anything I could offer you. I felt guilty for not being honest with you but convinced myself it was for the best. I wanted you to know me as the happy artist I am most of the time. I did not want to reveal the sad, grieving part of me.'

'I want to know all of you, to share your life – the good and the bad days,' Jane said quietly.

'But what's changed?' Cassie interrupted. 'Why have you brought us here now?'

'That was partly your doing,' Luciano said. 'You and

238

Lisa. Having you here in Lucca and seeing you with Jane has brought me such joy. I have begun to see that by meeting Jane, I have acquired a whole new family. I was sad that Frankie would never meet any of you and guilty that I had this wonderful life ahead of me when his was cut short. I was seized with the need to come back here, to make a kind of peace with the past.'

Jane nodded. Her eyes were pricking with tears.

'Yesterday, when you had all gone your separate ways, I drove out here. As I walked through the grounds, I felt Frankie's spirit. And instead of guilt I felt a kind of contentment. It was as if Frankie was giving me his blessing. The idea of marrying here had never entered my head but now it seemed the most obvious thing in the world. And, my darling Jane, I planned to present you with Villa Melograno as a surprise wedding gift. We can move here after we're married. I can see how much you love it.'

Jane couldn't speak at first; she was too overwhelmed. 'But I thought you were happy living in our apartment in Lucca.'

'Living in town suits me. But your happiness is more important. If you wish to live at Villa Melograno then that is what we will do. I spoke to Chiara yesterday and told her she could still store her pictures in a spare room and use the lemon house from time to time if that is okay with you. She's an established artist now, far less in need of my patronage . . . What is it, Jane? You look quite pale, my darling. Is there anything I can get you?'

Jane's head was spinning but suddenly everything began to make sense. No wonder Chiara had regarded her with suspicion; she must have suspected Jane to be a gold-digger whose forthcoming marriage might force her from the place that inspired her work.

'Jane, can I get you anything?' Luciano prompted.

'Actually, there is something – I would really like a large gin and tonic.'

'I can fetch that straight away,' Velia said.

'Drinks all round I think,' Matteo said. He squeezed Lisa's hand.

'A Prosecco please if you have one,' Cassie said.

'We have everything you can think of in the villa,' Luciano said. It was the most relaxed he had looked all day.

Velia returned with a tray. Jane used the glass stirrer to mix her gin and tonic. It smelt so good.

'We should have a toast,' Matteo said.

'To your new home,' Lisa suggested.

'No,' Jane said loudly.

Every face turned towards her.

'It's very kind and thoughtful of you,' Jane said, 'but I have no wish to live in this villa.'

'I thought you loved it.' Luciano frowned.

'I do.' It was true. The sweeping staircase, the high ceilings, the delicate frescoes, the lemon trees, the regal swans on the lake, the cool, mysterious woods. Villa Melagrano was enchanting. But it wasn't her home.

'It's the perfect place for our wedding, but . . .' Jane searched for the right words.

'It's very grand,' Lisa said.

Jane shot her a grateful look.

'Yes, very grand. A wonderful setting for a wedding or a special event and to visit from time to time, I'd like to do that. But I wouldn't feel right rattling around in a big place like this. Besides, I love our flat.'

'Even the rickety staircase, that old-fashioned kitchen, all my mess and the smell of paint?' Luciano said.

'All that.' Jane smiled. 'The villa is stunning. Who wouldn't want a peacock strutting past whilst they were eating breakfast, and the countryside is beautiful but the apartment is our home. And so is Lucca. I would miss so many things if we moved. Going to Giorgio's *pasticceria* for our breakfast; those evenings people-watching at Café Europa; popping into the gallery; cycling around the town; bumping into Livia and all my other new friends . . .'

And there were the things Jane did not say aloud: walking around the walls looking down on the town, filled with wonder that this was her new life; cycling around the narrow streets feeling incredibly free; spotting an artist at his easel and realising it was Luciano, too lost in concentration to notice anyone or anything except the scene he was capturing on canvas, and watching him silently from afar, her heart bursting with love. 'Do you mind that I don't want to move here?'

Luciano shook his head. 'Darling Jane, I did not think I could love you more.'

Matteo squeezed Lisa's hand. Even Cassie had a tear in her eye.

'Would you like another gin?' Velia said.

Jane looked at her empty glass, surprised. 'Oh, no . . . no thank you. One did the trick; my nerves are quite settled.'

'I feel terrible for having given you such a shock.' Luciano rubbed his bearded chin.

'I hope there's nothing else you want to share with us,' Jane joked.

'No, nothing. Now you know everything about me. No mysterious plans, no – how you say – skeletons in the cupboard.' Luciano spread his arms wide, his palms upwards. 'No more secrets, Jane. I promise.'

Jane felt so happy she dismissed the odd look that clouded Cassie's face.

Chapter Twenty-Seven

Jane took the coffee pot from the stove; her teapot was already resting on the iron trivet on the kitchen table.

Luciano's eyes lit up when he saw the paper bag from the *pasticceria*. He folded away his newspaper. 'Mmm, breakfast.' He rubbed his hands together.

Jane opened the bag; the sweet aroma was heavenly. She tipped three pastries onto a plate. A little cloud of icing sugar hovered briefly in the air.

'Aah, you're having one today. I didn't suppose for a moment you're allowing me three.'

'You can eat as many pastries as you like . . .'

'Your words are at odds with the look on your face, my darling. But I was only teasing. I like to see you enjoying these delicious *cornetti alla crema* once in a while. And I, regrettably, must try and curtail my appetite. I'll need to keep myself in shape when I have a new young wife.'

'Nearly seventy-one.' Jane smiled. She touched her auburn hair. She did feel younger since she'd covered up the grey and there were days with Luciano when she felt seventeen again.

'Who says I'm talking about you.' Luciano gave one of his booming laughs.

Quick as a flash, Jane grabbed the plate of pastries and held it above her head.

Luciano pushed back his chair. Jane stepped away.

'I'm not going to chase you around the flat, you're faster than me. But I know a way to get those pastries back.' His eyes gleamed. He reached out an arm.

'If you tickle me these are going to end up on the floor,' Jane said primly.

'And that would be a tragedy worthy of Puccini,' Luciano sighed. He sat down and put his head in his hands.

'Stop being so dramatic,' Jane giggled. She put the plate of pastries down.

'So, I'm forgiven.'

'Only because I don't want my tea to get cold.'

'Aah, tea in the morning – your peculiar English ways. What have I let myself in for?'

'One more comment like that and I'll take it into my head to eat two of those pastries.'

'*Mamma mia!* Now I am scared. I will need to be on my best behaviour.' He winked.

Jane ripped the corner off her pastry. Delicious.

Luciano's phone buzzed. 'I'll switch it off. No, wait, it's Viviana; she wants me to call.' He slapped his hand on his forehead. 'She left me a message yesterday whilst we were out at the villa. I completely forgot to call. I must be getting old.'

'Good thing you're getting a young wife.' Jane grinned. She sipped her tea.

Luciano strode up and down the kitchen, the phone clamped to his ear. Though Jane could just make out Viviana's voice at the other end of the line, the two Italians were talking so rapidly that she couldn't make head nor tail of the conversation. She knew it was good news. Luciano was beaming.

'I cannot believe it! No wonder Viviana wanted to speak to me yesterday. She would have called last night but she knew we were going out for dinner when we got back from the villa.'

'What is it?'

'Marvellous news! My painting of Chiesa San Michele has been sold.'

'The large one you only just finished?'

'Yes. Sold already!'

'That really is incredible.' Jane put her arms around him. He planted a kiss on her lips.

'In a way it is sad. I enjoyed looking at it hanging on the wall, knowing – at last – I had finally captured that tricky façade. And now it has gone – *poof!* – as if I imagined it all along.'

Jane nodded. She wasn't sure what to say. 'Perhaps you could paint it again, later in the summer when the light has changed.'

Luciano clapped his hands together. 'Yes! I could be like Monet, painting the same architecture again and again.'

'And those haystacks.' Jane remembered an exhibition at the Royal Academy many years before.

'Haystacks? I think I will leave that rustic kind of thing to Chiara. Now we must choose a couple of my other paintings that I can take along this morning to fill that large gap on the wall.'

'I'll come with you.' Jane stood up, brushing the pastry crumbs from her skirt.

'Are you not meeting the girls? It's your last whole day together.'

'I'll message them to meet me at the gallery. It will be much easier for you to hang the pictures with my help.'

'What would I do without you? Come upstairs, help me pick out a couple of pastels that you think would sell.'

'Shall I put that last pastry away for later if you're not going to eat it?' Jane picked up the empty paper bag.

'Put it away? *Mamma mia*, you are joking! I will eat it now. I'm not in that much of a rush.'

'Up a little.' Jane bit her lip. 'No, no, an inch to the right.'

'Jane! My arms are about to drop off!'

'Just half an inch . . . that's perfect.'

'At last.' Luciano gave a dramatic sigh. He stood back and looked at the two pictures. He turned to Jane and smiled. 'Thank you. You were right – it looks much better now the Palazzo Pfanner is above the Guinigi Tower. I would have hung them the other way around without your help.'

'They look great. Shall I help you with anything before the girls get here?'

'You could go out the back and put the coffee pot on. I might be too busy later to make one.'

Jane lit the small stove in the back room. She unscrewed the lid of the coffee canister. The shop doorbell jangled. Through the metal beaded curtain Jane could see a young woman clutching a large striped tote bag close to her body. It was the same girl who had come into the gallery a couple of days before.

The girl moved about the gallery fiddling with her hair, tucking a piece behind her ear and twisting the ends around her fingers. Jane poured Luciano's coffee. The girl was hovering awkwardly in front of Chiara's colourful painting of the Ponte Vecchio.

Jane brushed the beaded curtain aside. The girl jumped and gasped.

'Oh, hello again. Sorry, I did not mean to startle you.' Jane put Luciano's espresso on the shelf behind him. 'There you are, darling.'

'*Grazie*,' Luciano said. He addressed the girl: 'Are you looking for anything particular – a gift perhaps?'

Jane guessed Luciano was hoping that the girl would leave the gallery if she had no intention of making a purchase so that he could drink his coffee in peace.

The girl blinked rapidly. Her knuckles were pale where she tightly gripped the cloth handles of her bag. She glanced at the floor then at the big bear-like man by Jane's side.

'This is Luciano,' Jane said. 'Darling, this young lady came in the other day.'

'Are you really Luciano Zingaretti?'

'Indeed I am.' Luciano smiled encouragingly. 'How can I help?'

The girl tilted her head towards Jane. 'Could I speak to you alone?'

'There is nothing you can say to me that I would not want this lady to hear,' Luciano said firmly.

The girl fiddled with the edge of her bag. 'I don't really know how to say this.'

'Then say it any old how,' Luciano said.

'I think . . . I mean . . . I've come to see you because . . .' She glanced towards the door as if she might flee.

'Go on,' Luciano said softly.

The girl straightened her shoulders. She glanced once more at Jane. Then she turned back to Luciano.

'My name is Pia. I believe you're my grandfather.'

Jane gasped. Her hand flew to her mouth. It was only yesterday that Luciano had promised her that he had no more secrets. What more was she going to find out about the man she was due to marry?

Luciano stared at Pia. The gallery was silent. Outside, a child was crying in the piazza. Jane stood and waited for Luciano to speak.

'You believe I am your nonno,' he said at last.

Pia nodded.

'No!' He shook his head. 'My dear, I am afraid that is quite impossible. What on earth makes you think that?'

'This.' Pia reached into her large tote bag.

Jane tensed. For a split second she thought the girl was going to pull out a knife. What a foolish thing to imagine; she must be watching too much television.

Pia pulled out a large buff-coloured envelope.

'You have a document? Some sort of proof – this cannot be.' Luciano's voice was full of wonder.

Pia clutched the envelope tight to her chest. 'This is a sketch of my Nonna Concetta, drawn in 1965, exactly nine months before my mother was born, signed with the letter "L". Mamma believes the artist was her father.'

'How interesting, but I assure you this has nothing to do with me. Things were very different back in the 1960s. There weren't many opportunities for a young man to father a child, especially a shy, tubby boy like myself. I was far too self-conscious to speak to a girl I did not know. I had barely been kissed. Anything more than that was just a figment of my teenage imagination. But, please go ahead, show me what you have found.'

Pia loosened her grip on the envelope and handed it to Luciano. Her eyes darted nervously around the room. Jane felt nothing but pity for the poor girl, searching for the grandfather she had never known. She gave her a friendly smile.

Luciano opened the envelope and carefully pulled out the sketch. The colour drained from his face. He didn't need to say anything, it was obvious he recognised it at once.

Jane's heart sank. So much for his promises of no more secrets. She could hardly believe that he had concealed something else from her.

Luciano laid the portrait on the counter. It was drawn in the same type of blue pastel that he had used for his sketch of the *duomo* in Florence.

'You recognise this – you can't deny it,' Pia said.

'Yes, I do. The most beautiful girl.' Luciano smiled. 'Your nonna lived in Florence?'

'No, Concetta was from Naples. That is where Mamma and I live now, near the Piazza Plebiscito. You really had no idea you had a daughter, did you?' Pia's voice softened.

'I don't.'

'But you said you recognised this. How can you deny it?' Pia looked close to tears.

Jane looked at Luciano, searching for an explanation.

'Yes, I do recognise this. I dabbled in portraits once, but I was never as good as this. This is not my work; I only wish I had that talent. This was drawn by my brother Frankie.' Luciano turned the sketch over. 'And this little doodle, aah! This must be Biscotti, the little dog we used to have when we were children.'

'If my nonno was called Frankie, why would he sign it "L"?' Pia asked. Jane was wondering the same thing.

'My brother's name was Lanfranco but we never called him anything but Frankie. Perhaps that day he decided Lanfranco was more fitting for an artist, or maybe he was trying to sound more grown up, to impress your nonna.'

'Does he live in Lucca too? Could I meet him?' Pia said.

'How wonderful it would be if you could . . .' Luciano blinked and turned his head away.

'Frankie died when he was very young,' Jane said softly.

'Just a couple of weeks after he drew this.' Luciano shook his head.

'No wonder he didn't stay in touch with Nonna Concetta. He would never even have known he was to become a father. But will you tell me about him?'

'I would like to very much, for you have helped solve a mystery that always puzzled me. When we were going through his things, we found something in the jacket he was wearing the day he died. A train ticket to Naples. Our family always wondered about that. He had never mentioned going and as far as we know he did not know anybody there.'

'You think he was planning to meet my nonna?'

'I do not doubt it. And I am certain that if he knew she was expecting a baby, he would have done the right thing by her. Frankie always loved children. I am so sorry for my little brother and for your nonna. And for you of course.'

'For me?'

'That your search ends like this. That you have not found the grandfather you seek.'

'But I have found a great-uncle? Haven't I?'

'A great-uncle? Of course! How funny to think of myself that way. How wonderful it is to find I have a niece and great-niece after all this time. Your eyes, the line of your jaw . . . they are so much like my brother. It is almost as though I have a little bit of Frankie back in you. We are indeed relatives – you are a Zingaretti, there is no denying it! And soon you will have a great-aunt. This lady is my fiancée, Jane.'

'I'm so happy for you both. How wonderful that you have met!' Jane said.

Luciano picked up his phone. 'Let me see if I can get my colleague Alonzo to take my place in the shop this morning. We can go for a coffee in the piazza and afterwards I will dig out one of Frankie's old sketchbooks and you can see some more of his wonderful portraits – if you would like.'

'I'd love to if it's not too much trouble . . .'

'Trouble? It will be a pleasure.'

'The girls . . .' Jane said.

'They must come too if they like.' Luciano turned to Pia. 'Lisa and Cassie, Jane's nieces from England, are visiting Lucca. Hey, why are you crying?'

'I'm just being silly,' Pia sniffed. 'Since my nonna and papa died, it's just been Mamma and me. And now . . .'

'Now you have a whole new family! I think a hug is called for, don't you?' Luciano clasped Pia to his chest. Then Jane did the same. She looked up to see Lisa and Cassie in the doorway. Lisa looked slightly bemused. She couldn't read the expression on Cassie's face.

'Girls, we've just had the most wonderful surprise!' Jane exclaimed.

Luciano picked up his phone. 'Why don't you all grab some seats at Café Europa, Jane. I will ring Alonzo and join you as soon as I can. Oh, and I know I should not, but could you order me one of those wonderful peach *crostate* to go with my coffee. This calls for a celebration.'

'Honestly!' Jane tutted, but she couldn't help laughing.

Chapter Twenty-Eight

Cassie stretched out her legs. It was a pity they still looked so pasty and white but she was glad she had popped back to the hotel to change; it was so nice to feel the sun's warmth on her bare skin. She hadn't worn a skirt so short since she was a little girl. Lisa's face had been a picture when Cassie had plucked the green mini skirt from the sale rail in the boutique on Piazza Anfiteatro whilst they were killing time before meeting Aunt Jane.

What a strange morning it had been with Pia, the girl she'd met in the hotel bar, turning out to be Luciano's long-lost great-niece. Cassie thanked her lucky stars that she hadn't found an opportunity to confront Luciano about his past – it would have been so awkward. Everything had worked out for the best.

Luciano had taken everyone to Café Europa but after a while Cassie had made her excuses and slipped away. Maybe she was being a bit unsociable but she couldn't face playing happy families all morning. Jane had tried to persuade her to stay but when Cassie expressed a desire to walk the circumference of the old walls once more, Jane seemed to understand. Lisa had already disappeared, off somewhere with Matteo. What were they doing now? Holding hands in the botanical gardens? Kissing at the top of the Guinigi Tower? Or perhaps wrapped in each other's arms under Matteo's sheets?

Cassie shook her head to dispel the image. It was replaced by one of her sister – fully dressed – and her new lover toasting their relationship with a cold glass of wine under a plane tree at Da Giocomo's by the Piazza Napoleone. Cassie's face burnt as she remembered her own humiliation there: her clumsy pass, Alonzo's bewildered face.

It looked as though Lisa and Matteo were made for each other. How Cassie regretted her earlier disparaging remarks. She'd assumed Matteo was a charming chancer, like her own father, looking for a quick fling. How wrong she had been. Worse than that, she had flown to Italy with the express intention of putting a stop to Aunt Jane's wedding plans. How could she have been so interfering, so sure of herself, convinced that she knew all about a man she had never met? Jane and Luciano were happily planning their wedding, Lisa and Matteo were going to meet up in Prague. She was thrilled for all of them but what was she, Cassie, doing next? She was going home to pick out the right colour grouting for her Shades of Egypt floor tiles.

Cassie took her phone from her white shoulder bag. Paul's face smiled out from the screensaver. His blonde hair and sapphire-blue eyes were so different from Alonzo's dark looks. But Alonzo had been a fleeting fantasy. Paul was real.

She clicked on her photo library and found the pictures from their wedding day. How thrilled she looked. It truly had been the happiest day of her life. Paul looked so handsome in his charcoal-grey suit and he had worn that silk tie just to please her, even though he hated pink. Cassie had experienced a pang of guilt but the tie had matched the bridesmaids' dresses so perfectly.

Paul was a wonderful husband, as loyal and kind and hard-working as her late Uncle Eddie and she'd never doubted his love for her. She couldn't imagine getting home and putting her key in the lock and finding he wasn't there. Maybe she'd been attracted to him just because he was nothing like Dad; maybe she'd married him because he offered the security she'd longed for as a child. But that didn't mean that she didn't love him. She did love Paul, she was sure of that, but something in her had changed. Their ideas for the house no longer excited her; she wanted to tear up her five-year plan. Her conversations with Alonzo had left her wanting to make room in their lives for something unpredictable to happen; not a foolish dalliance with another man but something that would enhance their married life together. She wanted them to travel, expand their horizons, live a little. Could they do that together? She had to talk to Paul. He deserved her to be open and honest with him. Would he be hurt and confused? Or was there a small chance he would understand?

Alonzo usually completed an entire jewellery range before he brought his new pieces to Gallery Guinigi but this time he couldn't wait. He fumbled with the catch on the rose-gold vermeil chain as he arranged the necklace in one of the perspex cubes. His new jewellery collection was his most exciting and challenging yet. Although he was curious to discover his customers' reactions, he couldn't wait to get back to the studio, though his aching eyes were glad to take a break from peering through the magnifying glass and his fingers were stiff. Today, he should have been working on a tiny, intricate pair of gold wings set with tiny turquoise stones, but he couldn't leave Viviana to work singlehandedly now that Luciano had been called away.

A new family member – out of the blue! That didn't happen every day. How amazing it was for Luciano and

Jane to meet Pia after all this time, but how sad that Frankie had never lived to meet his granddaughter or discover that he was father to Pia's mother, Rosetta, now a grown woman. Life could be so cruel, but it could be kind too – Luciano was thrilled to discover he had a niece and great-niece living in Naples, just a couple of hundred kilometres away and Jane was too. Alonzo was so happy for them.

He slotted the matching earrings into the velour display stand and replaced the perspex lid. 'What do you think?'

Viviana came out from behind the small counter and stood opposite the display case. She studied the jewellery, her perfectly painted scarlet lips pressed together.

Alonzo twisted a button on his white linen shirt. Logically, it shouldn't matter if Viviana didn't like his new creations; no two people had the same response to a piece of jewellery or a work of art. But he was pouring his heart and soul into this new collection and Viviana had such exquisite taste. He really wanted her approval. He couldn't bear her inscrutable expression a moment longer.

'Well . . .'

Viviana clapped her hands together. '*Bravo!* Alonzo, these pieces are marvellous. So bold in design, but so elegantly realised. How do you do it?'

Alonzo grinned. It was worth leaving his studio today just to hear those words.

'I can't wait to see the whole range,' Viviana continued. 'But tell me – what inspired you this time?'

'Just a chance conversation.' Alonzo smiled.

'I think we've got a customer.'

Alonzo looked up as the man, who had been peering in the window, stepped towards the door. 'I can deal with him if you want to carry on with those orders out the back.'

'Sometimes I wish we had never started the online part of the business.' Viviana tutted and gave an exaggerated sigh.

Alonzo just smiled. He knew Viviana would soon be humming along to the radio as she wrapped and packed. The bell jangled. The customer hesitated in the doorway.

'*Buongiorno*. Please come in and look around, no obligation.' Alonzo always wondered why some people found Gallery Guinigi intimidating to enter even though they had striven to make it as friendly as possible. There was no right or wrong way to look at art as far as he was concerned.

'I cycled past that this morning.' The man spoke in English. He was looking at Luciano's new drawing of the Guinigi Tower.

Alonzo studied the man as he studied the pastel. He loved to observe people's reactions. This fellow was about Alonzo's age, late twenties, certainly no more than thirty. Clear blue eyes, a neat, straight nose – good-looking in a clean-cut very English way. He looked at Luciano's work with genuine appreciation.

'Wonderful picture.'

'Yes, the artist lives nearby, he is one of the co-owners of the gallery.'

The man nodded. He turned towards the jewellery display, fiddling with his trouser pocket and shifting slightly from foot to foot.

'Are you looking for anything in particular?' Alonzo hated asking that question but this man did give the impression that he needed some help and had entered the shop with a purchase in mind. So many people didn't; they browsed around the gallery as part of their holiday's entertainment and scuttled off looking guilty the moment Alonzo tried to engage them in conversation.

'Umm, yes, my wife . . .' The man chewed his bottom lip.

'You wish to buy a gift?' Alonzo said encouragingly.

The man's blue eyes brightened. 'Yes, for my wife, Cassie.'

Alonzo nodded. Cassie – that was a strange coincidence. 'A piece of jewellery?'

'Earrings, I thought.'

'A woman can never have too many.' Alonzo stretched out his arms, palms upwards.

'These are beautiful.' The man tapped a finger on the case that Alonzo had just closed.

'But you are not sure . . .'

'Cassie usually wears simple studs – nothing that dangles . . .'

Alonzo thought of Cassie's dainty pearl earrings. But the woman's name was just a coincidence. Cassie's husband was back in England.

'But these are so delicate. And the shape is perfect.'

'Would you like a closer look?' Alonzo was already opening the case. He unhooked one of the gold pyramids and handed it to the man before he had chance to decline. 'Rose-gold vermeil.'

'My wife loves anything Egyptian. She's even chosen it as a theme for our new kitchen.' He gave a what-can-you-do kind of shrug.

'Does your wife know you're here?' Alonzo couldn't help asking.

The man stiffened. 'Why do you ask that?'

'I don't know. Just a feeling.' Alonzo wished he hadn't spoken.

'My wife is visiting Lucca with her sister but she has no idea I've come to join her in Italy. I wanted to surprise her. But now I'm here . . .'

'You're not so sure?'

256

'When we've spoken on the phone, she's seemed a little
. . . oh, I don't know.' He shrugged.

'If you turn up with a gift, I'm sure she will be delighted
to see you.'

'Yes.' The man's frown lines softened. 'That was what
I was counting on.'

'As your wife is here in Lucca, there will be no problem
bringing these back if she does not like them. We offer a
full money-back guarantee, no quibbles.' Alonzo reached
for one of the branded gift boxes he kept under the counter.

'But whenever she's asked for earrings, she's always
chosen simple studs.' The man turned the piece of jewellery over. It glittered prettily in a shaft of sunlight.

'A man who buys a woman what she asks for cannot
go wrong. But a man who chooses something a woman
doesn't yet know she wants . . .' Alonzo let the rest of
the sentence hang in the air.

'I'll take them.'

Alonzo popped the gift box into a smart grey paper
bag and deftly tied an orange ribbon around it. His
Egyptian Nights range was going to be a hit. He handed
the man his personal business card. 'In case there's any
problem . . .'

The man read the card and slipped it inside his wallet.
'Thank you, *grazie*, Alonzo.'

'Thank you, Paul.'

The man hesitated in the doorway. 'How did you know
my name?'

Alonzo had to think quickly. 'It was on your credit card.'

'Of course.' The man smiled and closed the door.

Alonzo watched Cassie's husband walk away across the
Piazza Anfiteatro. He wondered if Paul would remember
that he had just paid in cash.

★

Cassie slipped her phone back into her bag and stood up. Two elderly gents immediately took advantage of the newly vacated bench. The younger-looking of the two helped his companion to sit down and prop up his stick. The older man pushed up his shirt sleeves and leant back. Cassie walked away. When she glanced back the old man's eyes were closed, his companion chatting on regardless.

Cassie walked slowly. There was plenty of time before she met the others for lunch. The thought of the freshly made *gnocchi* at Café Europa made her mouth water. She would try out a few new recipes when she got home. Paul loved to sample different dishes; he was adventurous in that respect. Cassie sighed. At least there was one positive change she could make without risking her marriage.

She walked on. A group of teenagers cycled past, calling out to each other and laughing. Cassie stepped to one side. A big golden dog, probably part Labrador, ran out from behind a tree, his lead trailing behind him. He bounced up to Cassie and leapt up, almost knocking her flying.

'Down!' Cassie shouted. She looked around for the owner to give them a few choice words. A curly-haired youngster, no older than eight, ran over and grabbed hold of the dog's lead. He bit his lip, looking up at Cassie with big brown eyes.

'It's okay,' Cassie said. The boy ran off giggling, the big animal half pulling him along. Cassie bent down to brush the dirt off her legs. At least she hadn't been wearing her white linen trousers.

She straightened up. A man was cycling towards her. From a distance he looked a bit like Paul. Cassie blinked. She looked again. The man was riding a tandem, quite possibly the one she and Alonzo had ridden just a few days before. She swore it was Paul, but of course it couldn't be. The Paul lookalike got closer. The resemblance really was uncanny. Cassie remembered a magazine article about doppelgangers; apparently everyone had someone walking around on earth who looked just like them. How creepy. She gave a little shiver.

The man on the tandem waved. He skidded to a halt right in front of her. He ran his hand through his tousled blonde hair.

'Cassie! Cassie, it's me.'

Cassie looked into her husband's bright blue eyes and gasped. 'Paul, what on earth are you doing here?'

'Well, that's a nice greeting!' Paul laughed. He swung his leg over the saddle and stood facing Cassie in the middle of the road. He leant forward, his lips touched hers. The fresh citrus scent of his aftershave was so familiar. He pulled her closer. The tandem clattered to the ground.

Someone shouted in Italian. Angry words.

'I think they're telling us to get out of the way.'

'Errm, yes.' It was all Cassie could say. She felt a bit weird as though she had just come round from fainting.

They stepped away from the path. 'Beautiful here, isn't it?' Paul said.

Cassie followed his gaze to the distant hills. 'What are you . . . I mean, er, I thought you were at work.'

'The MD was a bit surprised; I've never asked to take time off at the last minute before, but he didn't object.'

'But why?'

'I missed you. That's a good enough reason, isn't it? And I spoke to your Aunt Jane the other day and she thought you might be missing me too.' He looked at her with his sincere blue eyes.

Cassie couldn't help smiling. 'And this?' She patted the saddle.

'I thought I'd never find you if I had to scour the city on foot. Luckily I saw a bicycle hire place. Of course, I didn't expect to find something like this but when I saw it, I thought I might be able to persuade you to hop aboard. I knew you wouldn't approve if I arrived on my other form of transport.'

'You drove here?' Cassie couldn't imagine Paul negotiating the Italian traffic in a left-hand drive. 'Didn't you take a train from the airport?'

'I didn't do either.' Paul was grinning.

'You took a taxi?' She couldn't help wincing at the cost.

'Far worse. You're not going to like it.'

Cassie punched him playfully on the arm. 'Will you stop laughing and tell me!'

'Did I ever tell you you're cute when you're cross.' He dropped a kiss on her nose.

'You know I hate that.'

Paul lifted her hair away from her face and kissed the base of her neck. She felt a familiar tingle of pleasure.

'Mmm . . . you're not going to distract me so easily. How did you get here?'

'I hired a moped.'

'You rode a moped,' she said slowly. The thick medieval walls, the great plane trees and the paving beneath her feet were as solid as ever, but surely she was dreaming.

'I didn't walk down the motorway pushing it.'

Cassie gasped. 'But that's so dangerous.'

'I'm here in one piece, aren't I?'

Cassie caught sight of the time on her small gold watch. 'But what time did you land?'

'Oh, I flew out yesterday. I spent last night in Pisa. I

fancied looking around a bit. Lucky I got up early, there was quite a queue to go up the Leaning Tower.'

'You looked all round Pisa by yourself?'

'Well, you and Lisa have been gadding around Lucca without me. Why don't we go and grab that bench over there; you look like you could do with a sit down.'

Paul wheeled the tandem the few yards to the bench. She sat down thankfully.

'Better?'

'Yes.'

'Good.' He took her hand in his. It was warm and strong. She squeezed his fingers and looked up into his kind, handsome face. How she loved him. What madness had possessed her when she had fallen under Alonzo's spell?

'I'm glad you're here,' she said.

'So am I. You look great by the way. Different. I've always liked your hair loose. And this . . .' His eyes travelled to her bare legs.

She shifted slightly on the bench and tugged at the hem of her new green skirt. It looked ever so short now that she was sitting down. 'I fancied a change.'

'It suits you. You look more relaxed, less . . .'

'Uptight?'

'No, I'd never use that word about you. Less serious, I suppose. It's hard to imagine someone in a *Bella Italia* T-shirt having a five-year plan.'

'Or micro-scheduling.'

'Cassie . . .' Paul's voice changed. He suddenly looked so serious. 'We need to talk.'

'What about?' A cold feeling of dread enveloped her.

'I don't know how to say this, but I haven't been happy for a long time.'

Cassie's stomach clenched. She hadn't been physically unfaithful to Paul but she couldn't be sure that she wouldn't have taken her foolish fantasy further if Alonzo hadn't nipped it in the bud. She had been unfaithful in her heart and she regretted it terribly. But it was too late for regrets. This was her punishment. Paul wasn't happy. He didn't love her anymore. He'd flown out to Italy to tell her it was all over.

Chapter Twenty-Nine

'Oh . . .' Cassie looked down at the ground.

'Cassie, I don't want to say this, but I have to. And I need you to understand that none of this is your fault – it's me,' Paul said.

It's not you, it's me. The biggest cliché of them all. She could hardly believe she was hearing this.

'That micro-scheduling I was so keen on, it was a way of coping, a way of trying to make sense of my life, to take some control of where I was going . . . or not going. Then, one day whilst you were away, I was looking at those cooker hoods . . .'

Cassie felt a pang of guilt. All Paul's efforts to track down exactly what she wanted and she hadn't even bothered to click on the link.

'I was staring at the brochure and I felt so depressed. I thought, is this what my life is now – kitchen appliances? I know we had all those plans – and I was looking at the architect's drawings the other day and they're marvellous – but I want to call a halt to the whole thing.'

Paul fell silent. He sat on the bench staring into the distance. Cassie didn't respond. She was too choked up to speak.

'The family home, the children, I still want all those things – one day – honestly, Cassie, I do.'

'But not with me,' she mumbled.

'What do you mean "not with me"? Who else would I want them with, you daft thing? But right now I feel under so much pressure at work, like I'm a hamster scuttling round and round that wheel. All my life I've done the sensible thing: working my socks off to get good grades at school; studying finance to please my dad when I really fancied Ancient History; putting any bonuses I get towards paying off the mortgage and for what – Shades of Egypt floor tiles. I'd rather go to Egypt.' Paul sighed. He put his head in his hands.

Cassie exhaled. Her hands unclenched. 'You would?'

'Egypt, Morocco, Canada, the wilds of Alaska – wherever. I just want to live a little more before we have our kids. The firm's offered me the chance of a year's sabbatical – unpaid – of course. I turned it down. I know you'd hate the thought of lowering our income, but I've still got the chance to change my mind and . . .'

'Take it,' Cassie said.

'Take it?'

'Please take it. I'm supposed to transfer to our new office in six weeks' time. Maybe I could delay it . . . not for a year but maybe for a few months. We could travel together. I'd like that so much.'

'I wish I'd said something before,' Paul said. 'I was sure you were going to hate the thought of it.'

'I'm glad you waited.' Thank goodness he had. A week ago her reaction could have been so very different. She had Luciano and Aunt Jane and maybe even Alonzo to thank for that.

'Do you want to hop on the back of this bicycle? We could start our new adventures with a ride around the walls.'

Cassie looked at her watch. 'I reckon we can manage all the way round once, then we can meet the others back at

264

Piazza Anfiteatro for lunch. That's where Luciano's gallery, Gallery Guinigi, is.'

'Gallery Guinigi? I almost forgot.' Paul rummaged in his pocket. He took out a small grey box.

Cassie undid the orange ribbon. She held the rose-gold earrings in her palm. So delicate, they were unmistakably Alonzo's work.

'They're not your usual style. But maybe that's a good thing.' Paul glanced appreciatively at her bare legs again. 'Pyramids . . . so pretty.'

'They're from a new range inspired by ancient Egypt. I met the jeweller himself. He said he'd got the idea from a conversation with a friend.'

A friend – she'd happily settle for that.

'They're perfect. Can I wear them now? Would you help? I can take my studs out but I can't see to put these in.'

'Fiddly, aren't they.' Paul leant in close. 'There you are. A symbol of all the exciting things we've got in front of us.'

'A symbol of our future.'

And a reminder that she'd almost thrown it all away.

'You know something, Paul?'

'What's that?' He took her hand.

'I love you, Paul, I really do.'

'Well, I'm glad of that, Cassie, because I love you too.'

'For you.' Jane held out a foil-wrapped plate to Livia.

'For me? Oh, you didn't need to bring anything.' Viviana's mother lifted the corner of the foil. 'Mmm, my nose tells me what this is: *torta della nonna*. Delicious!'

'Viviana told me this was one of your favourites. It's Luciano's mother's recipe. It was a little fiddly but Pia showed me what to do. I wasn't sure what to bring . . .'

'Yourselves would have been enough. And flowers too!'

Lisa held out a bunch of gerberas, they looked so cheerful and bright.

'How pretty! So kind! Viviana, would you put these in water for me? And this must be Pia! I'm so happy to meet you!'

'Thank you so much for inviting me,' Pia said. She pivoted slightly awkwardly on one foot. Lisa's heart went out to her; meeting so many new people in the space of one day was a lot to take in.

'We insisted that Jane and Luciano brought you along,' Livia said. 'We couldn't have you spending your last evening in Lucca alone when all your new family is here. Now, do come through everyone, I think there's still some sun on the patio. I can't think why we're all still standing in the hallway.'

Lisa, Jane, Pia and Luciano followed Livia through the narrow kitchen to the back door, squeezing past Viviana, who was now filling a fluted vase from the tap over the butler sink. Matteo was already standing on the patio. He was opening a bottle of Campari.

'Perfect timing.' He grinned. 'I thought I'd wait out here, it looked a bit crowded in the hallway.'

'Wise man!' Luciano patted him on the arm.

'So good to see you all,' Matteo added. He kissed Jane and put his arms around Lisa. '*Ciao, bella!*'

'*Ciao*! Hi!' Lisa felt uncharacteristically shy kissing Matteo in front of everyone.

'Shall I pour?' Luciano said. He was eyeing up the open bottle and tray of empty glasses.

'Please do.' Matteo turned towards his mother. 'Is there anything else you need me to do?'

'No, darling, everything is under control. And Jane and Pia have brought a beautiful *torta della nonna* for dessert,' Livia said.

'They even made their own pastry with lemon zest grated in,' Lisa added.

'Sounds fantastic. I hope you can cook like that,' Matteo said.

Lisa had made a few pies and tarts over the years but she'd only ever used ready-rolled pastry and added a quick filling of chopped tinned fruit and squirty cream from a can.

'Hey, don't look so worried, I'm only kidding,' Matteo said. He leant forward and whispered in her ear, 'You're perfect already.'

Lisa glanced over Matteo's shoulder to where Viviana and Annika were standing hand in hand. Apart from 'hello', Lisa and Viviana hadn't spoken since Viviana had given her that awful dressing down in the street. Viviana smiled at her. It looked like a genuine smile, but Lisa couldn't help wondering what Matteo's sister might have to say for herself if the two girls found themselves alone.

'Such a beautiful evening,' Livia said.

'Perfect,' Lisa agreed. The last rays of sunshine were casting their warmth onto her bare arms; she did not yet need to slip on her denim jacket.

She had barely noticed the small patio on her last visit; her entire focus had been on Matteo. Now she took the opportunity to admire the pots of bright pink geraniums brightening the paving slabs, the purple bougainvillea cascading over one wall, and the roses that climbed up the others, as Livia proudly pointed out her favourite plants. More potted roses were clustered by the sunniest spot by the far wall. A black and white cat lounged at the foot of a cluster of sunflowers, their big yellow heads bobbing in the slight breeze.

'That's Bruno. He lives next door but he invites himself over here when he thinks our dog, Bella, isn't around,' Livia said.

'Aah, sweet.' Pia bent to stroke him.

'Mamma says he likes to come and smell the roses,' Matteo laughed.

'You might think it's funny but why shouldn't a cat enjoy the flowers.' Livia pretended to be offended. 'They have sensitive noses you know. This pink rose has a particularly wonderful perfume, don't you agree, Jane?'

Jane tucked her hair behind her ears and bent forward, her nose almost touching the petals. 'Mmm, heavenly! I love these old, scented varieties. I had a gorgeous white Rambling Rector at Sundial Cottage.'

'There's a fabulous rose garden at Cavriglia. It's too long since I last visited. We'll go together if you like.'

'I'd like that very much,' Jane said.

'Time for the *antipasti*, a few nibbles, as you say in England,' Livia said. 'It's warm enough to have it out here though we'll go inside for the next course.'

'I'll help, Mamma,' Matteo said. He squeezed Lisa's hand and followed his mother into the kitchen. He and Livia reappeared carrying two great trays laden with mushroom-topped squares of polenta scented with rosemary and sage; crunchy, twisted *grissini* and *polpettine di ceci*, the little fried balls made from chickpeas Lisa had discovered at Café Europa. Annika carried a blue platter piled up with half a dozen varieties of *crostini*. Bella followed behind, nose twitching. Lisa looked towards the patch of sunflowers; Bruno's tail was disappearing through a gap in the fence.

Luciano took a *crostino* loaded with chopped tomatoes. It was a good thing he was there to help put a dent in the mountain of food. He smiled at Lisa and pinged the waistband of his rose-pink trousers. 'Elastic – that's the trick!'

Lisa blushed. Had Luciano read her mind?

Pia laughed. She was beginning to look more relaxed. Luciano had that effect on everyone.

Lisa crunched into one of the crispy snacks. 'Delicious. It's a shame Cassie isn't here – she's missing out on quite a feast.'

'Of course your sister and her husband would have been very welcome,' Livia said. 'But your aunt insisted that she and Paul spent the evening alone together.'

'Quite right,' Luciano said. 'If a man flies all the way to Italy to surprise his wife, he deserves a romantic dinner for two.'

'I've never known Paul to be so spontaneous,' Lisa said.

'I don't know about that,' Jane said. 'Don't you remember the time when their car wouldn't start and he flagged down that ice-cream van and persuaded the driver to give him and Cassie a lift to your cousin's wedding. They pulled up outside the church with the chimes playing *Greensleeves* and half the guests thought it was part of the service.'

Lisa laughed; she had forgotten that. Perhaps she'd always judged Paul too harshly. And Cassie too. Just because Paul had a job in finance and a good pension scheme, she'd assumed Cassie had married him for security. But Paul had flown out to Italy just because he missed Cassie and he had presented her with those beautiful pyramid earrings too. Maybe absence did make the heart grow fonder; she certainly hoped it would have that effect on Matteo. It was only a few weeks until they would meet again but she was going to miss him so much.

'Penny for them,' Jane said.

Lisa just smiled.

'*Polpettine?*' Viviana held out a dish.

Jane took one of the golden morsels, bit into it and closed her eyes. 'Mmm . . . so good!'

'I am glad you think so; I made those myself,' Viviana said. She met Lisa's eyes and with an almost imperceptible movement of her head motioned for Lisa to follow her to the far corner of the patio.

'This is my favourite spot,' Viviana said. 'I used to spend hours sitting cross-legged leaning up against this fence reading or drawing when I was a child. This tiny little patch was mine; Matteo had the rest of this space for his ball games.'

Lisa gave a non-committal 'mmm'. She sipped her Campari and soda and waited for Viviana to say what she really wanted to say.

Viviana dropped her voice. 'I'm sorry about the other day . . . in the street. I shouldn't have spoken so harshly to you.'

'No, you were right. What you said was true. The way my father treated my mother was inexcusable but I shouldn't have allowed that to cloud my judgement for so many years. Matteo's nothing like Dad. I was so wrong.'

'But Matteo understands and now I do too. Everyone makes mistakes, Lisa. It is what we do next that matters.'

Lisa could feel a lump in her throat. She managed to mumble 'thank you'.

Viviana's brown eyes were full of warmth. 'No, I should thank you. I can see how happy you make him.'

'Talk of the devil,' Lisa said.

Matteo slipped his arm around her waist. 'Not sure I like my sister and my girlfriend plotting together.'

'You're too late to eavesdrop. I'm going to go and help Mamma and Annika finish sorting out the pasta,' Viviana said.

'So, what were you two talking about?'

'Nothing for you to worry about. And what's all this "girlfriend" stuff?' Lisa said.

'Isn't that what you are? I thought . . .' A shadow crossed Matteo's face.

'I'm just not used to it.'

'But it's okay to call you my girlfriend?'

'More than okay.' Lisa reached up and kissed him. This time she didn't care who was looking. She felt so happy she could float up into the evening sky.

Viviana called from the kitchen doorway: 'Is everyone ready to come inside?'

Luciano took Jane's hand. 'Livia has promised to make me her legendary penne with zucchini flowers. I hope she hasn't forgotten.'

'Come through to the living room everyone. I'm afraid it's a bit of a squash,' Livia said.

Lisa had to breathe in in order to navigate a path between the sofa and the end of the family's gate-leg table that had been moved into the centre of the room. Both its leaves had been extended to accommodate the party and the great array of dishes that Livia, Viviana and Annika had prepared. Matteo's thigh rested against Lisa's; he squeezed her leg under the table. She put one hand over his.

'Help yourselves to the *primi*. There's *penne ai fiori di zucca* and *risotto al chianti* – that's a very simple risotto with red wine and parmesan,' Livia said.

'And Livia makes the very best,' Luciano said. 'You take some first, Pia.' He handed her the serving spoon.

'Wherever Cassie and Paul eat tonight, they won't find anything as good as this,' Luciano added.

'That's very kind of you to say so, Luciano, but it's the company that makes a good meal even more than the food. I imagine that Cassie and her husband want nothing more than a quiet meal together,' Livia said.

'Did Paul manage to get a room in your hotel?' Matteo asked.

'Unfortunately, the Hotel Tosca is full so he will be staying with us tonight,' Jane said.

'Surely Lisa could stay here and let Cassie and Paul share the room,' Viviana said.

'Of course!' Livia exclaimed. 'Why didn't I think of that? Lisa, you would be most welcome, providing you are happy to share with Matteo, of course. We use that room as a guest room sometimes though it's full of Matteo's old things.'

Lisa flushed. She looked sideways at Matteo; his eyes were shining. 'Umm, yes, thank you.'

'That's all settled then, though I must warn you I get up early in the morning to go for a walk around the walls. It is probably because I am a very light sleeper.'

Lisa didn't know how to respond. Aunt Jane's lip twitched with amusement at Livia's unsubtle message. Matteo looked down at his plate.

'You are welcome to have a leisurely breakfast whilst I am out,' Livia added.

'Thank you,' Lisa replied. She shifted on the wooden dining chair.

'I think it's time for a toast,' Luciano said. He held up his glass of *Montecarlo rosso*.

'Of course. *Saluti!*' Matteo looked up, obviously relieved by the change of subject.

'To absent friends: Cassie and Paul,' Viviana said.

Luciano raised his glass. 'To my new great-niece Pia and to my darling wife-to-be. What a wonderful family I have. I truly am the luckiest man alive.'

Pia smiled shyly. Aunt Jane beamed with pleasure. How relaxed and happy she was, sipping her red wine with her fiancé, and new family and friends. It was a pity Cassie wasn't here to see how contented Jane looked tonight. But perhaps Cassie no longer needed persuading; she seemed to have forgotten all her objections to her aunt's forthcoming nuptials. Lisa wasn't sure what had changed Cassie's mind. Of course, her younger sister was relieved to discover that Luciano was far wealthier than any of them could have dreamt. But it was more than that. Cassie seemed softer. Italy had changed her.

Matteo's face was squashed up against the pillow, one arm rested along the dip in the sheet where the two single beds had been pushed together. He was breathing deeply. Birds were singing just outside the window but Lisa didn't dare open the shutter and peek out for fear of waking him. She lay very still listening to the muffled sounds of Livia moving around in the next room. A cupboard door shut with a soft thud. Matteo didn't stir.

A small rectangular clock with roman numerals confirmed Lisa's suspicions – it was very early, not yet six o'clock. She blinked a couple of times until her eyes adjusted to the dim light from the gap under the door. Above the bed, the lean faces of Italy's national football team stared down from a poster on the wall. One held the World Cup trophy aloft.

She twisted onto one side, leant over the edge of the bed, and studied the contents of the open nook in the bedside cabinet: some creamy books of sheet music, an old school atlas and a curly-edged biography of Roberto Baggio shared the space with dusty sunglasses, a set of screwdrivers and a plastic model of the Eiffel Tower. A framed photograph was lying on its back. Very carefully she slid her hand into the cabinet and pulled it out.

Lisa turned the picture over. Viviana and Matteo stood side by side. He looked about six, gap-toothed and mischievous, clutching his violin. Viviana was chic even then, in a plain navy dress with a white Peter Pan collar, her hair in a short bob not much different from her current hairstyle. Her hand was curled around a yellow pottery frog; she must have made it herself. Both children were so young yet you could already see how proud Matteo was of his violin and Viviana's artistic bent.

Matteo stirred in his sleep. Part of Lisa wanted to wake him up so that they could make the most of their final precious hours together before he left for Vienna and she, Cassie and Paul headed to Pisa Airport, but he looked so peaceful. She quietly slid the photograph back without waking him.

She lay still, staring at the ceiling, casting her mind back to the time when she and Cassie were the same age as the pair of siblings in Matteo's picture. When Cassie was six, she had been content to play quietly, hosting tea parties for Ele-pants and his friends, happy in her secure little world. Lisa had played outside whenever she could, climbing trees, making dens, dreaming of adventures.

The two sisters had been so different and yet they had been the best of friends. They had accepted each other's choices without criticism. They could learn to do that again. When Paul had turned up out of the blue yesterday, something in Lisa had shifted. Paul would never be Lisa's choice, but she could see how he suited Cassie, the way that Luciano – much to their surprise – suited Jane. Paul, Luciano and Matteo were all so different, but they had something in common. None of them were anything like Dad.

Her father's betrayal had influenced Lisa's life for too long. This time, she was going to take a chance on love. Besides, it was too late to change her mind. She had already given away her heart.

Matteo opened his eyes. A slow smile crossed his face. 'I thought I was dreaming, but you're really here.'

'Yes, I'm really here.' Lisa smiled. A strange, warm feeling enveloped her.

Chapter Thirty

'Have you really been eating all these cakes and pastries for breakfast?' Paul said. He picked up a sugar-dusted *cornetto* with the metal tongs and balanced it on his rather laden breakfast plate.

'I've been having fruit as well,' Cassie said primly. She made a show of arranging some slices of melon though there wasn't much room on her plate for them. 'The breakfast terrace is this way.'

She led Paul to the same small table that she and Lisa shared each morning. A sparrow hopped off the back of the chair as they approached and perched on the hedge that divided the terrace from the pavement. The tortoise-shell cat was basking in his usual spot by the base of the potted lemon tree.

'*Due cappuccini?*' the waiter queried.

'Yes, please,' Paul said.

The waiter did a double-take. He blinked and hesitated as if expecting Cassie's strange companion to vanish and an English lass in a loose, hippyish dress to materialise in Paul's place.

Cassie smiled. It was too early in the morning for explanations.

'Very good.' The waiter seemed about to say something else but he turned and walked away.

'I think we've got him completely confused,' Paul said.

'It was good of the hotel to let you take Lisa's place last night.'

'Luciano said the manager didn't take much persuading. Apparently he thought it was very romantic of me to turn up out of the blue like that.'

'It was.' Cassie smiled. She reached across the small table and rested her hand on Paul's. How small it looked. Paul linked his fingers through hers. Cassie's gold rings gleamed in the morning sunlight.

'And I was lucky Lisa was happy to relinquish her bed for the night, though of course I could have stayed with your Aunt Jane.'

'I don't think spending last night with Matteo was much of a hardship for her.'

'Your coffee?'

Cassie dropped Paul's hand and leant back so the waiter could put down the cups and saucers.

'*Grazie*,' Cassie said. She lifted the cup to her lips. 'Perfect.'

Paul took a sip of his drink. His nose wrinkled.

'Do you need sugar?' Cassie indicated the small dish of sachets printed with the Hotel Tosca's logo.

'What I need is a nice big mug of tea.'

'Oh, you should have said! You didn't have to order coffee.'

'When in Rome . . . and I thought you'd be disappointed if I asked for a pot of English Breakfast.' He shrugged.

'Of course, I wouldn't. Why should you think that?'

Paul leant across the table and lowered his voice. 'Last night you seemed rather keen on the new, adventurous version of me.'

Cassie felt her cheeks redden. She wasn't going to forget last night in a hurry. She ran her thumb across the back of his hand.

Paul smiled. 'Come on, let's get going. I want you to show me all your favourite places in Lucca before we go and meet the others.'

Aunt Jane looked at her watch.

'I'm sure Lisa will be here in a minute,' Luciano said.

Luciano's long shorts were banana-yellow, and a button was missing from his Hawaiian shirt. Cassie tried not to look at the profusion of dark wiry hair on his brown stomach. She looked at Jane but her aunt didn't appear to be at all embarrassed by her fiancé's eccentric appearance.

Paul's navy polo shirt and beige shorts were the same ones he wore on holiday year in year out. There was something kind of comforting about that. She caught him looking sideways at Luciano's garb. Paul winked back.

'Perhaps I should get some shorts like yours, Luciano.' Paul's face gave nothing away.

'They're from a shop just up the road in via Fillungo,' Luciano said.

'Though I'm not sure when you'd get the chance to wear them,' Jane added. She looked perfectly serious.

Cassie bit her lip to stop herself laughing. She feigned an interest in the pigeons hopping around searching for crumbs.

'Oh, here she is!' Jane said.

Cassie looked up. Lisa was walking across the Piazza Anfiteatro with Matteo. Matteo's striped scarf was knotted around the handle of her shoulder bag; her gypsy top was sliding off one slightly sunburnt shoulder. Matteo was holding a violin case and wheeling a battered navy-blue suitcase across the paving slabs.

Lisa waved.

'*Ciao!*' Matteo called as they approached.

'Sorry we're late, we were just . . .' Lisa tailed off; her face reddened.

'Saying goodbye,' Matteo supplied. He carefully placed the violin case on the ground. 'I'm going straight to the station. I have to fly to Vienna this afternoon.'

'Good luck with your concerts,' Jane said. 'Oh, you must meet Paul, Cassie's husband, before you go.'

Matteo stuck out his hand. 'Pleased to meet you. I've heard so much about you. I'm sorry I can't stay and join you.'

'Well, it won't be too long 'til we meet again. I assume you'll make it back to Lucca for Jane and Luciano's wedding.'

'I wouldn't miss it for the world. Lisa and Cassie's aunt is a very special person.'

'Oh, don't!' Aunt Jane squirmed.

'Come here!' Matteo embraced Jane then Luciano. He kissed Cassie on the cheek. Then he held Lisa close. 'I'll see you in three weeks' time. I'll be counting the days, you know.'

'I can't wait to see you again.' Lisa's voice quivered slightly.

Matteo leant in close and whispered something in her ear. Cassie couldn't hear what he said but from the look on her sister's face, she would bet anything it was 'I love you'.

Matteo walked away, his case rattling along behind him. Lisa's face crumpled. Matteo paused in the archway by Gallery Guinigi, looked over his shoulder and smiled. Then he disappeared from sight.

Cassie squeezed Lisa's hand. 'You'll see him again soon.'

'I know,' Lisa said. 'I really believe I will.'

'He's a lovely guy. I think you've finally got it right.'

Lisa laughed. 'All this time I've been running away from

commitment but now it's what I want. To have someone who thinks I'm special.'

'You've already got someone who thinks that. You're my big sister. You'll always be special to me.'

'Stop it! You're making me all emotional,' Lisa sniffed. 'You know, Cassie, meeting Pia after all this time has got me thinking about Dad's other daughter.'

'You think we should try and find her?'

'It shouldn't be hard. I found an address for her when we were clearing out Mum's things.'

'Why didn't you say?'

'I wasn't ready to meet her then and I was worried about upsetting you.'

'I think I'm ready now, don't you?' Cassie said.

'Funny isn't it, how much things have changed since we came out here.'

Cassie smiled. 'I used to hate any sort of change but I think these last few days I've changed for the better.'

'Don't change too much. I'd miss my bossy little sister.'

'And I'd miss my pain-in-the-backside big one.' Cassie grinned.

'Girls, girls!' Jane said.

'We're only teasing,' Lisa said. 'We've had a wonderful time here together.'

Jane beamed. 'Your mother would be so happy.'

'Now who fancies a quick drink before lunch, then to Umberto's,' Luciano interrupted. 'You'll need to eat something decent before your flight back to London. That airline food won't feed a mouse.'

'The team from Umberto's are going to do the catering for our wedding,' Jane added.

'Oh!' Cassie gasped so loudly that the others froze.

'Are you okay?' Jane said.

'Yes. I just realised how late it was getting. My watch must have stopped.' Cassie twisted Paul's wrist so that she could read the time on his.

'Quarter to twelve. We've got hours before we need to catch the train,' Paul said.

'It's not the train I'm worried about,' Cassie said. 'It's the shops in via Fillungo. Most of them will close up for lunch any minute.'

'Surely you don't need any more new clothes, though I do like the ones you've been buying.'

Cassie looked down at her green mini skirt. She hadn't been able to resist wearing it two days in a row. 'No, there's nothing I want to buy for myself but there's something I'm dying to show Aunt Jane. You don't mind if we disappear for a few minutes?'

'Not at all. You and Jane take your time,' Luciano said. 'When we're finished here Lisa and Paul and I can wander over to Umberto's and get a table. What are you going to want to drink? Sparkling water?'

'White wine, I think, as it's our last lunch here,' Cassie said.

'Me too,' Jane added.

'An excellent suggestion.' Luciano beamed. 'We can use it as an excuse to sample something we might have at the wedding. Now you two go and enjoy yourselves. If you're late back we'll just order another bottle.'

'So, what are we going to look at?' Jane asked.

'I can't tell you, I don't want to ruin the surprise,' Cassie said.

'Now I really am intrigued.' Jane adjusted her sunglasses and picked up her bag.

★

Pia could hear her neighbour's voice as soon as she turned into Vico Solitaria. Elena was leaning over her balcony, shouting and gesticulating with a wooden spoon. Mariella was carrying on her side of the conversation whilst pegging out her washing; her husband's large white underpants needed three pegs apiece.

'*Ciao*!' Pia called up, fumbling in the bottom of her bag for her keys.

Mariella swung around. She faced the street, arms akimbo. '*Ciao*! Pia, I am so glad you are here.'

'Mamma?' Pia tensed. The balcony doors to their flat were open and from the street nothing looked different.

'Oh, *carina*, it is not your mamma. I spoke to her just an hour ago. It is this crazy lady Elena I am worried about.' She tilted her head downwards.

'And it is poor Mariella's husband who needs help,' Elena shouted.

'Pah!' Mariella dismissed the comment with a flick of her hand. She plucked a string vest from her wash basket and pegged it to the line.

'You want to know what Mariella is doing now?' her neighbour demanded.

Pia nodded. She hoped it wouldn't take long; she was desperate to get indoors and tell Mamma everything she'd discovered.

'She is serving the roast vegetable sauce with linguine instead of penne. Everyone knows you need the ridges on the pasta to hold the sauce. Next she will be putting the meat sauce on the spaghetti.' Elena struck her palm against her forehead.

'My husband loves my linguine with vegetables.' Mariella jabbed another peg into a nightdress rather viciously.

'Fifty-three years old and she still knows nothing about cooking.'

'Nearly sixty and she cannot chop an onion.'

Pia took a step towards the door. She didn't have time to waste on her neighbours' great onion debate.

'Wait, Pia, we have not asked you – how was your trip?' Elena said.

'Wonderful, I have so much to tell Mamma.'

'Then what on earth are you doing out here?' Mariella tutted.

'Yes, don't hang around listening to us.' Elena waved her hands in the air. 'I will deal with this mad woman myself.'

Pia turned her key in the lock. She heaved her case up the stairs and opened the door to the flat. The smell of fried garlic wafted invitingly towards her. The sound of Rosetta's favourite singer, Andrea Bocelli, came from the kitchen. A woman's voice joined Andrea's. Mamma was adding her own contribution; she had a beautiful voice though Pia had not heard her singing for a long time.

'I'm home!' Pia called. She pushed her suitcase up against the wall next to Nonna's bureau, which dominated the narrow hallway as there was no space for it anywhere else.

The radio snapped off, there was a clatter of pans. Pia half ran into the kitchen. Rosetta's face was red, her hair was damp with steam despite the open window.

'Pia, you're home! I'm so happy to see you.' Rosetta squeezed her daughter tight. Pia hugged her back; Mamma felt a little less bony than she remembered.

Pia stepped back and looked at her mother's face. Rosetta's eyes were bright and her cheeks were less hollow. Perhaps it was Pia's imagination; Mamma couldn't have changed much over the last few days. Or maybe digging into the past had altered Pia's perception and reminded her that there was so much more to her mother than the illness that had recently defined her.

'Oh, Mamma, I missed you.'

'Not too much, I hope. I so much wanted you to enjoy yourself.'

'Oh, I did. Is that *melanzane* I can smell?'

'Yes, your favourite.' Rosetta held up a spoonful of aubergines for Pia's inspection, tipped it back into the dish and rested the metal ladle on an empty saucer. 'I can't wait to hear all about it. You've kept me in suspense too long. You've found him, haven't you?'

'I found out who your papa was but, oh Mamma, I am so very sorry . . . he passed away a long time ago, when he was very young. He died before you were born, even before Nonna Concetta knew she was expecting you. His family didn't know about Nonna so they would never have told her.'

'She must have thought he didn't want to see her again. She would have been too proud to try and track him down. My poor Mamma,' Rosetta sighed. 'I was so certain you had good news. When you phoned from Lucca, I was sure I could hear it in your voice.'

'I couldn't meet my real nonno, but I met his elder brother, your uncle, my great-uncle Luciano Zingaretti.'

'Luciano – how exciting. And my father, what was he called?'

'Frankie.'

'But the "L"?' Rosetta frowned.

'Lanfranco.'

'Luciano and Lanfranco, who would have thought it? Now tell me everything you know.'

'I hardly know where to start, there's so much to say.'

'Let's go through and sit on the couch and you can tell me everything. Shall I make some coffee?'

'Let me.' Pia was already unscrewing the lid of the stove-top pot. 'Go and sit down, Mamma, then we'll talk.'

Pia poured two cups of coffee. She sat down next to her mother on the old brown couch.

'I'd better start at the beginning . . .' Pia said.

Rosetta's eyes never left her daughter's face as Pia's tale unravelled.

'I was so upset when that creepy artist insisted his grand-father, Old Luigi, was your father. I couldn't bear to think of poor Nonna falling for such a horrible person.'

'No wonder you didn't say much that night when you called. I thought something must have happened, I could tell it in your voice.'

'I didn't know what to tell you, Mamma. That's why I didn't rush back. Thank goodness I got chatting to the man on the reception desk; without him I would never have gone to Lucca.'

'To think some funny little doodles on the back of the picture were a clue.' Rosetta shook her head in wonder.

'Luciano scanned in some old family photos and sent them to me.' Pia moved closer to her mother and took out her phone. 'Look, here's one of the two of them as young boys.'

'So sweet. Look at my papa's little cardigan.'

Pia scrolled across the screen. 'These were taken in Villa Melograno when Frankie was in his late teens.'

Rosetta took the phone and held it closer to her face. 'Such a handsome young man . . . Oh, in this one he's playing the piano; Nonna played too when she was young. Now I will be able to imagine them playing duets together.' Rosetta smiled.

'I wonder if they ever did . . .' Pia said. 'Oh, wait . . . I almost forgot. Luciano asked me to give you this.'

Rosetta took the small envelope. 'It's addressed to both of us but he said that you must open it.'

'I'm dying to tear it open but I think this deserves Nonna's special paper knife.'

'I'll go and fetch it from her bureau.' Pia stood up. Her mother continued to flick through the photos on the phone, a look of calm contentment on her face. Pia handed her mother the sandalwood knife, an elephant's head was carved on the handle. 'I wonder where Nonna got this,' she said.

'There's so many things we'll never know,' Rosetta sighed. She slipped the knife under the flap of the envelope and pulled out a card.

Tiny golden hearts scattered all over the coffee table. 'What on earth is it?' Rosetta began to read: *'Jane and Luciano request the pleasure* . . . a wedding invitation! How lovely!'

'I met his fiancée, Jane. She was so nice. I can't believe they've invited us. But . . .'

'I know what you're thinking, Pia, and I will be well enough to go, I'm sure of it. Because I've got something to show you too. That envelope, over there.'

'From the hospital?' Pia scanned the letter and looked up at her mother's smiling face. Tears pricked Pia's eyes. Tears of happiness.

'There's no guarantees,' Rosetta said. 'I'll have to have regular check-ups. But it looks like you and I will be going shopping soon.'

'Shopping?' It was the last thing on Pia's mind.

'We're going to a wedding. My uncle's and your great-uncle's. That calls for new outfits, don't you think.'

Pia thought of the contents of her student wardrobe and the elegant women in the streets of Lucca. 'Mamma, you are absolutely right.'

'Come on, Cassie, you can tell me now. Where are you taking me?' Jane said.

'That shoe shop on the corner of the street, the one with the green canopy. I do hope it hasn't already closed for lunch. Of course, you can always go back this afternoon after we've gone.'

'Oh, you mean Carlo Alessi.' Jane couldn't help feeling a bit disappointed. 'I only went in there a few days ago. They didn't have anything.'

'I know, but when I walked past yesterday there was a woman restocking the window display. I meant to tell you straight away but then Paul turned up and I clean forgot.'

'You seem happy to see him,' Jane said. 'That's quite a relief. I feared you might think I was being an interfering old biddy for calling him.'

'Honestly, Aunt Jane. How could you say such a thing? But what do you mean about ringing Paul? He said he'd called you.'

'Maybe he didn't want to get me into trouble.' Jane grinned. 'You know, Cassie,' she continued gently, 'I've always thought that you and Paul were made for each other. But sometimes, husbands and wives can start to take each other for granted. Especially if someone catches their eye.'

Cassie flushed. 'You mean Alonzo?'

'Of course.'

'Oh dear, was it that obvious? I've been such a fool, Jane. I was so busy planning our lives I forgot to look up and see where we were going. I was so busy thinking about the future I didn't see what was right in front of me. I made so many assumptions about what Paul wanted. I assumed I always knew what he was thinking. Then when I met Alonzo, I don't know what came over me. I'm so relieved it never went any further but I am glad Alonzo doesn't hate me.' Instinctively she touched one of her pyramid earrings.

'Far from it. If it makes you feel any better, I don't think your attraction was entirely one-sided. I could see from the way Alonzo looked at you but he realised almost straight away that you were married. But I understand your conversations inspired his latest collection. That's quite a compliment. It's not every day that a pink-cheeked English girl becomes a muse to an Italian jeweller.'

Cassie laughed. 'I guess not. But knowing Alonzo liked me a little too, I feel doubly guilty.'

'Oh, I wouldn't worry about that. I bumped into Viviana's mother this morning and she let slip that an old girlfriend of Alonzo's is moving back to Lucca. Apparently, there was some unfinished business between them. Viviana and Livia are convinced that she was the one who got away, so perhaps Alonzo will have someone to bring to our wedding after all.'

'I'm glad,' Cassie said. 'I really hope it works out for him. Oh, look, Jane, we're not too late, it looks like the shop's still open.'

'Careful, don't walk into the middle of the road like that, there's a couple of bicycles coming.' Jane pulled her niece out of the way. 'No shoes are worth getting mowed down for.'

'You haven't seen these! But joking aside, I think you're going to love them. Look – can you see them? There, in the left-hand corner of the window.'

Jane gasped. 'They're beautiful! Oh, just look at them.' How silly she was, it was only a pair of shoes but she could feel her heart racing.

'I know you were looking for a pair in white or cream, but don't you think they'll work perfectly?'

Cassie was right; it hadn't crossed Jane's mind to choose something metallic but the soft silver leather was so pretty and the motif in the centre where the straps crossed over was the exact same pink as the tiered skirt she had chosen.

'Come on, let's go in,' Cassie said. 'I can't wait for you to try them on.'

The assistant fetched Jane's size from the storeroom at the back of the shop. She held up one shoe for Jane's inspection. Jane nodded. The woman undid the dainty buckle on the delicate ankle strap and passed the shoe to Jane.

Jane carefully wiggled her foot into place and nodded. The assistant smiled and passed her the other shoe.

Jane stood up and took three paces across the shop floor towards the long mirror on the wall. The two-inch heel was easy to walk in and the leather was so soft and comfortable. She stood and looked in the mirror. The shoes were so pretty, fit for a princess.

'Oh, Cassie, they're just perfect.' She could feel tears in her eyes.

Cassie clasped her hands together. 'I just knew it as soon as I saw them!'

Jane handed over her credit card without even asking the price. The woman placed the shoe box reverentially into a large white carrier bag. As they walked back down the narrow street, Cassie slipped her arm through Jane's. 'It's so exciting. I'm so looking forward to the big day,' she said.

'You don't know how happy that makes me,' Jane said. 'It's funny, when you and Lisa first came to Lucca I got the impression you weren't too keen on me getting remarried.'

Cassie's big blue eyes widened. 'Really, Aunt Jane. Whatever gave you that idea?'

THE END

Acknowledgements

Firstly, thank you to my parents for our wonderful trips to Tuscany. We first rented a house in the tiny village of Gioviano more than twenty years ago. From there we made our first day trip to Lucca, starting a family love affair with the town that inspired *The Italian Fiancé*.

Thank you to my agent Camilla Shestopal of Shesto Literary for her calm demeanour and good sense. They say an editor's role is to 'help you write the book you think you have already written' and this certainly applies to Rhea Kurien, my editor, who provides such valuable insights and suggestions. Thank you also to the rest of the team at Orion.

I would not be a published author without the help of the Romantic Novelists' Association; I am so glad we can now meet in person again. Thanks to Tina Page, Nicola 'Sham' Geller, Eileen Goddard and my husband, Robert Wasey, for their early feedback. Finally, last but definitely not least, thank you to all my readers. It is always a boost to receive a fabulous review or encouraging comment, especially when I have just torn up a scene that is not working. I hope you all enjoy this book.

You can find me on Twitter: @VictoriaSWrites and Facebook: @VictoriaSpringfieldAuthor

Sun, sea and spaghetti . . .

Italy was Bluebell's dream destination but taking her granny's place on the *Loving and Knitting* magazine competition holiday she'd won wasn't quite what she'd had in mind. For one thing she didn't knit and for the other . . . well being single probably discounted her from the love category too. But a free holiday is a free holiday and it's the perfect escape from her lacklustre life.

Michela didn't think she'd be returning home to Italy so soon, a new job at her cousin's restaurant on the harbour of Positano was a dream gig, miles away from the grey London clouds. This time though, she vowed not to fall into old habits, Stefano was the past and now her future in her old hometown beckoned.

But under the Italian skies a whole host of possibilities await and maybe happy-ever-after is just a plane-ride away . . .

Under the Tuscan sun, the lives of three women are about to change forever . . .

Donna has been running the Bella Vista riding centre from her rambling farmhouse in Tuscany, taking in guests who enjoy the rolling Tuscan hills, home-grown vegetables and delicious pasta. It's been a decade since her husband Giovanni walked out, convinced she was having an affair. When the truth finally comes to light, can everything return to the way it was ten years ago? Or is it too late to start over?

When self-confessed workaholic Harriet takes an impromptu holiday to Tuscany, she quickly discovers that the relaxing yoga holiday she had been anticipating will be anything but. She's shocked when she's asked to swap her yoga mat and leggings for riding jodhpurs and a helmet! But the longer she stays at serene Bella Vista, the more she begins to rethink the way she's been living for so long . . .

Shy artist Jess has had a crush on Donna's son Marco from the first moment she saw him. This is her second summer at Bella Vista, and while it is a riding holiday, Jess was secretly hoping to pick up where they left off last summer – with an almost-kiss. But is Marco still interested or will this be a summer of sadness?

9 781398 712492